"Who are you anyway?" I asked.

"Andre," he said. "Private Investigator, but I'll do anything for money." He winked.

"You're not human," I said. "What are you?" I stretched out my Charmed senses and felt magic within him.

"I'm a vampire, princess. Same as you, but with a little extra dark superpower. I'm a full vamp though, and from what I can tell from your dismal amount of speed out there, you're half."

He dragged a chair from the wall and sat across from me.

"You have the Dark Charm?" I asked. "I should have figured; you ooze sleaze bag."

"And you have a little special magic up your sleeve too, don't you, princess? I bet you get a little hot now and then, don't you?"

I narrowed my eyes.

"And with a name like Karolina Dalca…I bet you've got enough training to back up that look you're giving me."

He knew my name, my powers, and where to find me. My eyes fell over his body, sizing him up as he sat across from me. Strong jaw, tall, six feet and maybe four inches, and muscular broad shoulders. I could take him—if I took him by surprise.

Praise for M. R. Noble

"This book grabs you by the throat and does not let go! A fast paced, enthralling journey through a hidden underworld of vampires, werewolves, and other beings of the night who wield a fascinating array of powers to devastating effect. Compared to the more stay-at-home-type of vampires and werewolves I know, these protagonists are pushed beyond the human limit. I highly recommend you acquire this book and hole up somewhere safe for the ride."

~Stuart Rutherford, actor from
What We Do In the Shadows

"Fans of Kim Harrison will be drawn into the imagery of Noble's first book of the Dark Eyes series. In between bouts of fighting and the intensity of paranormal, dark fantasy, there are moments of comedy that make this series opener a real page-turner."

~Booklist

Karolina Dalca, Dark Eyes

by

M. R. Noble

The Dark Eyes Series

This is a work of fiction. Names, characters, places, and incidents are either the product of the author's imagination or are used fictitiously, and any resemblance to actual persons living or dead, business establishments, events, or locales, is entirely coincidental.

Karolina Dalca, Dark Eyes

Contact Information: info@thewildrosepress.com

Cover Art by *Kristian Norris*

The Wild Rose Press, Inc.
PO Box 708
Adams Basin, NY 14410-0708
Visit us at www.thewildrosepress.com

Publishing History
First Black Rose Edition, 2020
Trade Paperback ISBN 978-1-5092-3278-9
Digital ISBN 978-1-5092-3279-6

The Dark Eyes Series
Published in the United States of America

Dedication

This book is dedicated to
every down-on-her-luck-woman out there
who needs a reminder that her inner strength
is the sharpest tool she has.

Acknowledgments

A special thanks to my sensei, who taught me that perseverance is a lifelong skill.

A scream from the rooftops thank you to Kirsten Koza, a brilliant writer, champion of wacky travel, friend, and humorist extraordinaire.

Thank you to my agent, Marisa Corvisiero, and my editor at the Wild Rose Press, Melanie Billings.

Thank you to the earliest reader, a fellow vampire enthusiast who encouraged me to "murder my darlings."

To my fellow members of the WCYR, *gratias vobis ago*.

Lastly, an emotional heartfelt thank you goes to my husband, friends, and family for their interest and support.

Chapter One
Karolina Dalca

I was born in Romania, but it never had the chance to be my home. Instead, I wound up in northern Ontario, completing an extra credit internship in my tiny town, staring down the face of an alleged flasher. I readied the paperwork before my mentor, Constable Danny, interviewed the perpetrator. It wasn't an ideal way to spend the summer, but my psychological profiling exam blew into flames—literally—and extra credit was the only way I would pass.

It was one-way glass, but as he looked ahead, it unnerved me to stand in his gaze.

My cell phone lit up with its silent ringtone. Mama called for the twentieth time. I hung up on her in an argument. She should've known better than to play with a vampire's mood—half vampire or not. Mama immigrated here with her parents to start a new life away from the crime of the 'old country.' After this morning, it was safe to assume violence was everywhere, even in the towns with dirt roads.

Still, she insisted the arms of the vampire underground were out of range—if I obeyed the rules of my father's kind. I grew up sheltered. The Charmed people of Romania stuck with their own. Grampa Dalca had an unnatural sense for people sneaking in and out of the house. I never knew if it was my family's earth magic at work or if it was just his lived experience. I would have been grounded double my age by now if I wasn't such a great negotiator.

Still, I was lucky to have a father figure to teach me to control my vampiric side and how to defend myself. As I looked down at the photos of evidence, the perp's bruised penis, it was clear he'd picked a little girl who'd been taught to give a swift kick to the nuts. Not many girls are.

Constable Danny primed the perpetrator to enter the interrogation room.

Control, I reminded myself. It was the mantra Grampa Dalca gave me. I fought for my independence my whole life, and I only got this far by staying in control…mostly. If I lost myself when they finally let me sit in on an interrogation, I would fail.

"Are you ready?" Danny asked me.

"I couldn't think of a nicer way to spend my summer than listening to you chat up perverts," I said with a royal inflection.

"Does that mean you're ready?" he asked, fighting a grin.

"Yes."

"All right, kid. Just observe the process for booking. We'll overlook the final paperwork when I'm done."

He called me *kid* all summer even though I've got boobs and I'm of legal drinking age.

Danny guided the perp into the interrogation room.

I trailed behind them.

The perp looked up at me and smiled. It was the type of smile which peels back one's skin with the sick feeling that he is liking what he sees. But nineteen is too old to be his type, way too old.

I thought of his provocation of the girl and the hairs on my arms stood at attention. A boiling feeling in my belly rose to my chest. My heart thumped like a battering ram against my ribcage. My fire magic pushed into my throat. I held it back, making my knees sink to the floor. This was my father's doing. I inherited the genes for fire magic from him, and if I knew him, I'd tell him what an ass it made him. I focused on my mantra and my earth magic. While I did, my vampiric senses slipped through my concentration.

The light blinded me. My hearing overwhelmed my ears. The beating hearts of those around me banged out like drums. My fangs slid down from the roof of my mouth. I was seconds away from the crippling thirst for blood. I concentrated on a bland memory of my childhood, sitting with my family by the fire. Forbidden to play with other kids, except Roman, Mama would make dolls out of clay which awoke with a breath of magic.

When I got older, I did what any teenager did—I rebelled. Going to Carleton University in Ottawa for Political Science, with the ambition of becoming an officer, was more than my family could take. Mama blamed the death of her parents on the fact their hearts couldn't take my leaving. Twenty-four-hour pneumonia was the real killer.

Thoughts of my family grounded me. I rose from my semi-crouched position.

The other officers' stares drilled into me.

But I knew how to portray my internal struggles as low blood sugar. My goals were simple. Stick to the rules of the law, whether this man deserved them or not, and don't reveal my powers.

"You can stay down on your knees if you want to, love," the perp said to me as he positioned his crotch closer to my face.

Before my eyes processed the flash, a rippling heat left my hands.

Then the perpetrator was screaming.

Danny seized the fire extinguisher and attempted to spray him as he ran flaming through the room.

The evaluating constable yanked a fire blanket from a first aid kit on the wall and tackled the perp to the ground. He wrapped the cloth around him snuffing out the fire and spreading the ashy remains of his coat across the checkered floor.

To my dismay, the pervert was okay. His clothing wasn't. His wrinkly rump laid sunny-side up on the floor, the image forever etched into my eyeballs.

****

Earth magic was a parboiled study of mine, but I was able to use my magic to spell the police sergeant into writing me up instead of firing me. They didn't know what caused the fire, only that it originated from my hands. I blundered through their memories with my magic. Hopefully, they weren't going home to their wives forgetting an anniversary or birthday. For the moment, I was safe and so was my internship. Which meant my measly income for university residence was secure.

I rolled my shoulders against the car seat, trying to release the tension from the day. I cranked the dial up on the radio and let the song "Ibiza" massage my sore spirit. Afternoon mist floated above the pine hills like steam and disappeared behind the curve of the road.

Movement caught my gaze. The trees jolted back and forth on a hill. Something big was out there. My tires kicked up rocks. I swerved, just missing a speed sign.

Pay attention, Karolina. Grandpa Dalca's words chimed into my head. I remembered his thick accent: *Does the dog wag the tail, or does the tail wag the dog?*

Taming my vampiric nature took years. My family picked up animal remains from the butcher and, if I rationed well, I kept my blood lust at bay. When I toted a padlocked deepfreeze to my dorm, I told my roommate I only ate game meat because it was ethically harvested. The backlash was she committed to the cause—not only did she want to use my freezer—posters started showing up in hallways. It was better than ripping her hipster neck out at night. Nothing was a substitute for blood from the source, and the night is catnip to Vampires. My shameful preference for bunnies was the only way I weathered through most nights. It was the cost of abstaining from human blood.

I arrived at the main road. Just a little longer and I'd be at home with my mother.

The question was what would coax her into finishing our previous conversation?

I turned into the parking lot of Mama's favorite sweet shop and checked my makeup. My eyes looked like two melted blackbirds in a nest of hair. I hit the showers after my shift, but I only had time for a quick body rinse. There was no denying the day I had.

I got out anyway. I walked into the store and a tingling draped my shoulders. The familiar feel of magic. The doorframe had orphic markings carved into the top—an ancient custom of the Charmed people. Our house was full of them too; it was how we identified our own.

The store clerk was behind the counter.

I waved, and then took a moment to review the trinkets for sale. Some carved plaques hung from twine between packaged incense and a taxidermy albino falcon. The falcon's eye shone like liquid still flowed within its body. The first plaque read *Charmed with earth, know your worth, for no one can go forth*.

The Earth Charm was the most common inherited magic, but one could invoke it too. Those Wicca parties advertised at your local occult shop were no joke. The Water Charm was used by spiritual humans, like priests and shaman. The Air Charm was hard-won if one wasn't born with it, and Fire even more so.

I flipped to the next plaque. This one read *Beware of shadow that consumes, your soul it dooms, unless the light you love exhumes*. I shivered at the memory of Mama's terrifying fables. Just like the elements, there are also the Light and Dark Charm. Sparking the Dark Charm takes an intense act of malice, and I would have to want its power. The more extreme version is Shadow Forging. I didn't want to think of the acts I'd have to commit to Forge. The change would shred my soul and rip apart my body…

The Light Charm is much more pleasant. Whenever I read a story in the newspaper about a miracle, Mama said it was the magic of a person with the Light Charm.

I paid for a box of candies and wished the shopkeeper a good day.

I turned the corner just outside the door and faced Roman Lupei. Our families emigrated from Romania to

Canada at the same time—naturally they converted into extended family—and our parents dreamed one day our relationship would be more.

Now, he tried to make their dreams a reality. When we were a couple of lanky teens, I would've laughed. But after high school graduation, he'd learned his father's trade and became a carpenter. The family business was his now—and so was the body of an Olympian.

"Hey, super chick," he said.

"You wanna be the bad guy?" I asked, my voice flat.

He fiddled with his keychain, a creepy piece of bone set into a bronze disk. I hated it. He pocketed his keys, putting the old trinket out of sight.

"Some guy was asking around for you today," he said. "Saw him at the coffee shop when I was there." His dark hair reflected the now setting sun, giving it an auburn hue. A golden glow faded from his eyes, and I knew the tip of the sun had just set behind me.

"Tom," I said.

He grunted and shook his head. "He doesn't have your number, so he resorts to tracking you down in your hometown?" he asked. "What a loser."

Tom wasn't a stalker. We were in the same program at university, and he was interning in the next town over. I stopped responding to his texts a while ago. Fighting the urge to plunge my fangs into his artery while we made out really put a damper on things.

I'll probably die a virgin.

"We weren't serious," I said.

"Looked like he wanted to be," he said.

"I stopped talking to him a while ago."

"So, you ghosted him? Next time I see him around I'll tell him to send a carrier pigeon."

I rolled my eyes. "Listen, now's not the time, Ro."

"Why? Did something happen today? Is it the cravings? Do you need blood?" His hand brushed my hips, trying to draw me into his whispers. It would've have been a fatal idea, if the cravings were a problem at this moment.

He waited for my response and put his hand into my hair, grabbing a hand full. He let the strands run through his fingers.

The gesture sent an invisible caress down my back. Why was he doing this? He knew my secret. He knew seducing a hungry vampire was volunteering for a bloodbath.

"You're lucky I gorged this morning."

"I'm not scared," he said. "Are you admitting it's not the blood that has you red faced?"

I should have retreated, but I looked up and saw his chest rise and fall. The image of it without a shirt traipsed into my head, and then I was leaning against him. My eyes continued upward and…stopped. In the heat of the moment, I couldn't get farther than his neck.

Carotid artery be dammed.

"I'm just stressed," I said. "I've got to run, Ro. Mama's waiting for me." I shifted out of his arms and stepped around him.

"Okay, I'll drop off the wood for the reno at your house on my way home," he said.

I walked to the car trying to combat thoughts of Roman without clothes. My blood pumped hard behind my ears. I slammed the door shut and cracked a window. The cool breeze felt good on my face. *Shit.* I tossed the box of candies on the passenger's seat. *Besides wanting to be a blood bag, what did he want? To ruin our friendship over a lay?* Even if we could have sex, I didn't want to end up like one of the washed-up cheerleaders who screamed at him for not calling the next day.

On the drive home, I followed the edge of the forest ridge. We lived a half-hour from town. It was the price of an amazing view.

I drove up to our century-old home. Next to the historical plaque was a sign which read *Dalca* tilted sideways toward the ground. The September wind struck again. Dalca is my mother's family name; it's Romanian for *lightning*. Grandpa Dalca liked to brag it was the magic of our family blood which made us so lethal. He told me I had to fight like lightning itself.

I stooped to fix the sign, and then paused to eye the walkway. The weeds overtook the flagstone pattern which had been my summer project.

Mama and I had spent the last two years renovating the house. It was my way of spending time with her after my grandparents died. A way of telling her I was still here. It was almost done, but she kept coming up with trivial tasks. My heart told me she was afraid I wouldn't be around much after.

I caught chill as the wind rose, carrying an early winter breeze. It rustled through the woods across from our house.

"Hey Mama!" I called as I stepped inside.

She stood over the stove, stirring some sort of red saucy stew. The house smelled of meat, nutmeg, and cloves.

A new can of cooking oil spray was on the counter.

My bane and my savior. From the ripe age of two, my clothes had a habit of smoldering into flames on my skin when I threw a tantrum. *Talk about the terrible twos*. Raising a Fire Charmed child wasn't easy. It'd cost Mama a lot of patience and extra cash spent on kids' clothes. She'd come up with the idea of bewitching a can of kitchen spray as a magical fire-retardant. While most women put on their make-up in the morning, I had to spray down all my clothes.

I warmed myself over the fireplace's fading embers, which dimmed to darkness. The hum of the power in my chest swelled forward, sensing its fallen comrades in the hearth, and restless from the half release at the police station. I held out my hands and dropped my control. Fire unfurled from my arms and into the fireplace.

The flames exploded outward, licking up the surrounding walls and into my face. I jumped back with a scream.

Mama gasped. "Karolina! When will you learn? You can't use your magic if you can't control it!"

The flames died down as quickly as they arrived, leaving only charred streaks on either side of the hearth. *I can control it. I just need more practice.* I sighed, already accepting the responsibility of painting over the black marks—again.

"You're better off using the earth magic I taught you," she said.

"I'm not giving into the gypsy stereotype," I said. "Earth magic is all healing and love potions. Maybe I'll grow a mole on my face too while I'm at it."

A hunk of meat thumped against the cutting board.

"What's that on the table?" she asked and eyed the

box of candies.

"A peace offering," I said.

"You don't need a peace offering for a fight that's already over," she said. "What date do you start back at school?"

"I'm due back on campus in two weeks." I flopped down on the couch, brainstorming how to approach the subject of my father again.

"Mama? Do you have any other family left I haven't met?"

"Just Auntie Miruna in Romania," she said.

I looked over the couch and saw she had pursed her lips. She knew what I was about to get at. My fingers fidgeted with my necklace. It was the only item I had of my father's. A pendant of braided gold, all three shades intertwined into the shape of an oval. Set inside was a ruby. It didn't melt under heat like regular jewelry, which added more to the mystery of my father. I hadn't taken it off since Mama gave it to me.

"If you had more family out there in the world, wouldn't you want to know?" I asked her.

"It depends, my darling girl, if they are people worth knowing," she said.

"If they help me understand who my father was, what he was like…then it's worth it."

"There are some things you're better off not knowing, Karolina."

"Every daughter needs to know about her father! I can't believe you don't know anything else about him. You can try to keep it from me all you want, but I will find out."

She'd tried convincing me my father was an injured Russian vampire who dropped unconscious on her doorstep in Romania. She nursed him with her healing magic and her nineteen-year-old self was apparently seduced in the process. *No qualms over giving it up before marriage for her.*

"How many times do I have to tell you, Karolina? He died. He died the day after I met him, I have nothing else to tell you," she said. "I was lucky enough to have my parents to care for me and come with me to Canada."

"How could you fall in love with a man in one day?" I yelled. "What is it you're protecting me from?" I gripped the spine of the couch, crunching it inward. "Mama, I have fire magic. The women in your family always had earth magic to be healers, the men were fighters, my fire originated with my father! If I could contact his family, maybe they could teach me more control."

"It's out of the question," she said.

"What if something ever happened to you, Mama? Who would I turn to?"

"The Lupei family will always care for you like you're their own." She looked so satisfied with her answer, that my frustration—and my fire—threatened to explode.

The Lupeis were like family, but I wasn't one of their own. They would never know what it meant to be a vampire. We could share the sunlight, religious temples, and even a poutine, but if they cut their finger—they'd never share the lust to suck the blood from it like honey from a pixie stick. They wouldn't know what it's like to have inhuman strength or a fear of silver. And they wouldn't understand how it feels to never know your own kind.

The vampire underground—akin to a mafia—had a foreboding reputation. Mama had filled my head with stories of vampires who let their egos run rampant at nightfall. If one got caught killing a human or exposing our kind, the underground would deal with the indiscretion. A vampire could disappear overnight if they weren't worth the cost of interceding with the authorities. But this was based on Mama's word—and I already knew she lied about my father. Never knowing another vampire was more frightening than any of Mama's cautionary tales.

"Mama, I love you, more than anything in this world, and I know you're looking out for me, but the Lupeis are not family. I know they're gypsy too, maybe even Charmed, but I'm half vampire. I need to be with my own people!"

Moonrise was surely coming.

She looked back to her recipe book. "The Lupeis love you like a daughter. Roman loves you."

I snorted. "Roman loves a lot of girls."

"Plus," she said. "The Lupeis know who to contact if it comes to it, and you have an emergency box in the backyard."

"Oh Mama." I held my head in my hand. "How much more stereotypical can you get? I'll never dig up that old box."

I lay down on the couch again, looked up at the ceiling, and accepted today's defeat. Even through the closed windows, the strong wind's howl was coming through. It sounded almost human.

The outside wall to the kitchen exploded into the house.

With blinding white light, wood and debris sailed

through the air like missiles. Stunned and blinded, the heavy wood crashed into me. The impact drove me back, flipping me off the couch and onto the floor.

Coldness rushed to my head and the vision drained from my eyes.

Chapter Two
The Fire

My skull could have been a split melon, were it not for the blood throbbing in my temples. I opened my eyes. The room twirled like a merry-go-round of splintered wood and drywall. An acidy taste gushed into my mouth.

The front of the house was blown open. A gust of wind scattered snow on the smoldering debris inside. The cool air of the phenomenon shocked my skin. The cold steadied the room long enough for me to stand. There was another quaking blast. A flare of light. I dropped to my knees. A whooshing overhead made my spine bristle. I twisted. A thick ribbon of lightning hummed above me like a surging river.

The electricity zapped into the opposite wall and sent drywall shooting through the air.

My body unfroze. I tucked and rolled across the rubble and landed behind our upturned sofa.

"Mama!" I cried.

Wreckage encircled me. Piles of timber were strewn across the floor; she could have been buried beneath any one of them. Shrieks cut through the night air like a dying animal. I cringed and crouched low. I wanted to stay—to hide.

Courage, Karolina. Grandpa Dalca's voice played in my mind.

"Mama!" I called and sprinted out into the open.

A crackling boom shook the ground behind me. I called up my vampiric senses and skidded behind the next pile. As I turned to look at the couch, now blasted apart and set aflame, another sizzling bolt soared toward me.

I dove forward into another roll and felt the scorching prickle of electricity narrowly miss my feet.

A man's voice called just outside the broken wall. "Bronwyn! The swarm is getting away. Aim to the woods!"

A blast sounded opposite our house, and I could hear the crashing of trees.

I dashed to the next pile and searched the rubble. My hand grazed an object, warm and soft. I threw a piece of drywall away to find Mama's face grimacing underneath.

"Karo," she said.

I could smell the blood before I spotted it and my fangs burst through the roof of my mouth. Hunger surged through me—and I hated myself for it. Her shirt was soaked in crimson, which had leaked through the fabric and pooled onto the floor.

"Run," she said. "Run now."

"No, Mama, not without you."

"You have to, darling. Go now, while you can. Stay away from the Forged."

"The Forged?" I wanted to scream. "Shadow Forged?" I shook her in a bout of panic, then repulsed by myself, swept the hair from her face. "They're not real, Mama, not here. I'm going to get you out of here. Everything will be fine."

"Run!" Her eyes bulged as she looked over my

shoulder.

I turned my head.

A dark shadow glided toward us like a spider, puncturing a trail of holes into the floorboards. It sprang into the air, revealing a twisted human face in place of a spider's head. I screamed. It landed on me. High on the adrenaline thumping behind my ears, I grabbed a leg on either side of it. My foot kicked up and I rolled backward throwing it off.

Like a centipede it folded in half and changed direction midair.

I seized a nearby two-by-four and rammed the weapon through its chest. My hand slid all the way inside. Its innards were like jelly mixed with tar. The texture repulsed my hunger, like it knew the flesh between my fingers was an abomination. I yanked my hand from its unmoving carcass and the murky outline of its skin faded. Its arachnid body was made of an assortment of human parts—like a spider who'd been created on Frankenstein's table. Its skin crumbled like sand and collapsed in on itself.

There was movement at the front of our house. A blonde woman blustered into view outside the broken wall. A gale of swirling snow encased her. Balls of light surrounded her hands, making her look like a candle in a snow globe. She extended her palms and the light turned into beams of lightning which crisscrossed in front of her. She propelled the bolts into a group of Shadow Forged, delving a trench in their wake.

A redheaded man charged behind her. "Bronwyn, left!" he cried. "Protect the innocents in the house!" He smashed a glowing axe into a Forged that lunged at him. An orb of piercing light emanated from his other hand, which he rose over his head and slammed down into a Forged. The ground shuddered with a sonic boom. Light circled outward, carrying the smell of burnt tar through the air.

When the man's back was turned, the woman he'd called Bronwyn turned to face us. A hardness moved across her face like a stone mask. Her gaze fixated on me. Snow swirled around her like a frozen whirlwind. She flung her hands forward.

A bolt of lightning coursed through the air.

I rose slightly from my crouch at Mama's side while fixated on the redheaded warrior—leaving me wide open. *Training aside, a rookie was still a rookie.*

Something slammed into my side just before the bolt touched my chest knocking me to the ground.

The world curtained white.

Mama screamed beside me.

I scrambled toward her, and a rancid smell filled the air. I'd never smelled the scent before, but its presence made my body tremble. I met her side and my vision faded back, but I couldn't bear to touch what was left.

The blast had stripped her beauty from her face. The features we shared were gone, and so was the life from her body. She lay shriveled, like she'd been put through a microwave.

I wailed and folded to the floor. My breath fluttered back and forth, neither inhaling nor exhaling.

"Ma-m!" I cried.

The floorboards beneath my fingertips smoked and crumbled to coals. Fire rushed up my forearms. Like a bomb detonated inside of me—my whole body erupted into flames.

A white blast hurtled at me.

The bolt met my fire. Flames plumed around me. Rather than frying under the heat of the lightning, I pummeled into the floor, burning a pothole into the foundation. The concrete liquefied. I sank deeper until the force of the blast was gone. My hands clawed their way back up the hole and then I was barreling toward the woman.

The scene around me, our burning house, the woods outside, all blended into obscurity. All I could see was the woman who killed my mother. I leapt into the air. Her hands glowed, conjuring another bolt of lightning.

A blazing light reflected into my eyes off her breastplate. For an instant, I was faced with the burning image of myself. An orb of fire encircled me like an explosion inside a sphere of glass.

Bronwyn rolled backward, escaping the flames as I fell. She swung her arm and snow gathered in front of her, solidifying into an ice wall.

The wall steamed into the air on contact.

She threw both hands outward and a frigid gale rushed to form an ice shield.

I burned into the ice squall, shoving toward her with each step.

"You killed her!" I screamed.

I thought of Mama's face, and a white-hot pain overtook my senses. Fire flared outward in an amber flash, sucking the oxygen from the air, and tearing the leaves from the trees.

She flew backward from the burst, her armored legs scorched black. Her scream cut through the noise of battle. She hit the ground and scrambled back—just as I crouched to lunge.

"Bronwyn!" The redheaded man screamed and charged me from the side, abandoning a pile of Forged falling to ash. The air around him crackled with electricity. His glowing hands thrust outward.

A bolt of lightning three feet across thundered toward my chest.

I crossed my forearms in a panicked block. The liquid flames around me concentrated into a center shield, swelling out into a stream. The blows collided midair and the ground blackened beneath the meeting of the elements.

An instant later, the flames I forced into a stream propelled back. An electrical firestorm hurtled into me.

My shoulders braced.

I skidded across the dirt into the garden, right through the juniper bushes I always hated. My legs locked. The shrubs tore into the air after being sizzled in half. Hunks of clay liquefied and sprayed at my back. I dug my heels down and slowed. I muscled my arms forward against the blast. I lunged deeper to keep my foothold in the dirt, but the fireball advanced with each passing second. I poured more power into the stream, keeping it at bay, but the force was too great.

Tears rimmed my eyes. I had to draw more power.

My skills with fire magic had been lazy and uncontrolled, but I knew it was fueled by my emotions. I thought of my mother. That she was gone.

A boiling heat rolled off my body. The horrific image of her as I crawled to her side replayed in my mind. Rage. Unyielding and uncontrollable, it seethed from me.

The flames around me darkened, the deep hues

weaved through the fire.

The blast soared toward the man.

"Lukas!" Bronwyn cried.

He dropped his guard and rolled across the ground to her.

The blast hurtled into the grass where he once stood and shook the earth as it formed a fiery crater.

They clasped hands. A blinding white light flashed out around them with a hiss, and then collapsed in on itself. When the light faded, they were gone.

I stood staring where they once were. My flames diminished. My body shook with sudden weakness. I looked back. Flames engulfed the house and roared into the night. Mama's body burning with it.

I stumbled closer to the fire, but it bellowed kicking out flames. The heat burned my skin the nearer I got. A crash echoed out as the roof collapsed. Wood flew across the driveway. My heart beat wildly.

I can't get to you, Mama.

Tears streamed down my chin. A heaviness set in on my muscles. I gave into exhaustion and fell to my knees. All I could do was stare at the burning flames.

Chapter Three
Hunger Calls

Smoke billowed up from the falling timbers. The firelight played patterns of gold against the dark plumes. A thought broke through my numbness. Smoke. Neighbors would notice the smoke and call the fire department. The firefighters would be here soon. The police would come with the firefighters.

My tears blurred the scene of our burning home. To say a woman blew up my house with a light beam and I accidentally set it on fire—was insane. Even if I used my magic, I couldn't smooth this over. I would be blamed for my mother's death. I would be charged with murder.

Run. I had to run. But how could I even get away? My keys, wallet, and cell phone would burn to ash with Mama.

"No," I said.

Giving into despair wasn't an option. Grandpa Dalca raised me to be stronger. Mama hadn't given up her life for me to huddle into a ball and cry. She'd even planned for this very moment. The box.

I willed my legs of lead off the ground, commanding my limbs to work. I ran around the heat of the flaming house and into the backyard. My fingers raked the dirt as I frantically threw clumps of grass out of my way. Clay wedged under my fingernails and rocks scraped my skin, but the fear of living behind bars was more painful.

Metal gleamed in the dirt.

I snatched it up, only to shriek and drop it. The corners of the wooden box were silver. Charmed markings were carved into the wood. I looked down to see the silver pattern burned into my skin. I whipped off my jacket, wrapped the box inside, and dashed into the woods. I ran hard, putting distance between the house and myself. My lungs burned. I tapped into my vampiric strength. My senses shot alive with the thrill of the speed and the fear of falling prey to the manhunt that might yet pursue me.

Everything that happened took mere minutes to occur. Darkness cloaked the trees around me. My eyes struggled against the eerie night. My ears tuned into the sounds of the forest. I stretched my senses farther—the faint sounds of sirens. My muscles burned as wind and branches rushed by.

A root caught my foot and I flew to the ground. The force of my run surged my body into a violent roll. I rag-dolled down a slope. The impact at the bottom of the hill drove the breath from my lungs. The crickets silenced. I peeled my eyelids open and my vampiric senses worked to adjust my eyes to the blackness. The shapes of the trees stood out clearer. The back of my neck and head were swollen, pulsing from the whiplash of the tumble. My body ached. *The box*. I felt for it along the ground and tightened my jacket around it.

I continued through the woods at a light jog. This time not sacrificing my vampiric agility for speed. My right leg throbbed. I touched my jeans. No blood. Movement helped with the pain, so I upped the pace.

Had it been ten minutes yet? Surely the first responders were at my house now. If they picked up my trail they would have to follow on foot.

My run continued to the edge of our land, and I slipped under our neighbor's wire fence. The neighbor's woods were twenty acres. Then, there was a wildlife conservation and a hunting reserve. I made a pact with myself. I would keep running for at least another two hours. A craving for fresh blood flared with the exertion, but after all the bloodshed, I couldn't will myself to hurt a rabbit or a raccoon.

My mind tuned out as I ran. I lost track of my sense of time. The pine needles were slowly painted white with moonlight, and I could feel the force of my familiar friend rising. If the moon was almost above me, I had been running for hours. I used my heightened sense of smell to try to avoid any directions which smelled like two-week-old garbage, the stench of bear. When I stopped to smell the air, a fresh gust hit me in the face. I fell over in a tangled mess on the dirt, and then crawled onto the smooth terrain underneath the canopy of a red pine. Only then, did I do the math.

The emergency responders would put out the fire first. Then they'd look for our bodies. *Then…*my throat closed. They would find Mama's remains. If they discovered my body wasn't in the heap with Mama's, they'd look for me. If they couldn't find me, they'd form a search party. I would be the prime suspect, or the suspected victim of a kidnapping. The helicopters could pick up a heat source on infrared, but the search team would have to go on foot to catch me in here—which gave me another little lead. If they needed to run DNA tests on the remains to see whose they were, it would give me at least a day. *My internship was good for something.*

I could get away with building a fire tonight.

I searched the surrounding area, feeling around for dead wood which wasn't too wet. I constructed a little tinder tepee and I sat crossed-legged in front of it. I summoned my magic to start the fire and held my hands out. They remained damp and unlit in the darkness. I struggled for a moment, squinting my eyes and tried to force my will. Nothing. Bruised, cold, and exhausted, I sat there. After setting fire to our home and laying waste to our yard, I couldn't even produce a flame?

The emptiness in my chest started to fill with anger. A tiny ball of warmth grew inside me. I thrust the feeling into my palms. Magic hummed down to my hands glowing faintly in the dark. A spark formed on the wood. I dipped my head down and blew, stoking the flame to catch the rest of the wood. A circle of light immersed me and the surrounding dirt. I leaned back against the tree trunk in the fire's warmth, trying to fill the hollow feeling in my chest. The quiet of the surrounding woods taunted me, as if screaming, "you are alone."

A wolf howl echoed out in the distance. I closed my eyes and listened. Branches rustled in the wind. Another howl sounded from miles away. It was hard to believe that, before dawn, despite the miles between them, they'd meet each other. I looked up and felt the magnetic lure of the full moon above me. Its company was unusually empty. Despite the fire, a shiver crept through the night air.

I fumbled with the sleeves of my jacket—avoiding the silver—and unwrapped the wooden chest the size of a jewelry box. I ran my fingers over the carved wood again, remembering what Mama fought to teach me. Learning the tools of earth magic was Mama's dullest lesson, but some of the symbols I recognized as wards—spells of protection. I used a corner of my jacket to undo the catch and opened the lid. Stillness. Not even a faint glow. Since the box was meant for Mama and me, perhaps by nothing happening it did its job of telling friend from foe?

The top layer of the box was a can of cooking spray and thick stacks of money. I counted four bundles of Canadian one-hundred-dollar bills. The stacks were heavy in my hands. I guessed they totaled at least eight-thousand dollars. My passport and birth certificate were underneath. My back straightened. The next row was six stacks of Russian rubles, marked one thousand rubles per bill. I placed them on the ground, and then leaned forward holding the last remaining item in the firelight. It was a torn piece of paper which read *Kurortniy Bulevard 14, Kislovodsk 357700, Russia.*

The paper was hard cardstock, but it felt so delicate in my hand, it might disintegrate under my touch. At last, I had a clue. I read the address repeatedly, each time coming up with a different scenario where I appear at the address and my father's family takes me into their arms. Assuming the address was connected to my father was reasonable—given the country—but thoughts of a loving family were indulgent. I packed up the box and lay down with it tight against my chest like a teddy bear. I told myself I could have an hour to rest and sleep.

****

I blinked at the dying fire. The moon was in the

southern sky. I had slept for hours. The exhalation of a large snout drew my gaze across the fire. A strange smell hung in the air. I crept to a sitting position.

A low reverberating growl sounded out. Glowing eyes appeared above the fire. Clawed paws skulked out of the darkness and into the dim light of the embers. A brown wolf emerged, baring a huge snarling snout. Its threatening stance registered in my brain. It wasn't a wolf. It was too big. Its legs were too long, disfigured at the joint hinges. The mouth was too large. Foam dripped from its snarl, exposing its long-jagged fangs.

I sat, staring down the werewolf.

The beast's weight shifted to its hind legs. I jumped up on one knee. My senses flooded in. The werewolf sprang. I braced myself and leaped forward, intercepting it midair. My hands planted on the underside of its belly. In one motion, I gathered the strength I had and tossed the wolf over my shoulder.

It slammed against a tree trunk and fell sprawling to the ground. The werewolf's eyes blazed with need, hunger. It circled me. Its jaws darted toward my leg repeatedly. Sidestepping its bite and hammering my fist into its neck was my defense. But our dance grew tiresome. It yelped when I landed another blow. As our stalemate continued, my footing faltered. My guard drooped.

The werewolf charged me head on. Its eyes shone in the firelight, looking brown rather than yellow. Its gawky legs were uncoordinated, elongating as they tore through the dirt. Patches of hair fell in hunks from its skin.

This time I had no defenses. Dead tired, I held my forearms in front of my face as the wolf hurled into me.

I fell onto my back, and the werewolf dove for my neck.

I fought against its now fluidly changing body, trying to keep my neck from its bite range. Its large jaws shortened and morphed into something between human and wolf. They snapped like a rabid dog's jaws, inches from my face. I closed my eyes in reflex, but the sting of its teeth in my throat never landed. I shoved back on its shoulders of pure muscle, now covered with smooth skin. I opened my eyes and gasped, caught in the gaze of beautiful amber brown eyes.

It was Roman, panting and covered in sweat from the transformation. He trembled as he shifted his weight to look down at me. "Karo, oh my God, I could have killed you," he said. "What the hell are you doing here?"

"I…" I looked down and saw his bare chest. I gazed down farther. He was completely naked. My face heated.

"I'm on the run," I said.

"On the run from what? What are you doing in the middle of nowhere?" Roman wiped my cheek where I could feel dirt stuck to my dried tears.

I stared at him. "You're a werewolf."

He stroked my hair with his thumb. "Really, Karo..." he whispered. "I thought you always knew." His touch, his concern, all broke through the shock—and it was exactly what I needed.

I kissed him.

He froze, then kissed me back.

His hands trailed down my body, and since my vampiric senses were still alive, his touch felt extreme. My clothes dropped off in a haze. The horrors in my mind melted away. The night heightened my sense of smell and taste, which made his skin a salty wonderland. My fangs barely poked through the roof of my mouth. Too weak with exhaustion and not quite blood-starved enough to be ravenous. Instead of dominating him in a fit of blood lust, I let him take control of my body.

He held me down. Where my body bucked against him, he squeezed harder. His mouth traveled to my chest and then between my legs. I writhed against the forest floor. My hips searched for his, but he held me back.

"Not yet." His words came on a heated breath.

His closeness was torture, until he finally slid inside me.

****

I awoke in Roman's warm arms. His heat kept the chill of the morning dew away, until this moment. The sun's dim light peeked through the trees. Bird song broke the forest silence.

Roman brushed the hair out of my face. "Karo, I have a tent nearby; let's go get ready there, okay?" He rubbed his hand up and down my arm to warm me.

"Okay," I said and rustled through the leaves for my clothes and the box.

Roman, looking like a nudist park ranger, led me fifteen minutes away from my camp. He had a high-end tent and a campfire cook site set up, making it look like camping naked in the woods was a regular occurrence for him. The back of his Jeep held enough gear to furnish a wolf's den.

"Looks like I imposed on your plans." I nodded to his set up.

He laughed. “You *were* a surprise.”

He helped me into his tent, and I dropped down on the plush sleeping bag. He sprawled out on his back with his arms crossed behind his head, letting the old Roman swag resurface. He took a moment to study me, then nudged me to him. I rested my head on his chest and absorbed his warmth.

“Karo, I need to know what’s going on with you,” he said. “But first I need to say something.” He took a deep breath. “I’ve wanted that for a really long time. When you showed up last night you were all I could smell. As a wolf, it drove me crazy. I had to have you. I wanted to consume you. You have no idea how frightening it was, but I fought it somehow. I changed back to a human under the full moon. That’s never happened before.”

The longer I waited, the more tension grew in his chest.

“Last night was…surreal,” I said. “But you have no idea what’s happened. I’m in trouble, and I need our friendship now more than anything.” I backed away.

“You have it,” he said. “I promise you. Now what’s wrong?”

I told him everything.

“They’ll run a DNA test on the human remains in the house, and when they find out it’s only Mama, I’ll be the number one suspect,” I said. “Best case scenario they’ll think I’ve been kidnapped. That gives me a day, maybe two tops.”

“Maybe DNA testing will give you weeks, you don’t know,” he said. “Dyads hunt the Forged. They protect people. What bothers me is why the Forged are here.”

"A rush order of DNA takes a day. It was part of station orientation. The Dyads are not the good guys here. That witch killed Mama. How the hell do you know about Dyads, Roman? Where were you last night?"

"What?"

"I said where were you? You said you were coming by and you never came. Instead, I find you out here. You're a werewolf. You never told me. You say you thought I knew, but that's bullshit. Like it would ever come up in conversation—hey, Karo, I turned into a wolf last night—how's it going? You're defending the beings who killed Mama. How much do you know, Ro?"

"My priority is keeping you safe, Karo" he said. "If there's more Forged out there, I need to know. I'm sorry Ana's gone. I loved her too. But my family made promises to yours, and I intend to keep them."

"And the rest?"

"I couldn't come by," he said. "Not after seeing that guy looking for you and hearing you guys dated. I needed to shift, I was jealous, and I didn't want my anger to get the best of me."

"And the rest?"

"All the supernaturals know the Dyads! They're the good guys, Karo. What happened last night was a tragic accident—but still an *accident.* It's a big bad world out there. Your mom didn't want you to be a part of the undergrounds. It's dangerous."

So, everyone knows but me.

"Why didn't you tell me you're a werewolf?"

"My last name is Lupei, Karo. I have a duty to uphold. A whole pack to be loyal to."

"You lie to me, yet expect me to embrace you as family?" I said.

"We are, Karo. There's nothing I wouldn't do for you." He took the moment to immerse me back into his arms.

I was angry, but I let him hold me. "You think the Forged were there for Mama?"

More silence. His muscles tensed underneath me. Even after he'd been caught lying, he was still keeping secrets from me.

"There's something else. I opened my emergency box," I said and listed off the contents. "The only living relatives of Mama's are in Romania," I said. "I think the Russian address is someone who can help me. Why else would Mama put it in? Maybe they're affiliated with my father? I think the only way to know is to go there and find out."

"I would only use that as a last resort," he said. "You have no idea who this person in Russia is. For all we know, he or she may be sending the Shadow Forged after you. They're always controlled by a master."

"Mama wouldn't have put it in there if she thought they'd hurt me," I said. "Even if it's dangerous, it's my only lead. The way it is now I have two days max, but if I make it to Russia, I'll have more time to clear my name."

Roman dropped back down on his back and put his hands over his face. "Fine. Then I'm coming with you."

No. I lay back down on his chest to hide my expression. Knowing what I knew now, I wasn't sure if I could trust Roman. If we traveled to Russia together, would he help me find the truth he'd helped Mama keep me from? No, he wouldn't. Neither would he stay behind willingly.

"Okay, but Ro? Can we just sleep for another hour? I'm so tired. I need more sleep before we leave. Please?"

"All right. One hour." He wrapped his arms around me.

I nuzzled my face against his chest.

"Goodnight, dark eyes," he whispered and kissed my forehead. He closed his eyes.

Oh Ro, you're going to be furious. I summoned as much earth magic as I could muster while I lay in his arms. Focusing my will, I remembered the sleep spell my mother had taught me. A tingling sensation started at my toes and cascaded up my body. After building the power up to a climax, I breathed out, feeling the tingle leave my skin in Roman's direction.

I opened my eyes, and there was a faint glow around his body. It worked. I leaned over him and touched my lips to his mouth. I had a moment's guilt for judging Mama for her night of passion with my father when they met. I now knew firsthand how easily it could happen. *Like mother like daughter.*

I put on Roman's sweater and threw an energy bar, the box, and some water into a nearby backpack. The scent of him cloaked the fabric at my chin. As I climbed the nearest hill, I hoped he wouldn't hate me too much for leaving him. I was furious with him, but I didn't hate him.

I looked out over the hill and set my sights southeast for Ottawa. I would collect whatever belongings I could from my dorm and flee the country. I didn't know how yet, but I would go to Russia.

Chapter Four
Stranger Danger

Six hours had passed. I dripped with sweat from my journey. The sun shone high, radiating heat down on my forehead through the gaps in the pines. The heavy pack on my back dug into my shoulders. I walked sluggishly. My chest heaved from the heavy run I just abandoned. My heart beat in my throat.

No one at the O.P.P. station could complain about me not doing search and rescue training anymore. I ran more in the past nineteen hours than I ever had in my life. This was not how I expected to spend the day after I first had sex. I always imagined myself at a historical resort for a romantic weekend getaway. Maybe sipping champagne in a bathrobe, getting ready for a couples' massage with the man of my dreams. Hauling ass through the Canadian wilderness, dirty, sweaty, and about to drop dead—wasn't what I had in mind.

I took the water bottle out of my pack and swished the liquid around in my bone-dry mouth, then guzzled some down. The sleep spell I hit Roman with was meant to last eight hours. But since the spell guidelines couldn't account for lazy students, he could wake up at any minute.

I forced my soggy walk into a jog. The plan was to be close to boarding a plane by now but trekking through the forest lining the Ottawa river was harder than I imagined. I forced my legs to kick out one after the other in a slow run. Ahead, the forest floor gave way to a worn walking trail. I followed the path to a dead end of shrubs. Bursting out of the woods, I staggered onto a cement sidewalk in the suburbs.

A family of three with a stroller gasped. They looked at me like I was a cave man who stepped out of a time machine. Apparently, my time in the woods hadn't done me any favors.

"Sorry," I said and folded in half to catch my breath.

They kept their distance walking around me. The woman with the stroller whispered to her husband. I worked to look normal, while panting, and walked down the sidewalk.

A taxicab rounded the corner up ahead. I flagged down the cabby. He smiled as he approached, until he was close enough to see the dirt on my clothes. Then the look he gave made me want to jump into the nearest shower. Once he spotted the hundred-dollar bill in my hand, however, he jerked his head to the backseat.

I hurled myself into the cab before anyone else could see me. "Carleton dorms, Grenville, please," I said. Forty-five minutes later, we entered the campus grounds.

"Right here is fine, keep the change," I said.

I stepped out of the cab and tossed my borrowed pack on the ground. Carleton University was nothing like the historical buildings of the University of Ottawa. For every dull brown brick the Carleton buildings had, there was an old retired KGB or CIA agent for a professor to go with it. It was part of the charm.

I peeled off Roman's sweater and let the cool wind

hit my skin. Then I slung the bag over my back again, hoping to blend in. A quick glance around the campus told me it was mostly deserted during the lingering end of summer. The occasional person's voice quietly chimed in the distance.

I walked toward my dorm, Grenville, the only place left which had my belongings. Being covered in mud at the airport wasn't incognito, and I wasn't about to show my face on a store camera. Spread against the side of the building, I paused to listen. Everything was silent—except for the breeze against the grass.

I rushed the corner, ready to sprint in and out.

A low whistle broke the quiet. "Wouldn't do that if I were you."

I spun toward the wall and caught sight of a tall, black-haired man leaning against the bricks. "Oh yeah? Why's that?" I asked. My eyes surveyed him for a badge. A day ago, I dreamed of being an officer. Now I was afraid of seeing one.

"They're waiting for you in there," he said. "I'm here to help." His blue eyes studied me back. His face was young and almost boyish, like it'd been frozen in time compared to his athletic body. The accent he had was slight and hard to place.

"Who is?" I asked and stepped into the building's shadow.

His body blurred and streaked forward, so fast, that in the time it took for me to draw a breath, he'd jarred to a halt before me. My hair blew back over my shoulders.

"You're not normal," I said.

"Thank you?" he asked. "Neither are you, princess. If you want my help, we have to move—now."

"I don't know who you're calling princess, but I'm not going anywhere with you."

"Fine," he said, "but I'm leaving, because no amount of money is worth dying for a stubborn brat."

Dying. He turned to leave, but I stretched for his arm. "What money? You're being paid for me? By whom?"

"That's none of your concern, but what should be is how quickly we get the hell out of here," he said.

He presented me with answers, and who was I to look a gift monster in the mouth. "Lead the way," I said. Instead, he snagged my waist and threw me over his shoulder. I huffed out a breath when my stomach hit like a sack of bricks. He held me in place like I was paper light. I was small, but being half vampire, I was pure muscle. Whatever he was, he had unnatural strength too.

The world blurred around me the instant he ran. His feet turned up hunks of grass, and a second later my neck jolted when he stopped in the cover of the next building. I kicked my legs out while he rounded the corner, and he threw me down.

"Fine, but you better run your ass off," he said.

I followed and called up my vampiric agility. But no matter how hard I ran, I lagged behind. We took cover again, and then he led me to the Frontenac dorm. He paused at his reflection in the window—fixed his mop of a haircut—and then walked inside. He shot a look at the young lady, a rezdon, behind the front desk. She blushed and buzzed us through the doors. When I joined him at the elevator, he hit the button.

"How do you have a room here?" I asked.

"They rent out the empty dorm rooms in the

summer. It was the best place to stay close to your dorm and keep a low profile."

"What are you, some kind of detective?" I asked.

"Close," he said.

The elevator door beeped open and I followed him in. My face reflected at me in the steel doors. I touched a patch of hickeys on my neck. Guilt and butterflies swirled in my guts, but I reminded myself Roman could show up at any time to try to drag me back into our hometown. I imagined meeting his wolf form again wouldn't end as pleasantly as the last time.

When we got off, he opened the door at the end of the hall, and we hurried inside.

I threw off the backpack and melted into the closest chair. I kicked off my shoes and lay limp for a moment, closing my eyes. I had the uneasy feeling of someone staring at me. I snapped my head up and caught him eyeing up my body.

"Who are you anyway?" I asked.

"Andre," he said. "Private Investigator, but I'll do anything for money." He winked.

"You're not human," I said. "What are you?" I stretched out my Charmed senses and felt magic within him.

"I'm a vampire, princess. Same as you, but with a little extra dark superpower. I'm a full vamp though, and from what I can tell from your dismal amount of speed out there, you're half."

He dragged a chair from the wall and sat across from me.

"You have the Dark Charm?" I asked. "I should have figured; you ooze sleaze bag."

"And you have a little special magic up your sleeve

too, don't you, princess? I bet you get a little hot now and then, don't you?"

I narrowed my eyes.

"And with a name like Karolina Dalca…I bet you've got enough training to back up that look you're giving me."

He knew my name, my powers, and where to find me. My eyes fell over his body, sizing him up as he sat across from me. Strong jaw, tall, six feet and maybe four inches, and muscular broad shoulders. I could take him—if I took him by surprise.

I leapt from my chair, snatched his front chair legs, and flipped him over. He landed on his back with a thud. I advanced and mounted him with one knee over his throat. "Who hired you?" I leaned more weight into his neck. "Why are you here? Who's looking for me? Who sent the Forged?"

He choked out a noise. "I can't speak, ease up."

I released my hold.

He wrapped an arm around my thigh and slammed me to the ground. He was on top of me, pinning down my shoulders and hips in the time it took to blink. His cologne flooded my sense of smell. I fought for an opening, but every strike I made he caught and forced to the ground. Panic birthed a fury in me. I attempted to lash out any way I could.

"Stop struggling. I'm not going to hurt you," he said. "Plus, you have the smell of wolf on you; I can't stand being this close to you for long."

With my struggle, I felt the fire spark inside my chest. Heat hummed through the air toward him. He flinched back and flicked his eyes down to me. In that instant they'd changed from blue to swirling black pools.

"You smell. You are going to take a shower to calm down. Then you are going to come out and have a civil conversation with me," he said.

My insides screamed as he let me up, and I robotically walked into the bathroom. I tried to close the door, but my body wasn't my own. Instead my limbs hung at my side, and the door stayed open. Andre watched, sitting back in his chair with one eyebrow raised as I stripped down.

"Sorry," he said. "Wasn't much time to be specific."

Every instinct in my body recoiled, but my hands kept completing the task they'd been ordered. I stepped into the shower, red-faced with nothing but my necklace on. At least there was a shower curtain, so my shattered dignity had a momentary place to hide. The hot water hit my skin, igniting it with pleasure. After hours in the woods, a shower was a moment of bliss. My rib cage bore a huge bruise which matched the one on my leg. I unwrapped the tiny hotel toiletries, my body still on autopilot.

When I finished, I opened the curtain and stepped out. Water soaked the floor as I walked toward him. My cheeks burned with heat. I tried to will one of my arms to snatch a towel on the way out the door, but they just felt numb. I stopped before him, water pooling at my feet on ground.

"Miss Dalca, would you please sit down?" he asked.

"Yes, of course. Thank you, Andre." I felt like a droid, following dutifully while my instincts wanted the opposite. I fought to draw up my earth magic. Focusing my will, I called to it, but the Charm didn't answer. Andre never specified how long our civilized conversation was going to last.

A warm sensation passed over my skin and my senses snapped back under my control. My arm jolted with the delayed message from my brain, and I lunged off my seat for a towel. I wrapped it around myself frantically.

His eyes turned back to blue as he laughed. "I'm glad your need for a towel won over your need to strangle me. You really are just a baby vampy."

I was so angry my hands shook. My fangs broke through the roof of my mouth, and my skin crawled with the need to tear him apart.

"Is being naked really that embarrassing for you?" he asked.

"You're here for a reason," I said. "You were hired to come here. Why? By whom?"

"I've been hired by a benefactor to find you," he said, "and retrieve the appropriate verification of your identity. Once that's been completed, I'm to deliver you out of the country to my benefactor."

I believed the person who hired him might be someone who could help, but unless it was the person at the address, I would be wary. Still, Andre shared a valuable truth—he needed me. I also had a ride out of the country. My toes began to tingle with a familiar sensation. It was my earth magic I summoned. *I need more time*.

"What type of verification do you need?" I asked and paced the perimeter of his reach, careful not to look at his eyes.

"Your birth records, and your mother's birth-certificate," he said.

Interesting. Mine alone wasn't enough. "And how do you plan on getting those things?" I could feel the magic building in my chest. I focused on a protective spell, and hoped I remembered it right.

"You're going to tell me," he said. "Or even better, give them to me, and don't think I can't feel what you're doing right now."

He launched from the chair, his mouth wide and fangs gleaming, causing me to flinch. Within my pause he'd closed the distance. His frightening black eyes reappeared, and he slammed me up against the wall. "Tell me where to find the certificates," he said.

But he was too late.

I let go of the climaxed power in fear, the second he'd sprung from the chair. Now, I stared down the dark pools of his eyes and felt their lure, but my own magic hummed within me. My body was my own. I laughed in his face. "Aw Andre, I wish I could," I said. "But my house burned down and I'm on the run. If you want my help, you're going to help me first."

"How about, I just rip your throat out instead?" His body shook, and the air crackled around him. Veins of violet lightning streamed across his body, shocking my skin where we touched.

"Now now, Andre, you can't touch the cargo," I said. "Your benefactor didn't go through all this trouble for you to deposit my dead body." I hoped.

The dark lightning around him grew, hitting my skin like needle pricks. He held me against the wall, and the drywall cracked behind me. His black eyes honed in on my neck. His face grew closer with each pulse in my throat, which boomed like a drum in my ears. My instinct was to fight—but incinerating my ride out of the country wasn't ideal.

He ran his lips down my neck, sending goosebumps sprawling across my skin.

"If…this is going to work," I said.

He paused at the base of my throat.

"Then we need to make a deal," I said.

He laughed and the wet of his mouth touched my skin.

"You can't…" I said.

"No?" he asked.

I cringed at my own stammering voice. Pleading wouldn't help. "Do it," I said. "Do it and see what your benefactor does to you." I was bluffing, but I forced more power into my voice. "What will the big bad Andre do then?"

He tore himself away, punching his fist into the wall. The violet electricity which coated his skin flew from him in a sizzling blast. It burned like a comet into the drywall and a chemical smell filled the air. A large charred crater was all that remained on the wall. He extended his hand to the ceiling and ripped the fire alarm off before the smoke wafted up against the panels, then sat down.

"What are your demands?" he asked.

As gracefully as I could manage in a towel, I sat down. "I want the name of your benefactor. I need to know what's going on, his interest in me. If you give me this, then I will go with you willingly. But first you have to use your crazy mind powers to get my stuff from my dorm." It felt silly to tack on, but I needed my clothes.

"Fine, but ladies first," he said. "Where are the

certificates?"

"Benefactor first or you don't get them," I said.

"Your uncle. Now, where?" he said.

What the hell type of uncle hires him? I eyed the leather duffle bag by the bed. I needed more information on this man. I needed to know his story was true.

"In my pack beside you, in the wooden box at the top," I said.

He rummaged through the bag, then a gold sphere of light burst outward. With a whooshing noise he flew from his chair and collided with the ceiling. His body fell back to the ground with a thump, and lay limp on the floor.

I just killed my only lead.

Chapter Five
Cat Nip

Shit, shit, shit. I scrambled over to him. *Please be breathing*. I shoved his chest, hoping it would recoil. It didn't.

"Come on. You're not dead," I said.

After a grueling second, his rib cage expanded. His breathing was sluggish, and from the slack in his face—I knew he was out cold.

Private Investigator my ass. I unzipped his bag and saw a bunch of folded dress shirts. Nestled between them I could see the spine of a black leather book. It glittered under the lamp, like it was covered with dried blood. I picked up the book.

A blistering pain ripped up my arm. My hand clamped around the book locking it in my grasp. I flailed, unable to let go. Smoke seethed from the pages, gathering in a ball around my fist. The vapor plume shot outward, slamming me against the wooden desk. My fingertips blackened. The darkness sped up my arm in streaks, feeling like hot knives cutting my skin. I screamed.

"Andre!" I stumbled toward him and collapsed to my knees. "Andre! Wake up!" I shook him. The pain felt like poison overtaking my senses. I buckled to the floor beside him. "Andre, please!" I tried to shove him again, but my arms contorted against my chest. I kicked at him. "Andre! Wake up!"

His eyes opened. He jerked his head to the side, squishing his cheek against the floor.

"Andre!"

He looked to my face, and then to the book in my hand. "Pay back'sss a bitch."

"You bastard. Help me!"

He rolled onto his side. His legs hung limp as he wormed toward me. With each wheeze, his face looked more paralyzed and bloated.

"Hurry," I cried.

He moaned and dragged himself to my shoulder. "Drink me," he said. The veins in his neck bulged making him look like a giant toad.

"No," I cried, "use your magic."

"Drink," he said.

My body seized. I jerked forward and faceplanted against his chest. With all my strength I lifted my head into the nook of his neck. My fangs popped through the roof of my mouth. I opened my jaws and let my fangs sink into his swollen artery.

His blood tasted like salted caramel. My eyes rolled back into my head. I swallowed him down. The pain I felt washed away, and my body felt like it was thawing into the carpet. All that existed was the blood and the need for more.

Andre moaned in my ear. My hand entwined in his hair. I sucked harder. He shoved me away and I landed on my back, panting. The book had fallen from my hand and lay beside me.

"Oh…my…God," I said.

"Your turn, sweetheart," he said as saliva dripped from his mouth. His skin looked sickly green.

"But you're better," I lied. "It's fading."

"The earth spell is wearing off but I'm weak. I need blood to heal," he said.

"But I've never been bitten before."

He propped himself up against the bed. "Karolina, I need it."

"No, you'll drain me dry."

"I'm not eight years old anymore," he said and yanked me onto his lap. "It won't hurt, you'll love it."

"Fine. But I'm only doing this because I need you to—"

He drove his fangs into my neck.

Pure unrefined ecstasy exploded from the veins in my throat and coursed through my body. My back arched, and I trembled in orgasmic pleasure. He held me tightly against his chest, tugging my hips into his. The towel around me loosened as his hand ran up my back to my neck. My head tilted in a moan. A tingle arose from his skin, alike the sensation of my own magic but stronger and pulsing. Where my thighs lay against him the feeling overtook me again, and I cried out. The warmth of my own magic poured out over our bodies.

He jerked his face from my neck.

I looked up at him, breathless.

His boyish face had returned, and he licked up the blood droplets that trickled from his mouth.

"You taste—so good," he said. "Like fire and sunshine. Chili pepper and cinnamon." He looked down at me and paused…staring at my lips.

I peeled some sweaty hair from my face and dismounted him, averting my gaze from the huge bulge in his jeans.

"Why do we taste like that?" I asked.

"When you drink from another being you taste their soul, their essence," he said.

I survived most of my life on animal blood. My family had caught rabbits in the backyard, and their sweet taste was a flavor I'd gotten used to.

"I need a second," I said and got up.

He cleared his throat. "Before you do, can I please have your certificate, or we don't have a deal."

I picked up the box from the floor and held out my birth certificate.

"Nice trick with the box," he said and yanked the paper from my hand. He looked down at it. "It's just yours."

"It's all I have," I said.

His lips narrowed into a thin line. "It'll do for now," he said and walked out of the room.

I sat down in one of the chairs which remained upright. The room was trashed. My hand absentmindedly found the remote on the coffee table and I turned on the TV. A news announcer was telling a story about a mauling last night: "Police reports state the people were mauled by unidentified animal talons, but amongst the wounds human bite marks were found, baffling crime scene investigators. A detailed report to be broadcast tonight at eight."

****

A little while later Andre returned. "Your stuff," he said, and dropped a cardboard box full of clothes at my feet. On top were my finest lace bras and panties. I shouldn't have been surprised.

"We need to talk," I said. "But first I'm going to change."

I took the first couple pieces of clothes and stepped into the bathroom. Then I turned the lock and ditched the towel. When I got to the mirror I gasped. The bruises on my chest were gone. I tossed my hair back to look at my neck. All traces of Roman's kisses had disappeared. I felt two round scabs on my artery. Only Andre's fang punctures had remained.

Vampire blood could heal.

His blood hadn't broken the spell; it had healed me physically. This knowledge arrived too late, and at a price. Mama was gone. I broke a vow to Grandpa Dalca. I hadn't drunk from a person before, and I hadn't expected to…love it. *It's just another vampire*, I told myself. I closed my eyes and rested my hands on the sink. When I opened them again, my ruby necklace caught the light. Fire danced inside the gem. I clutched it, feeling its pattern against my palm. I had family, an uncle. Andre could get me out of the country.

I yanked on the lace and threw on the pair of jeans and sparkly tank-top. When I walked back into the room, Andre was lying down on his bed watching TV.

"I need to tell you something. I didn't just run away. I'm a fugitive. Or will be."

"What?"

"I may be named a person of interest, if not the main suspect shortly. We have very little time to get out of Canada before it will be impossible for me to cross the border."

"Because your house burned down?" He raised a brow. "Not uncommon for a fire user?"

"Yesterday, the Forged showed up at my house. The Dyads followed." My jaw clenched. "There was a battle and my mother died."

Sadness flashed across his face. He looked down at his hands. "I'm sorry."

"That was eighteen hours ago," I said.

"I'm smuggling a fugitive over the border if we wait much longer?" he asked.

"Yeah," I said.

He took an ancient flip-phone out of his inner coat pocket and started dialing. He spoke in Russian to the recipient on the other end, and after a moment he flipped it closed. I kept my face blank when I recognized the language.

"The nineties called. They want their phone back?" I asked.

"Very funny. We're getting a plane out of here," he said. "When was the last time you saw the Forged?" He threw some clothes into his bag and zipped it up.

"When Mama died. Where are we going?"

"Romania," he said.

"*Romania?*"

"I need to check in with my contacts there. What about the Dyads?" he continued.

"The same time. Don't they only show up when the Forged are around?"

"They say that, but I'm not one to trust the rah-rah Dyad propaganda," he said. "No organization should be given that much power unchecked. Next they'll be the ones running your government."

"What do you mean?" I asked.

"The Dyads own half the buildings in Ottawa. Their headquarters are out of Greenland, but they've recently made a great deal of money in penny stocks. They expanded their enterprise to Ottawa real estate and the publishing industry in Iceland."

I grunted. "That's absurd."

"It's the way things are now, princess. The world is changing, and so are the power struggles amongst the undergrounds."

"Does every supernatural race have an underground?" I asked.

"All of them. I'm surprised you don't know, since your campus is full of underground agents. Ottawa's a capital city, there are diplomats from everywhere," he said and walked to the door.

"I knew it existed," I said. "But, excluding the Charmed and the attack from yesterday, you're the second supernatural I've met." Roman wasn't his concern.

"Oh yeah? Why did you reek of wolf then?" He opened the door. "Forewarning. All the wolf race wants is a strong mate to make super-human wolf babies with. If you're not messing around with the pack leader himself, you'll just be passed over to him by one of his minions."

I scoffed. "You don't even know him. He's been loyal to my family since the day we were born."

"Oh yeah? Why's he not here with you now?"

"None of your business," I said.

"Sure. I rest my case." He stepped out into the hallway.

"Where are you going?"

"*We* are taking a cab to the airport."

I put on my dirty boots and stepped out into the hall. A quick glance back at the black hole in the wall reminded me of who I made a deal with.

"You know, if this is going to work, you'll have to stop attacking me and start trusting me," he said.

I clutched the straps on my backpack and looked up at him. "How about this? When I know I can trust you, I'll stop trying to get the jump on you."

"Well, *trust* me when I say those boots aren't low profile," he said.

I looked down and harrumphed. He was right.

"I'll call for a cab and see if I can get you a new pair," he said. "What's your size?"

He walked down the hall, took out his retro phone, and started dialing.

Chapter Six
Into the Night

A black unmarked cab picked us up and drove us to the Ottawa International Airport. The driver scanned the road under his baseball cap, and a few times he caught me looking at him in the mirror. We entered the drop off lane. "Best of luck," he said to Andre. "Boots are in the back."

"Thanks for the favor, Nikki," Andre said.

Nikki. I would remember his name.

We got out and I put on the finest pair of caramel riding boots I ever saw. They were the same style as my ruined ones but were of the quality I only fantasized about buying. I didn't know if Andre paid attention to my style or if it was pure fluke. We headed to the VIP entrance of the airport. I walked past the baggage check and fought the urge to spring into a run.

"Play it cool, princess," he said. "Act like I'm your sugar daddy taking you to Europe."

"More like pain in the ass chaperone who I can't wait to ditch."

"Ouch," he said.

We made it all the way to customs before my clothes started to dampen with sweat. I got my passport out when I caught sight of the security check. A heavyset man stood by the metal detectors.

"Passports, please," said the customs agent.

The agent swiped them and handed them back to us. "This way, please," the heavy man said. He held his arms away from the customs channel and toward a side room. His Russian accent was thick.

Andre appeared calm, but he gave me a slight nod. I queued my vampiric sense up.

"Just routine screening," the customs guard said.

"Yes, of course," Andre replied.

The guard led the way for us, and we politely followed him. I kept pace with Andre, staying at his side rather than behind. My hand grazed his by chance and I felt a shocking prickle.

We entered a door marked 'Security Office' and the smell of blood enthralled my senses. My fangs glided halfway down from the roof of my mouth. I glanced at Andre. His gaze was fixated on the guard's back like a cat, his fangs freely exposed.

In the middle of the room I could see the interrogation area clearly. A fleshy object lay just within the door. It was an outstretched human arm. The smell of not only blood, but death drifted to my nose. The security door echoed as it slammed shut behind us.

Andre darted behind me in a streak of violet.

I stomped down on the back of the guard's knee.

He cried out in pain and buckled to the ground. Recovering quickly, he pivoted on his injured knee and rose on his good leg, thrusting his weight forward. He shot back at me swinging his fist like a cannonball. His eyes bulged. His fangs spread wide, looking like he'd rip my throat out.

I recoiled into fighter's stance, back to back against Andre.

As the massive guard rushed me, I caught his wrist

with a two-handed block. I twisted my hands and used the momentum of the blow to dislocate his arm. In one smooth motion, I glided over his shoulder, and drove my elbow with all my weight into his jawbone.

He dropped face first.

I regained my position against Andre's back, and his magic tingled through my clothes. We moved together in a circle. My focus shifted to his opponents. A man lay on the ground with his throat pulsing blood on the tile. Two men remained. One was blond with a lean build. The other had a dark complexion and braids to his ears. They spoke in Russian, summoning sparks of darkness from thin air into their palms.

Andre's magic flared out around me, the violet lightning weaving together into an orb-like shield.

The vampires thrust their arms forward. Streams of black lightning shot from their hands and sizzled through the air. They hammered into Andre's shield. The impact drove us back against the wall.

I hit the concrete flat. My spine rattled against the steel and drywall, but I held form, thankfully, because the moment Andre hit the wall he bounced back and charged them. I struggled to remain alongside him, trailing in the outskirts of his orb. He moved so fast his outline blurred as he ran. He lunged and hammered his fist into the blond's front knee, sending him crumpling to the floor. Then he drove his heel into his diaphragm. Andre's mouth dove to his throat.

"Nooo!" I cried. It was against my vampire instinct, but I didn't want to be a part of slaughtering these men. If an opponent was down and not getting up, it was enough.

My breath jarred from my lungs as the large man

with braids slammed into me.

I was flung to my back in the seconds of shock. Before I recovered, he was on top of me pinning down my hands. I attempted to buck him off by using the strength in my hips, but he was too strong. His fangs gleamed in fluorescent lights as his face darted to my neck. I panicked. My skin erupted in flame.

In a flash of color, Andre flew at him from behind. He grabbed him from the back in a chokehold, and the vampire's eyes bulged. He kicked out and grasped at Andre, but Andre continued to hold his neck tight. In thirty seconds, the vamp grew limp.

"Your morals are going to get you killed," Andre said. He let go of the vampire, who hit the ground with a thud.

I looked at the blond. He was unconscious but breathing. I rose to my feet.

"Open up. Police!" Insistent rapping came from the other side of the door.

"Come on, princess. It's time to go." Andre blasted the camera with a lightning bolt, and a flickering light traveled through all the wiring making it smoke. Next, he did the smoke alarm. We took off running.

Dozens of footsteps echoed from where we exited.

Andre took my hand and propelled me out the backdoor. We ran through the small VIP waiting area. Cries for us to stop echoed at our heels.

"A-one," Andre said while we ran.

"Sir, you have to slow down. Surely your pilot will wait!" a flight attendant in a blue suit called out as we dashed by her and through the doors. Down a carbon fold-out hallway, there was a metal airplane door which opened with our approaching footsteps. We hustled through the hatch. A flight attendant slammed it shut behind us.

We cut our sprint to a halt inside the entrance cabin. I dug my heels in to avoid crashing into Andre's back. I panted to catch my breath and choked on my own saliva when the gaudy plane décor gleamed in my face. This had to be a joke.

The floor was clad in bright cobalt-blue carpet, and the lights on the walls sparkled gold. In front of us was a small kitchenette with black marble counters. Black velvet curtains hung in the doorways at the front and back of the plane.

"Heya Smoke, glad you could make it. We're all queued up. I'll tell the pilot it's lift off," said the flight attendant. He walked into the front behind a velvet curtain.

"It's Smoke, eh?"

"Wow, Canadian's really do say 'eh'," Andre said and walked to the kitchenette. He turned around and his sparkly white teeth were crimson. I winced as the image of the third vampire with his throat ripped out flashed into my head. What had Andre said? *My morals will get me killed.*

He ran his face under the tap and rinsed the blood away. Not only did I feel the siren song of hunger inside myself, with more than a woman's intuition, I could sense it in him. A low vibration emanated off him. It hit me in waves, promising me excitement and release. The need to feed felt equivalent to the thrill of being alive.

I opened the velvet curtain and stepped into the seating area.

There were rows of black leather chairs positioned to face the big screen on the wall to my back. A few coffee tables were bolted to the ground. On my right there was a full-size bar.

"Okay, passengers. We're taking off. Sit down and fasten your seat belts. We'll be in the air in a second!"

I picked a spot by the big screen and was fumbling with the seatbelt when Andre entered.

"First time flying?" he asked.

I leaned back in the chair and closed my eyes. "Yes."

He sat down beside me and clicked his belt on. "Then you'll need this." He handed me a piece of gum. The plane's engines abruptly blasted out a whirling noise. Andre took out his phone and powered it down.

"What's the deal with your phone anyways? It's old," I said.

He stuffed it into his pocket. "There wasn't much selection in Ukraine after the conflict with Russia."

"Oh." I remembered some of the side conversations in my Russian politics class. "What has it been, four years ago now since Russia helped the separatists?"

He faced me. "Yeah, but I'm talking about the one in 1992. Though, it was nothing compared to the one in 1920."

Wow. Andre looked like he was rolling up to twenty-one, but what he'd just told me would mean he was over ninety years old. How long would I have made it before my friends started to notice I didn't age like them? The embittered timelessness in which Andre carried himself now clicked into perspective. He'd lived through the worst of the world wars, the tank battles of Ukraine, and Chernobyl.

"You're from Ukraine. Do you have family there

still?"

"No, Karolina."

"Where are they?" I asked.

He looked down. "I don't want to talk about it," he said.

"Okay."

A coolness hit me. Then a sensation reminded me of one thing, and one thing only—the way I felt after Mama died. I carried the feeling in the pit of my stomach since. *Revenge*.

Nine hours later, I awoke to an empty seat. I looked over and found Andre at the front of the plane. He was opening a compartment concealed in the wall. He punched in a code on the metal dial pad. With a beep, the electronic lock unlatched, and the door opened. Stacks of money in a multitude of colors sat inside.

"You have Romanian money in there?"

"Yeah," he said and held up a stack marked *Lei*, "I have whatever I need to get you to your uncle." He slipped the cash inside his inner coat pocket.

"I see," I said. His words were mundane enough, but the indifference in which he said them, reminded me I was his objective. Healing me back at the dorms had been necessary for his survival. The room felt colder again, and the chill was coming from Andre himself.

The plane speaker buzzed to life. "Agent Smoke, prepare for landing. Hang on tight—we're coming in hot!"

Agent. He said Agent. I sat back in the seat upright. Gears thumped beneath my feet and the landing gear dropped along with my stomach.

Andre handed me another piece of gum. He hadn't

looked at me since I awoke. I felt my jaw tighten. Deciding to test my new hypothesis, I concentrated on my inner senses, and parsed out the one which was new. I could feel him with it. When I closed my eyes, I knew where he was sitting from memory, but I could also *feel* him. In my mind he stood out like a beacon in a black void. I probed out with my newfound power and nudged toward him, only to slam into an invisible icy wall.

My eyes snapped open.

Andre was glaring at me.

I looked down.

Chapter Seven
Romania: The Home of Folklore

"Where's your passport?" Andre asked.

"It's in my pocket. Why?" The plane door opened and music from the airport traveled down the fold-out hallway, beckoning me to my mother's homeland.

"Switch it to your inner coat pocket," he said. "The gypsies around the airport will have it sold on the black market before you realize it's gone."

I forgot about Europe's reputation for 'Travelers': gypsies who roam the land pickpocketing to get by. Not everyone from Roma descent was like the stereotype; both my grandma and grandpa's side had a long, proud history in Romania.

"I forgot," I said, and slipped my passport into my inner pocket.

"Call your magic up, not the fire," he said. "Usually if they feel the Charmed in you, they'll leave you alone."

I called my earth magic and made a face when I felt its tingle in my toes right away. With all its use, earth magic and I were developing a fairly steady relationship.

The airport was modern for a country famous for olden vampires and medieval castles. The floor and walls were smooth cream tiles, with a mix of honey-colored wood. White chairs lined the boarding areas like shiny leather teeth. We walked along a bar lit up with blue neon lights. At the end of the counter, a three-person band acted as a magnet for airplane passengers.

The DJ spun disks on the equipment, creating a masterpiece of electronic booms. His partner played an electric violin; his face lit with passion as his fingers blurred across the strings. Finally, a dark-haired beauty sang out in Romanian. Her siren voice haunted me as it pierced through the violin and bass melody.

When we passed them, I felt the vibration of the Charm in their music. The woman shot me a cheeky smile between words. A man emptied the entire contents of his traveler's pouch into a guitar case. His companions danced with their pockets inside out while sweat dripped from their brows. Others sipped cocktails like zombies as they waited for their flights…if they could break away from the spell at all.

Romanian words flashed in neon on a computer screen which hung above the hallway. Underneath, the English translation read *Welcome to Bucharest.*

We walked down the length of the airport. I scanned the crowd the way my Crime and Intelligence Analysis course taught me, taking note of the activity around me through my peripheral vision. When we arrived at the opposite end of the building, Andre stopped at a desk labeled *Autonom*. A sign in the vast universal language was beside it—a stick figure standing beside a car.

"Give me a minute," he said.

"Yeah."

Andre returned a few moments later. "Let's go," he said. His pocket buzzed as we rode the elevator down. He took out his phone. A voice spoke in Romanian on the other end and he replied with the same perfect pronunciation. Jealousy bit at me. He could speak it and I couldn't. Mama had forgone speaking her language to me. Wanting me to fit in with the other kids, she'd only spoken English at home. The snippets I learned were from my grandparents.

He flicked the phone shut and we headed into the parking garage.

"How many languages do you speak?" I asked.

"Fluently? Five. English, Romanian, Ukrainian, Russian, and Italian," he said. "You start by learning small amounts as you travel around."

"I can mostly speak one language," I said. "I was going to choose some intro language courses for my electives at university this year. Try to get a little more culture under my belt."

"The best way to learn a language, Karolina, is to be immersed in it." Andre tried to take my hand, but I crossed my arms.

A sleek black car rolled up, with the word *Dacia* mounted on the front of it.

The valet opened the door. "*Doamnă,*" he said.

It took me a moment to realize he was waiting for me.

"After you," Andre said.

"I can't remember the word for thank you," I said as the driver took our bags and handed Andre the keys.

"*Mulţumesc,*" Andre said. He got into the seat and slid his hands lovingly over the steering wheel. "Hello, gorgeous." He turned the key and purred when the engine revved to life. We roared onto the speedway where a large arch glowed in the distance at the center of a roundabout clustered with trees.

"What type of car is this?" I asked.

"It's a 2014 Dacia 1300 concept," he said. "It's made in Romania. I try to drive a car that's made in the country I'm visiting."

I wondered how many countries his work had carried him to. "I'm excited to see my family's homeland," I said.

"I'm glad I could show it to you," he said.

Too nice. He was looking at me the way he had in the dorm. The dash clock read *4:30 a.m.*, only a few more hours until sunrise. We passed under a pedway connecting a cluster of stark buildings which shadowed the dead area of Ceausescu's rule. The road brightened deeper into the capital. I turned to the window and watched the lights of the city blur by like falling snow among the people. "Why are there so many pedestrians still out?" I asked.

"You're in Europe's party capital, little vampy. The bars close at six in the morning here." He jerked the car. An oncoming car glanced by us and blared its horn.

"The city isn't what I expected," I said, and rolled down the window, letting the dance music from the streets fill the car. Andre turned down a narrow road, laced with historical stone buildings, which soon turned into restaurants and nightclubs. I studied the architecture. Some buildings were medieval, with high pitches and carvings of wolves or angels. Others were midcentury modern. The blend of old and new was exciting, like I too could build on what once was. I loved Romania for that promise.

Andre swerved again to avoid a pothole. Once straight in the road, he rolled down his window, and hung his palm out into the rush of the oncoming air. His dark locks blew back, and he rested his head against the seat. He relaxed in the motion of the rushing wind. I decided, in this moment, he was in love with Romania.

We turned down a crumbling cobblestone street and stopped outside the doors of a restaurant. The sign read *Rosu Foame*. I leaned over him to look at the building. It was made of ancient gray stone, with windowpanes in an iron cross pattern. The candles inside danced in the restaurant windows with the pulse of the music.

"It's our check point," he said. "Let's head inside for a bite."

"I'm down," I said, ignoring the pun.

A man in a black jacket opened my door for me. When I got out, a red object stepped into the light of the restaurant. It was a woman in a short red dress and gray fur. Her black makeup was smudged, and she beat her fists wildly against the chest of the man she was with. He took her by her twiggy wrist and whispered in her ear.

I shortened the distance between the couple and myself, my hand almost close enough to rip the man off her.

I was jarred back toward the car.

Andre had taken my arm and guided me back to the car at freakish speed. I rolled my elbow out of his hold and faced him.

"She's a junkie," he said. "Look at the track marks on her arms. He's probably a concerned family member."

I looked at her again. She and the man walked into the darkness of the alleyway. She swung her arms as she walked, showing angry needle-like wounds scabbed over on her forearms. I cringed. My experience of living in Ottawa for university showed me that criminal drug rings were the sad reflection of any city that punished addicts as criminals, and Romania wouldn't be an exception.

"I didn't consider it was a family member," I said.

"Let's head in."

He gave me his arm and I took it, for formality. We crossed the threshold of the restaurant door, and I felt a drape of magic. The pungent odor of lavender slapped me in the face. I looked up above the door and saw foreign carvings at the top. The ceiling had more of the markings carved into the heavy timber columns.

The maître d' approached us and spoke Romanian to Andre.

"For two," Andre said.

The man took the hint and switched to English. "Right this way, please." He led us to a private booth in the back and gestured for me to be seated first.

"Now what?" I asked

"I meet my contact, and you eat. Relax," he said.

"You won't eat?"

"I'm a full vamp remember? I barely eat food."

"I feel sorry for you."

He lit up, and I'll admit it, he had a nice smile. Nice teeth, nice mouth…nice eyes. His gaze felt like velvet against my skin. I looked down. If he'd used his power again, I couldn't tell. His eyes were still blue, but I didn't know if he had more subtle talents. I hoped my spell was still in place.

"I'll relax if you tell me more about yourself," I said. "On the plane, I heard the call on the speaker. He called you *agent Smo—"*

"Shhhh. Don't say that here. There are others who may know that name." He leaned in. "Pretend we're on a date. Yes, he said agent," he whispered, audible only to my vampiric hearing.

I leaned in to whisper. "To be an agent means you are an emissary, P.I.s work on contract. An agent means you are a part of an organization."

He shuddered when my lips accidently touched his ear. "Careful, sweetheart. I've lost a lot of blood to you and I'm starving."

"You're wanting me to act like we're on a date. So, if you want me to play along, you have to give me a little more info to work with."

"I sparked the Dark Charm when I was eight," he whispered. "After that your uncle, Loukin, took me in. I've been his top man ever since."

"I see." So, my uncle and Andre were a part of the underground.

"Plus, he wouldn't have trusted just anyone to retrieve you." He attempted to meet my gaze again, but I wouldn't risk his compulsion, or my stomach fluttering. *Sunrise was coming*, I told myself.

"What? You're saying you're Mr. Impulse Control?" I played at a laugh, but it sounded breathy.

"Yes."

I remembered the trashed residence-room and wondered if he considered that restraint. "Doesn't say much for the rest of them," I said. "Why just one man?"

"Stealth." He leaned closer.

"What makes me so important?"

"Maybe if you're good, I'll tell you," he said.

"Maybe I'll be good if you tell me. And Andre, I can be *so* good." It was too far, but the words just flowed out.

"There's some information I can't share, no matter what the reward," he said and leaned back against the booth. "I think it's time we ordered, don't you?"

My face burned.

The waiter approached us and asked for our order.

"I'll try a glass of the house's special blend," Andre said.

"I'll have the merlot please."

"Excellent. I'll leave the menus with you and will be back in a moment with your drinks."

I felt the blood starting to leave my cheeks. "Can you help me with the menu?" I asked Andre.

"Of course, Miss Dal—" he stopped mid sentence. "What should I call you?"

I said the first thing that snapped to mind. "Dark Eyes."

"That's all you got?"

"Better than yours," I said.

He helped me find the Romanian translation of mushroom and bacon stuffed beef, *muschi poiana*, on the menu. Then he downed his wine in two gulps and set the glass on the table. When the waiter returned, Andre ordered a bottle of the house special for himself and placed my order.

I felt woozy from the thick lavender scent.

The waiter delivered my food and the bottle of wine for Andre. Andre poured a glass and downed the whole thing in one gulp. "I'll be back in a second," he said and disappeared into the back of the restaurant.

The room blurred. I hadn't had much wine. My food steamed in front of me. Two days of hunger turned in my stomach.

Halfway through my meal, my senses were still foggy.

A feeling of anger zinged through my chest. I gasped. It was Andre; with my new sense, I could feel it was him. Like before on the plane, I felt him in the distance. His emotions flooded into me. His rage balled inside of my chest making my heart beat in my throat. In the fleeting seconds I called to my new power to feel for more details, but the sensations washed blank. I composed myself, but the room spun through the haze of the lavender. I felt drunk.

Andre sat down just as I finished. He had a spare wine glass with him. He set the glass down beside his and filled them with the house special.

"Hey," he said and slid the second glass over to me. "I want you to try this wine, It's really good."

Buzzed, full of food, and warm with comfort, I took the glass. I held it to my nose, but all I could smell was lavender. I took a sip. An explosion of flavor washed over my tongue. If desperation and intoxication had a palate this was it, and they tasted *good.* Fangs burst through the roof of my mouth. Deep rattling hunger turned in my stomach, then disgust. The owner of the blood had a soul riddled with despair.

My hand trembled and let go of the glass. It fell and shattered on the table. Everyone turned to us for a moment. The waiter rushed over, but the blood inside the glass already soaked outward across the white tablecloth like a crimson ink blotch.

"I told you," I said, "I don't drink human blood."

"Come on, Karolina, you drank mine. How is this any different?"

The waiter placed a white napkin over the spill and

cleared away the glass.

"It is. What we did with each other was different. You can't say that it was equal to this," I said and gestured to the bottle.

"Aw, little vampy," he said. "What? Are you going to say what we did was special?"

"Yes, I tasted your soul."

He looked away. "So have a lot of girls, sweetheart, and to be honest, your flavor is a bit much."

"Where?" I whispered. "Where does the blood come from?"

He met my gaze.

A chill ran over my skin. The context of the situation set in. This restaurant had bottled human blood. The lavender. It covered up the smell of blood, vampiric senses and all. I called up my vampiric eyesight, but it was blurry. I concentrated, but all my senses were numbed. The markings. The restaurant was spelled. I peered at the closest table; it had a bottle marked the *house special* on it. I looked to another, then another. They were all the same. Outrage lit a fire inside me.

"Where?" I yelled.

Everyone stopped and stared at our table.

Andre looked back at me tight-lipped.

Fine. I leapt from my seat and headed for the kitchen, wobbling on my legs as the room teettered. A waiter appeared and blocked my path. My protective instinct took over. There may be people in there. They could be bleeding to death at this moment. He held up an arm to shove my shoulder back.

"Wrong move, buddy," I said.

He yelped as I broke his arm.

I charged for the door and kicked it open. It swung back on its hinges as I ran into the room. A man at the stove rushed over, Romanian erupting from his lips like rapid fire. I shoved past him into the back of the kitchen. Two skinny men were on the ground with their arms covered in bruises. They lay on the floor with needles in their arms, murmuring desperate praises to each other and encouragement to keep going. The needles were connected to a rubber tube which was placed in the top of a wine bottle.

The back door gaped open. More frail men and women stood in a line-up. They scratched the scabs on their forearms, while a husky man at the door handed them cash. The breeze from outside blew at the dirty clothes of the two on the ground, clinging the fabric against their soggy skin.

The house special.

I crossed the distance to the man with the cash and tapped him on the shoulder. He turned his head, and I punched him in the nose. Blood sprayed like a fire hydrant as he collapsed to the ground. I recognized some Romanian profanities that Grandpa Dalca used to let slip.

"Charming," I said.

I turned to the two on the ground and plucked the needles from their arms. Taking some nearby cloth napkins, I applied pressure. They yelled at me while I did, but they had lost too much blood to fight back.

A hand clamped down on my arm and hauled me upward; my back cracked, and I cried out in pain. The force of the grab took me off my feet and out the backdoor. I crashed through the people in the line-up on the way out.

Chapter Eight
Lightning Storm

I hit the cobblestone street with a thud. Rolling with the impact took some of the weight, but my shoulder still throbbed against the cool stone. The alleyway was dark. Its narrow street, with medieval buildings, which were once a royal palace, birthed concrete apartments like they had quaked through the crumbling rubble. The old town felt like a minotaur's maze. Thunder rumbled behind me, and the hairs on my neck stood erect.

I sprang to my feet to face my attacker, and the junkies from the line-up scattered. Andre walked toward me.

"What are you thinking? Are you out of your mind? Do you know how many Romanian vampire dignitaries just witnessed your little scene in there?" He closed the distance between us in a flash and clutched me by the scruff of my jacket. He was so angry; lines on his face appeared for the first time.

I swept my wrists out and down into his forearms. My blow broke his grasp and I stumbled back. "I would never prey off the sick and weak!"

"You could have gotten us killed in there, Karolina!" He shoved me. "Move! You blew our cover!"

"We need to call the police!"

“No!” His movement blurred. He snatched me around the waist. “We’re leaving, God damn it!”

I fought against him, but his grip was ironclad. He carried me kicking down the alleyway. While I struggled, a shadow crept across the cobblestone. I looked up to see the tail of a coat slip from sight on the roof ledge high above. On the eaves lining the roofs, I caught glimpses of silhouettes against the skyline.

“Andre…”

“I said no, Karolina!”

“*Andre*.” The alleyway gave way to a courtyard ahead. Gargoyles glowered down at us from the roofs above. Bodies stirred among the stone guardians.

“Andre!”

“What?”

“We’re being ambushed,” I whispered.

“I hope your little scene was worth it, Karolina.”

Men and women leapt from the rooftops baring fangs. The silence broke from the sounds of their clothing fluttering in the wind as they fell to the ground. A fluid stream of black lightning blazed past us and reverberated into the ground. Clumps of rock blasted into shards around us. I dodged a hunk of stone. The air filled with the charred smell of rock and sulfur.

Instead of the surrounding people gawking at the noise, the streets cleared. The shutters slapped closed on the apartments lining the square. Except for one. A face hovered in the window, with a look of quiet indifference before it disappeared. There was no help for us here.

The vampires rose from their crouched positions, untouched. Their black hollow gazes fixed on me as they walked toward us. Darkness crept up from the earth and air around them, like a menacing fog. The blackness spiraled into their hands and swelled.

I spun my head, looking for an opening in the crowd. Andre stood by my side. I didn't need to count our opponents to know it was too many. I clasped his hand and yanked him into a run. My arm jolted in its socket. He remained unmoved. I turned and hauled on him.

We were surrounded.

Andre swooped to a low crouch with his arms spread wide in front of me. His lips stripped back in a feral hiss. A crackling ball of violet lightning soared outward from him and immersed us in a large circular shield.

Our attackers each called up their own forms of magic. Black lightning crackled to life in the hands of some. Others swirled dark smoke back and forth in their palms. One man's face twisted as he morphed the dirt into gleaming chunks of dark metal. A threatening mace formed between his hands. It floated in front of him in a fluid motion.

A bolt of black lightning collided with our shield with a crash. More stones soared to the roofs.

Andre held one hand in a cupped position, in the other he molded a ball of violet electricity. Without warning, he dropped and rolled beyond the walls of the shield. He raised one hand unleashing the energy ball into a whip of lightning. It sizzled through the air at flashing speed, cutting through a cluster of vampires, and cracked out to the side. Their steaming halved bodies fell to the ground.

A torrent of attacks smashed into the orb around me.

One vampire threw a punch at Andre, but he sidestepped the vampire and cut off his head with a crack of his whip. Another charged toward Andre's chest. Andre's free hand flashed to the vamp's neck and crushed his windpipe.

The orb around me jarred to the side when Andre moved his empty cupped hand. I sprinted to stay within its protective shield.

The mob of vampires rushed to Andre and he disappeared from my view. His lightning whip cut through the air as black smoke and lightning shot in from the crowd. The stone square flashed like a continuous strobe light, filling with the smells of flesh, blood, and smoke.

A lonely bystander rushed into the square screaming "police" into a cellphone, only to be plucked up by a nearby vampire and devoured. The man's backpack fell to the ground, his American flag badge covered in his own blood.

Light reflected off the gleaming mace that floated from the horde. The vampire who had stared me down stepped from the crowd. He flashed forward, twisting his body to the side, and sent the mace smashing into the orb.

The shield jarred backward. I smashed into the ground. My head hit the stone. Warm liquid trickled down my neck, and a pungent iron smell turned my stomach. Through my spotty vision the shield appeared to be intact above my head, but the edge of the dome prickled against my upper thighs. My lower legs lay outside the shield, exposed.

The jagged points of the mace tore through my skin. My voice shrilled into a scream. I recoiled my legs. My nerves erupted in agony. Behind the safety of the shield, scarlet rippled in a pool around me.

Andre's scream echoed against the stone walls of the square.

He'd sacrificed himself for me. Guilt chewed its way up my stomach. A ribbon of blood pulsed from my legs.

The vampire with the mace sent it high into the air.

A switch deep inside of me flicked off, and in the moment of kill or be killed, my morality disappeared.

As the mace smashed down into the shield a second time the electricity dissipated around me. I rose on my mangled legs, as a molten ball of fire. The mace melted above me and steamed into the air. My attacker sucked more dark magic from the earth into his hands and hurled it my way, but the chunks of metal perished in the circle of flames.

I walked forward.

He retreated from the heat and attempted to form a shield of dark metallic debris around himself. He failed. The flames consumed his horrible face. My legs shook with strain and threatened to buckle from the agony of my wounds, but I continued, forcing the last bit of energy from my exsanguinated muscles. I stepped through him. His body evaporated. The putrid smell of burning flesh cloaked my face as I walked. I headed into the middle of the horde, where tiny flashes of violet lightning were still flaring.

The world around me grew hazy. Shadows started to creep in the corners of my eyes. More elemental attacks tainted with the dark charm soared into my flames. The blood flow at my ankles slowed to a trickle, but I kept moving. The smell of charred flesh got stronger and more rancid the farther I walked into the crowd. They dove over one another to escape my path.

My knees buckled. Total body weakness overtook me. My flames shrank inward with each passing second.

Andre stepped out from a heap of downed vampires. Blood seeped from his mouth. His shirt was shreds of fabric now. A chunk of flesh was missing from his torso, but raw angry threads of skin were slowly filling in. He'd fed off his attackers to heal. A path of bodies cut a line through the mob. They advanced like barracuda on the pocket of space their fallen comrades just created. Andre was progressing my way.

He fought savagely, tearing apart vampires with his hands. Purple electricity crackled around him. He shot out barbs of lightning sporadically. It sizzled as it pierced through the vampires, cutting them to pieces as they fell.

I crawled to him. The last of my fire diminished.

He fell to my side. The electricity surrounding him snapped up into a small sphere around us.

I threw my arms around his neck. "You were right, I'm sorry."

He wrapped an arm around my waist as his other hand surveyed my wounds. The Vampires beat against the tiny shield surrounding us. It flickered with each blow. Andre would be out of magic soon too.

"No. I'm sorry," he said, and bit down on his wrist. Blood dripped to the ground. He placed his wrist on my mouth, and I drank. Cracks of lightning struck the ground at the edge of the sphere, chipping away the stone street beneath us. The enraged faces of the vampires looked in, blocking out the view of the courtyard. They continued their assault on the shield. It buckled and shrank tighter around us.

"I was worried you'd die when the shield fell," he said and searched the back of my head with his fingers, making me wince. "I was trying to get to you."

"If I used my fire sooner, we may have gotten out of here." I hesitated. "You were right. My morals got us killed."

"Shushhh," he said. "You'll be okay." He held his wrist up to my mouth again. I started to drink but stopped after a few seconds. I would deplete his strength. I turned my gaze to the shield and the frightening faces outside it, my tongue thick with the rich flavor of his blood.

"How long can you hold it for?" I asked.

"A couple more minutes," he said.

I retreated from his wrist. The bleeding had clotted, and I felt some of my wounds beginning to close. If this really was the end, then I would embrace it. I looked up at Andre and our faces drew closer.

A ground shaking roar echoed out around us.

I yanked myself from Andre.

The vampires surrounding us screamed. They turned their backs to our shield, engaging in battle with a large beast that hurled through the crowd. With a deep snarl the beast circled around. It smashed through them, tearing and flattening them to the ground. Muddy-red liquid splattered against the cobblestone. The vampires closest to the orb were plucked from where they stood with horrifying screams. My nails dug into Andre's arms.

A ghostly calm ensued. The huffing of a snout

broke the placid stillness. Andre and I sat still under the shelter of the now fading shield. The beast prowled over to us crunching on the bodies of the fallen vampires. It stopped to snuff at a pile of rocks and guts. I peered through the pulsing wall of electricity at the creature.

It rose on its hinged hind legs, with disproportionately long arms and claws shaped like talons. It had the face of a wolf I recognized, a mouth too big and full of razor-sharp teeth. The beast's hairy leather skin started to transform.

I had witnessed this change before. *Roman.* I held my breath.

The body of the creature shifted like water, rippling as it changed form. Hair fell from its skin, leaving it smooth and silky. Its form shrank down to the size of a muscular man. He turned his back to us and walked to the corner of the square. He picked up clothes from the mouth of an alleyway in the far-away corner of the courtyard.

I rose from the fading shield.

Andre gently took my hand when I was halfway through.

I turned to him.

He raised an eyebrow at me. "Friend of yours?"

Chapter Nine
Three's Company

Orange and red streaked the dark blue sky. The amber light of the sun crept over the roofs of the courtyard, angling its rays onto the walls of the square. The naked man slipped on boxers, and then a pair of blue jeans from the pile of clothes. I would have known that olive-skinned ass anywhere. I walked toward him. My footsteps sounded like Velcro against the scarlet cobblestone. It reminded me of stomping cranberries at the Ottawa festival last year. Except it wasn't cranberries beneath me now. It was the blood of fifty men. There's no way Roman could have saved us, that he could even be here.

"Ro," I said.

Roman turned around, crunching on a bone beneath his feet. The low sound of sirens rang off in the distance. He assessed my wounds, traveling upward from the healing cuts on my legs, and stopping at my neck—where Andre's bite marks had scabbed over. He glowered at my throat. I shifted my hair to hide the marks.

Roman looked from my neck to over my shoulder. I felt Andre's presence approaching from behind. Roman gestured to me, to the bodies, to Andre. "What the *fuck,* Karo?"

"It's not what it looks like," I said.

"Oh, you must be the friend Karolina told me about," Andre said. His voice was cheery as he blustered between us and stuck out his hand to Roman. "The one she said I would love to meet."

Roman's face turned deadpan, then rebooted. "Nice to meet you, buddy," he said and clasped Andre's hand. They shook and Andre tried to take his hand back, but he couldn't get it out of Roman's grasp. With a tiny motion, Roman crushed Andre's hand.

Andre gasped. Both men jumped to action. The air flew from my lungs. Roman wound up to punch Andre in the face. Andre's other hand was inches from Roman's jaw. I did the only thing I could think of in a millisecond and jumped between them.

Andre's fist glanced off Roman's jaw as I landed on Roman's arm.

Roman's fist stopped the moment I entered proximity of the fight. He slipped his arm around me instead of punching Andre and plucked me free from the danger zone.

I placed both hands on his chest. I shoved at him, but it was like trying to budge a brick wall.

"Ro!" I shouted.

He carried me out of the way.

"Can we have a sec!"

He proceeded to drop me on the ground, but I wrapped my arms around his shoulders. "Ro, please!"

He stopped trying to yank me off him and I shifted my face to his, still holding him in my arms.

"Fine," he said.

I guided him back toward the privacy of the mouth of an alleyway. Andre cursed in the background. I looked to him for a moment and saw his hand hanging limp and deformed. I turned to Roman.

"Make sure you kids make it quick!" Andre's voiced echoed into the alley. "We have to get out of here!"

"What are you doing here, Ro? How did you find me?"

"I tracked your scent to the airport, Karo. An air flight attendant confirmed a couple left a pile of bodies behind them when they boarded a private flight to Romania."

"You tracked my scent all the way here? You realize that's crazy, right? I'm not going to complain about you saving us, but you just showed up and slaughtered fifty vampires. How the hell did you hide your strength all our lives?

"*Us*. What the hell, Karo. Who the hell is that guy? And what do you think you're doing? You could have died today. I told you going after the address in Russia was extremely dangerous, so you just go charging off by yourself?"

"It was my only lead and you know it. I couldn't stay in Canada."

"So, you thought you'd run off alone, or with a stranger? Who is he, Karo?"

"He was hired by my uncle, Loukin, to find me."

"Nabakov," he said. "So, you know about him now."

I hovered my face close to his. "I know a lot of things now, Roman." I made a mental note of my father's family name.

"Not enough."

"Then tell me."

"No. The more I tell you, the more you'll go

running off into trouble."

"I'm a big girl, Roman; I can choose to run into trouble if I want to."

He put his hands on my shoulders and looked me in the eyes. "Karo, these people aren't like you. They're killers. They feed off people for fun. If you fed off people last night, I understand you only did what you had to."

"No! I would never feed off a human."

"You might want to wipe the blood from your mouth, before you say that."

I wiped my lips. "It's not what you think. I didn't drink human blood." I rushed the words out without thinking.

He froze. "Whose blood is it?" His expression darkened. "Is it his?"

I averted my gaze.

He held my face gruffly in his hands. "Did you let him drink from you?"

"We needed to heal," I said.

His grip tightened. "Did you feed off each other?"

I shoved him away. "It's not a big deal, Ro. It's something all vampires do. You wouldn't understand."

Roman walked up beside me.

I turned my head to avoid his gaze, but it still burned into my side.

"I understand a lot more than you think, Karolina," he said and turned to the courtyard. "You have no idea what you've done."

I leaned back against the stone wall and took a long, deep breath. My body shivered against the dewy stone. I knew what I had done; I killed people tonight. I told myself it was self-defense; it was acceptable. But the truth was, taking another life, vampire or not, could have sparked the Dark Charm. Roman's words played in my head. *You have no idea what you've done*. It was true. Andre and I shared a type of magic now. I just didn't know what that power was yet.

I turned the corner and walked back into the square. Roman was watching the entrance from the street. Andre sat crouched sucking blood out of a fallen vampire. His crushed hand had morphed back to form. In a sick way, I had to commend him. It'd never occurred to me to drink from a corpse, nor could I compel myself to do it.

The sunlight angled into the courtyard just enough to touch the ground. The bodies of the vampire mob burst into dust upon the contact of the sun, like cherry bombs going off all around us. Andre gagged. The vampire he had been feeding on had turned to sand within his hands. He spat ash out of his mouth. Roman laughed, but he was cut short by the approaching sound of sirens.

"We have to get out of here," I said.

Andre got to his feet. "It was nice to meet you, poochie. We'll be leaving now!"

"No, Andre. From now on, where I go he goes." I turned to Roman. "That is, if you want to come with us?"

"I'm a man of my word, but we gotta ditch the leech," Roman said.

"No. We need him. He's been hired to take me to my uncle." They opened their mouths to protest, but I cut them off. "Whether you like it or not, we have no time. I'm calling the shots now. Both of you seem to have an agenda, and if you don't want me going rogue, then you'll do what I say. The way I see it, if one of you tries to force me into his plan, you'll be stopped by the other. So, unless you want me sneaking away while the two of you have a showdown, we're doing things my way."

"Well, Miss Dalca. I'm impressed," Andre said.

Roman glared at me.

Flashing lights turned the corner of the square. The three of us sprinted out of sight down the alleyway to the restaurant. Andre led us around the side of the building. I tensed and called up my senses, ready for an attack. Andre handed the keys and some Romanian bills to the valet just about to check off shift. We took cover in the restaurant entrance. The wait wasn't long, but there was nothing like multiple attempts on a lady's life to put a sense of urgency in her step.

The car rolled up.

Andre jumped in the driver's side and left Roman and me standing in front of the one remaining seat.

"Just sit in my lap, Karo," Roman said. He sat down in the seat and parted his legs for me to sit between them. I sat down and leaned back against his chest. He was so warm. After the events of the evening, I felt like I could sink right into him. Roman closed the car door and buckled the seat belt across my hips.

Andre shifted the car into gear and jerked the vehicle onto the road, making Roman's head smack against the glass of the window. The engine thundered. Our bodies pressed into the seat as the buildings streamed by.

"Pothole," Andre said.

"I'm sure," said Roman.

Andre had no tender caress for the Dacia this drive.

I had the feeling Andre was fickle with his women, cars included. A prickling feeling crept off him and over the seat to my leg. I concentrated and explored my new sense, the burning sensation tingling against my skin intensely. I focused on what emotion made me feel that way. Anger…or was it jealously? It halted. I probed outward only to feel the wall in place again.

"We need a place to hide. Any ideas?" Andre asked.

So far, I managed not to endanger the last remaining member of my mother's family, but I was out of options. "Just for a few hours?"

"Sure," Andre said.

"Auntie Miruna's house."

"Where is it?"

"Constanta, on the Black Sea," Roman said.

I gave Andre the address. "Ro, when you took down all those vampires, how did their magic not hurt you?"

"Dark magic doesn't work on werewolves."

"Really?" I asked.

"Yeah. Only earth magic can work on werewolves, since we're of the earth," he said and looked out at the clay colored hills as they rolled by. They were part of a sprawling burnt orange ocean, but still a reminder of the pine mounds back home.

"Don't forget about light magic, Poochie," Andre said.

"What do you mean?" I asked.

"Told you, princess, I'm not all bad. I've sparked the Light and Dark Charm."

"Trying to say you can take me?" Roman asked Andre.

"So," I said, "the Earth Charm and Light Charm are the only elements which can affect you? Why would the magic of your own people be your weakness?"

"It prevents corruption," Roman said. "Those in the pack born without the wolf gene keep us in check. Since I was born a wolf, I can't use magic the same way you do, Karo."

"Huh." It made sense. If Roman had the Charm like I did, I would have felt it a long time ago. His power lay in his strength. Strength even Andre, a full vampire, couldn't overpower. But Andre had the Light Charm.

I analyzed the details of the attack. The magical assaults were all shades of black, but Andre's magic had been dark purple. I hadn't thought of the detail until now. Andre had completed a selfless act so pure; he'd sparked the Light Charm. I couldn't imagine him capable of it. Everything he'd done so far had been for personal gain, including saving my life.

"Well," I said. "I'm going to get some sleep while I have the chance."

Roman's hand slid up and down my arm. "Get some rest."

More waves of sensation traveled through the air from Andre. I couldn't tell if it burned or if it was just so cold it burned. I ignored the feelings and closed my eyes. I rested in the warmth of Roman's body. "Ro," I said.

"Yeah?"

"What happened with the police in Canada? Is there a warrant for my arrest?" I asked.

"You're wanted now, Karo. They'll arrest you if you go back."

****

The car jostled me awake. The landscape flashed before me. High cliffs emerged from coral-colored sand, speckled with rocks and weeds. The mounds of earth gave way to patches of arid greenery at the base. A white bird flew parallel to the hills, its chalk feathers reflecting the warm hues of the rock. We were closer to the coast.

I tilted my head back and let the sun warm my face. Through my eye lashes I caught another reflection in the car's side mirror. I locked eyes with Andre. He had watched me within the angle of the mirror. I averted my gaze and straightened in my seat. Roman stretched his arms above his head as I adjusted.

"How long was I out for?" I asked.

"Whole ride," Roman said.

"We'll be arriving at Constanta, in fifteen," Andre said.

We turned off the long desert highway. Wind rattled the trees, the moist coast air painting the surrounding land in evergreens and palms. The Dacia cruised into downtown Constanta, engine warm and purring after the highway drive. The sun shone against the church domes and steeples. Aqua blue water sparkled in the sun behind the city skyline. Concrete buildings alternated between historical manors, like they'd been dropped from the sky on the old city. Like the fairy-tale which once was, would slowly be stomped out.

"The old stuff is gorgeous," Roman whispered.

"I know," I said.

Andre turned the car down the sharp corners of the street. We passed the city center and headed closer to the edge of the harbor. We rolled up to a white and red stone manor. It had large white columns which extended skyward three stories. Atop the columns sat gray stone lions. They didn't look real, but rather felt so real I waited for them to stir. It was the famous Lion House, an old masonic temple.

"Great Auntie Miruna lives here?" I asked.

"No," Andre said, "The Lion House was for the men. She's across the street."

I looked to the left and saw a white stone mansion with opera style balconies at every window. The railings were carved stone, making every deep bay window look like an ornate cloud. The manor was four stories high, giving the top floor a view of the ocean over the Lion House.

Andre turned off the car and popped the trunk.

I sat humbled for a moment. Then clicked off the seat belt. Powdery white stairs led to a double door entrance. Each step I ascended presented another question. *Would she know me? Would she turn me away?* On the top step the doorbell seemed daunting, but I rang it anyway.

Roman and Andre's footsteps followed me up the stairs.

I stood up straight and hit the button again. My heartrate spiked at the sound of movement inside.

Chapter Ten
Aunt Miruna Albesuc

One of the large doors swung open. A white-haired woman with olive skin stood tall in the threshold of her home. She gazed at the three of us, then focused on me. Her face lit with a warm smile that I never expected to see again. It was the smile that I so often saw on my mother. My eyes brimmed with tears as Great Auntie Miruna threw her arms around me.

When she backed off, she straightened me out in front of her. "You have the taint of death around you, child. Quick, come in."

She ushered us through the door, and I almost lost my footing when I passed through a humming wall of power at the threshold. Once inside her foyer, I looked up above the doorframe. It was the most ornate magical carving I ever saw. The plaque was wood with swirling lines of gold laid into it. Whoever had made the protection ward spent weeks on its creation. I never felt a threshold so guarded before.

Miruna took my hand. She wore her hair secured back in an orderly fashion, and her clothes were modest and functional. The same principal was applied to her home. It was tidy and well kept, but the antique furniture wasn't gaudy or overindulgent. I wondered how a woman of her age managed to keep up with all the housework.

“I’m so happy to see you,” I said.

She squeezed my hand. “I always saw you in my dreams.” Her expression turned troubled. “You have a darkness around you, my child. What battle did you enter which forced you to take lives?”

I froze. “Vampires attacked us, ones that are working for someone who wants me dead. Probably the same person who sent Shadow Forged to our house in Canada.” I braced myself. “Mama’s dead.”

She nodded and closed her eyes. Then spoke in Romanian and crossed herself.

“Did you know?” I asked her.

“Your mother visited me in a dream,” she said. “She asked me to look out for you. Around her head was a crown of light. I hoped it wasn’t the case, but it seems her spirit came to say goodbye.”

Her words plucked a cord of envy. Mama always said Miruna was the most powerful white witch she’d known; it could be why she’d been contacted by Mama’s spirit and I hadn’t. Miruna always seemed like a folk tale to me, a heroine I heard about but never met. Now, she stood in front of me.

“I’m sorry I didn’t call to tell you sooner.”

“No, I’m sorry, child. If anyone tries to take your life, you fight, Karolina. You are a Dalca! You fight till your dying breath.” She slammed her fist on the front hall table, making Andre and Roman jump.

“I promise.”

It felt good to have another person in my corner—even if it was a ninety-plus woman who couldn’t fight anymore. I just hoped we had gotten lost quickly enough from Bucharest, so no vampires could have trailed us here.

"Come to the kitchen. Let me fix the three of you some lunch and tea."

"Thank you, Mrs. Albesuc," Roman said.

Andre dropped our bags by the front hall table. Miruna squinted at his chest as she walked by. Her scowl faded by the time we got to the kitchen. She filled a copper kettle and placed it on the stove. I took some heavy cooking platters out of the fridge and put them into the oven to help her, but she smacked my hands away. We sat down. The room flooded with a meaty spice aroma which made my mouth water.

"Now." She took the squealing kettle off the stove. "You must be Roman."

"Yes Ma'am," he said.

"You have your father's eyes," she said. "And you?" she asked Andre. "Who is this stranger accompanying my niece?"

"Andre, Mrs. Albesuc."

"Andre who? It's Miss, I never married."

"Andre Zima, Ms. Albesuc."

Miruna placed a hand on her heart and sucked in a breath. She patted him on the shoulder. He took the teacup from her outstretched hand, and she turned his chin to her face. "Bless you, child. May you come back to us one day."

Andre swallowed his tea, along with any facial expression which could reveal what Miruna spoke about.

She sat down and the small chat began. I dipped a cookie in my tea. A hunk landed on my shirt and I flicked back my hair to wipe myself clean. I felt the weight of Miruna's gaze on my neck. A tiny smile formed on her lips.

"Pardon me, Ms. Albesuc, for speaking about business so soon," Andre said, "but we're under pursuit. I have been charged with the task of taking Karolina to her uncle in Kislovodsk. We require the late Ms. Dalca's birth-certificate to prove Karolina's identity."

Kislovodsk was the same city on the address from my box. If it wasn't the address Mama had intended me receive sanctuary at, it was close.

"What makes you think I have it?" Miruna asked.

"Again, please excuse my direct demeanor. We know Ms. Dalca fled Romania unexpectedly from this location, shortly after Karolina was born."

The bastard. He knew it was here all along.

"I do not tell lies," she said. "So, I will tell you. But I will also state my opinion on the matter. Karolina, I do have your mother's birth certificate, but I do not think you should go. In Russia there are things your mother made an oath to protect you from. You yourself said there have already been attempts on your life." She paused. "But if you, Karolina Dalca, want to discover your birthright, then I will not stop you."

"What do you mean, discover my birthright?"

"It is not for me to tell, child. Your father's family is yours to discover. But they are not my family. And you have been forewarned."

Seeing my aunt had warmed my heart more than I imagined, but deep inside of me was a void. A void which yearned to know where the other half of me was derived from. I wondered what features I had from my father's side. If they saw me, would they know me like she had? There was also the issue of my Fire Charm. I needed to learn more control. I couldn't continue to live my life afraid of my own powers.

"I'm sorry, Auntie. I have to go."

She took a deep breath and nodded. "Then the three of you will rest here before you set out in the morning. This is still our family home, Karolina, and you are expected to come here any time you please."

"Thank you."

"Now let me see your legs. They're still injured." She held out her hands expectantly.

"How can you tell?"

"From the flow of your aura. All living things have energy, a life force, and of course a soul." She gestured to her stomach, her head, and her heart.

"Body, mind, and soul," Andre said.

"When you become a skilled practitioner of light magic, child, you will start to see the essence of life, and when you're ready, the soul." She rolled up her sleeves. "Now, let me see those legs."

I laid my legs across her lap.

She rubbed her hands together like she tried to warm them and then hovered them above me. She didn't meditate or take a moment to call her magic forth; it just came. The second she put her hands over my legs, her palms glowed with white light. It didn't tingle like dark magic, or Andre's mix of light and dark. It just felt warm, like the sun's rays on my skin.

She took her hands away and the aching pain I had tried to ignore drifted away.

"That's amazing!" I lifted my legs back and inspected them.

"Your turn." She faced Andre.

"Oh." He held up his hands and shook his head. "My hand is completely healed. No need."

"That's not where you are injured, and if you are

traveling with Karolina, you need to be well."

Roman laughed as Andre recoiled from her approaching hands.

Andre searched for a way around her. "I feel fine, Ma'am, I swear." He almost made it out of his seat, but she was a spry old thing—and managed to block his path. She planted her hands on his chest, and the breath left his lungs. His eyes grew wide as her hands lit up with light again. He leaned back, breathing rapid and hitched. Avoiding my eyes, he stared at the ceiling. She backed away and he leaned forward against the table.

"There. That wasn't so bad," she said.

"Yeah," Andre said. "Thanks." He looked as pale as Miruna's china.

I looked at Roman; he made no attempts to hide his amusement. "You just wait until it's your turn," I said.

"I'm a wolf, Karo," he said. "I heal myself."

Miruna put a steaming plate of stew and dumplings on the table. The afternoon was full of laughter and stories of our family history. I learned Albesuc was Romanian for 'White.' My grandmother's family were known throughout Romanian history for their abilities in light magic. Miruna's manor had always been our family home. Before my grandparents and my mother fled to Canada, they lived here. In fact, this house was how my grandparents had met. Grandpa Dalca used to come and go from the Lion House across the street. Grandma Dalca used to watch him every time from her balcony, until one day he had finally gathered enough courage to knock on her door. They'd been together ever since.

The light in the kitchen window glowed orange. Sunlight slowly slipped away along the horizon as

Roman washed the dishes. He always had to be first, and tonight he beat me to dish duty as his victory.

Andre picked over his food. At first, I worried whatever Miruna had done to Andre made him sick, but after an hour he started to steady. Looking less pale, he sat rigid in his chair, tapping his fingers against the wood as he watched the sky darken. Any suggestions of him eating more was a moot point. He needed blood to satiate his hunger. The rich flavor of caramel slid into my mind. A warm rush flared up from my stomach.

Andre's gaze flicked up to mine.

"Well the sun's down," Roman said. "You should get some rest for tomorrow." He found the dishcloth and started to dry the dishes.

"I'm a vampire, not a two-year-old," I said.

Miruna gestured to the hallway door. "Yes, but you're also half gypsy, and we have much to talk about. Let me show you to your room, and I'll get your mother's birth certificate."

"Sounds great," I said.

Miruna paused. "Oh Roman, you'll be in the bedroom at the foot of the stairs." Then she turned to Andre. "You'll be at the farthest end of the hall."

"Don't worry, Ms. Albesuc," Andre said, "I'll be on my best behavior."

She took my hand and led me into the hallway. I picked up my pack on the way to the stairs. The dark hardwood creaked under our steps. We climbed the staircase. Pictures of all the Albesucs before us loomed down at me as my hand glided along the polished banister.

The room she assigned me faced the inner city. The lights of the concrete buildings now burned like lanterns in the night. The room was full of wooden trunks and bookcases. A canopy bed sat against the wall. The covers and draping were all white lace, which reminded me of a young girl's bedroom.

"It was your mother's room," Miruna said.

I ran my fingers over the bed covers. "It's beautiful. Exactly what I would have pictured."

She walked to the wooden trunk at the foot of the bed. She opened it, exposing large carvings on its lid. I searched my pack, brought out the wooden box, and examined it.

"The markings are the same."

"Yes, your grandmother and I had the same teacher," she said.

"Your mother?"

She nodded. "The way each family learns and practices their Charm is different." Her hand traced the carvings on the trunk lid. "You will be able to tell when it's our family's light or earth magic from the similarity in the markings." She rummaged through the trunk and found a book. "It's handed down to the next generation." She snapped the trunk lid shut and held it up. "When they're ready."

The book was covered in the same markings as the trunk and box, with a leather string wound around it.

"Seems to be a theme here," I said.

"It's protected. Only our family can remove the string."

Before my escapade, I would have laughed. But after the pain Andre's book had inflicted on me, I knew anything was possible. "What will it do to them?"

"A person may try to remove the string which binds it." She grinned. "But they will change their mind before they touch it."

"I see." It was much nicer than the spell on my emergency box. "What is the book about?"

"It's a book of the Light Charm, Karolina. A family heirloom. I have no use for it anymore, and it seems you could do with a little more strength for your journey." She handed it to me.

"But I don't have the Light Charm."

"Yes, you do," she said. "You started to develop it at birth. You were always such a loving, passionate little girl. All you must do is invoke it. Your mother's birth certificate is inside." She left the room and closed the door behind her.

Damn. Mama was bad for talking in gypsy riddles. She must have learned it from Miruna. I sat down on the trunk and unwound the security string. I flipped open the front cover. A drawing of an intricate sun was on the first page. Underneath it was a saying in Romanian beautifully handwritten, *O stea poate deveni un soare sub presiunea întunericului.*

I would have known it spelled backward. My mother always said the phrase to me as a child. It was her catch phrase when she wanted me to have the courage to follow my own heart.

"A star becomes a sun, under the pressure of darkness," I said.

One day, I ran home from school in tears after the new kid got ambushed after school. Max, the child whose parents dressed him in ripped jeans and worn sneakers, had to outdo the others and hit him in the head with a rock. They all scattered and ran home. Except the new kid. I had hobbled him home to his parents.

I had begged Mama to call the bullies' parents. She asked me what I did when the beating transpired. I was so angry that she put the responsibility on my shoulders. When I told her I stood by, she said the phrase to me again. When I still didn't understand she told me to be my own hero. Inside of all of us was the potential for greatness—all it took was a change in perspective. When I cried and told her I was afraid, she nodded and said, "You can burn brighter than they can, if you have to."

In a moment, my six-year-old self decided I would be a police officer one day. I would protect people. When I got to high school and reflected again, I decided her parenting skills were seriously lacking. Looking back now, I understood what she tried to groom me for. She wanted to give me the skills to stand up to the type of people who existed in the undergrounds—where the murder of innocent people was the byproduct of their crime rings.

"*O stea poate deveni un soare sub presiunea întunericului,*" I said. My attempt at a Romanian accent butchered the phrase, but hearing the words spoken aloud made me feel like Mama was here again, like anything was possible. Sparking the Light Charm could be possible.

I turned the page. The was no page numbers or table of contents. Some of the pages had only markings, carvings which when drawn had a magical purpose. The first few pages explained the dynamics of light magic. Its purpose to defend, heal, or protect. The essence of light magic came from the human will to protect, love, and create. I already knew these principals, but eventually I got to the coveted material.

I read in detail the various spells used with the Light Charm: one of which was used to protect this house. Light wards were the strongest forms of protection on a dwelling. They were not easily broken and could only be dismantled by another light user. Foreboding reputation aside, this is how Miruna must have stayed safe all these years.

The grandfather clock chimed for the third time. I thought it was broken, but when I looked at the hands, I realized three hours had elapsed without me noticing. I squandered the opportunity to bank sleep while I could, and I still hadn't learned how to invoke the Light Charm. I flipped my way through to the end. It was all just more spells.

Getting up felt painful for my stiff muscles. I placed my new book into my pack and got into bed. A floral nightgown had been folded underneath the covers for me. In the darkness, I contemplated hypothetical ways I could try to spark the Light Charm, none of which would be successful, since preplanned acts were never genuine and riddled with self-interest. In my case, I was full-fledged desperate for the Light Charm.

Light magic could be stronger than any other magic a person could possess. I think it gave truth to the principal 'love is stronger than hate,' which one innately knew. Full vampires were stronger than I was. Roman was stronger than any vampire. The only way I could get an edge was through magic. Conundrum. How could I spark the Light Charm? Back to the beginning I circled.

I rolled over and got tangled in the sheets. How could Andre have sparked it and not me?

My blood rushed at the thought of his name.

Hunger turned in my stomach. My heartbeat pulsed in my ears. *No*, I told myself. It was just his nighttime proximity, made worse since the blood exchange. At sunrise it would go away. *Learn to ignore it*. I ran my hand down my stomach restlessly, and my skin ignited. There was another way to control my appetite. My hand trailed along my thigh. The way Andre had looked at me in the car popped into my head. *No, no. Don't think about that*. Our encounter in the dorm flooded into my memory.

There was a small creak in the hallway. I summed up my new sense and propelled it outward. I felt Andre's presence at the far end of the hall, around his door. I gulped. I felt further. Andre's emotions immersed me. He was in his own personal hell. A crushing pain erupted in my chest, the type of pain I felt when Mama died. My body heated, and I had an all-consuming need for someone, anyone—anything—to take the pain away. A cold force blew across the room and slammed into me, knocking me back into my pillow.

The sensations were gone.

I shot up to a sitting position. Panting and covered with sweat. My own feelings returned to my body. I wiped my hair from my face, and my breathing started to slow. Whatever Miruna had attempted to heal in Andre, she needed to go back for a second round. I flipped off the covers and touched a foot to the ground. If I check on him, would he let me in? The phenomenon of the cold wall wasn't new. He had the advantage of knowing how to shut me out, while I was still trying to understand our new bond. Whatever he felt, he wanted to go through it alone.

I relaxed, focusing on the feeling of home the Albesuc house gave me. My chest soon felt heavy. I drifted into the dreamy stage of consciousness just before sleep. As my mind rolled into blankness, the floorboards creaked at the foot of the stairs.

"We can't let her go," Roman whispered.

A female voice whispered back. I jerked. *Wake up*. I fought against the hazy paralysis of sleep. *Wake up*. In my head my arms moved as I struggled out of the bed, but physically my body relaxed further against the soft sheets. My breathing slowed, and my thoughts blurred into darkness. I slipped into a deep imageless sleep.

Chapter Eleven
The Ocean's Call

"Coff-ee…" I grumbled my best zombie impression as my feet shuffled across the floor. Miruna called out something from the sunroom. I felt my way around the kitchen and squinted against the morning sun. Coffee ran down my hand when I attempted to pour it into a mug. I unstuck one of my eyelids which had been cemented together. With the vision of both eyes, I managed to get my coffee in the cup this time. On my way to see Miruna I lifted a pastry off a platter.

"Where are the men?" I asked and sank onto the couch beside her while she read the newspaper. I stuffed a piece of coffee-soaked pastry into my mouth.

"Outside, doing some chores for me."

I choked on some coffee. She really was a white witch if she had managed to get Roman and Andre working together. "Do you have anyone to help you with the chores regularly?"

"There is a young lady who comes to help me with the cleaning."

"If I was staying…I could help you with the house."

"It's the price I paid, Karolina, for not having children."

"What do to you mean?"

She put down her paper and looked across the

street to the Lion House. "Your grandma wasn't the only one who loved a man."

I looked at the stone lions staring down at us. "He used to come and go from the Lion House too?"

She nodded. "I was young and ambitious. When he first called on me, I turned him away. It just made him love me more. I had plans, Karolina, and I chose power over love."

I couldn't bear the sadness in her eyes. "You're known to be the strongest white witch in Romania. I would say you accomplished a lot."

"It's true. I took the path less traveled by, and I've saved a lot of lives." She looked back to the Lion House. "But my warrior man and I vowed we would save those lives *together*. He was killed before we married."

"I'm so sorry," I said. "How did he die?"

"Protecting our neighbors from members of a Russian vampire gang passing through the city."

This story was getting worse and worse. Another loved one claimed by the underground. The conflicts between supernatural societies was the main cause of death for our kind. Whether they were vampire or human, it was all the same, needless death. My hands felt cold.

Like she had read my mind, her mood switched to cheery. "Your grandma, on the other hand, married right away. She was devoted to her home life and had your mother. Her earth magic was exceptional. She even opened up an apothecary and sold Charmed medicine."

"They didn't use light magic?" I wondered why I'd never seen Mama use it.

"It takes an extreme act of sacrifice to trigger the

Light Charm. It is the dark circumstance of war which puts people in such a position. One must be brave enough to take a stand against the destruction it breeds."

I leaned in. "When you make that choice, you invoke it?"

She nodded. "Your mother and grandma were never exposed to a situation where such a choice would be forced."

I remembered Grandpa's teachings over all those years. "Grandpa was the warrior in our family, not Mama and Grandma."

She held up a finger. "But the Light Charm was always in them, Karolina. It's in everyone from the moment they're born. It's important to know all its teachings. Should you ever be faced with a choice, you'll make the right one."

A star becomes a sun, under the pressure of darkness. My family made sure their children were raised to make the noble choice, should they be faced with such atrocities.

"Shit." I held my forehead in my hands. "I'll never spark it, because I want to."

"So, you are resolved to go to Russia?"

I nodded.

Her eyes glistened. "And so, we will see, child. If you are like me, or if you are like your mother. There is no shame in either one."

"And Grandma?"

She laughed. "You have a good heart, child, but you have too much fire in your soul to be her image."

"Maybe I won't have to choose between love and power."

"Hmmm," she said. "You would be original indeed."

I couldn't remember a time when I felt the type of love Miruna had. Eternal love. The kind which keeps one going when one is ninety and alone. Roman and I had a friendship built on a platonic love, with desire as a recent addition, but its title was still one I couldn't place.

Miruna stared at me. "It's not too late. You and Roman could always choose to stay here."

The door hinges squeaked in the front hall. Roman and Andre walked into the hallway, shirtless and covered in sweat.

"You owe me a bottle of vodka," Andre said and kicked off his shoes.

"The only reason you beat me was because you used your magic," Roman said. "I would like to see how you match against me without it."

Miruna got up off the couch. "Gentlemen, is the wall at the back of the house reinforced?"

"Yes Ma'am," Roman said and interlocked his hands against his belt buckle. His dirty jeans hung low, showing off the lower curve of his abdomen.

"I added some rebar into the concrete mix. It could withstand any attack thrown at it now," Andre said. He leaned against the doorway and his thick shoulder muscles glistened in the window's sunbeam.

Miruna had a point—there is merit in the idea of staying put and enjoying my present company.

"I'm glad you got the job done so quickly," Miruna said.

"Nothing like a little healthy competition," Andre said and smacked Roman on the back.

"Thank you for helping an old woman." On the way out of the room she glanced over her shoulder. "Oh, Karolina. I thought about your dilemma."

I stood to join them.

"Maybe there is another drawing you forward on your journey." She left the room. I realized her loafers and shawl were just camouflage; she was a devious old woman.

"What's that about?" Roman asked.

"Nothing."

Andre cracked his neck. "We've been here too long. Do you have the certificate?"

I nodded.

"Good," he said. "We'll head back to Bucharest, hop on a plane, and mission complete."

"No," I said.

Andre looked down at me. "What do you mean?"

"We almost lost our lives back in Bucharest," I said. "They'll be looking for us now, and even with Roman's strength, it's not worth risking another fight. From what I've learned about magic, tracking spells are ineffective over water. Whoever is sending the vampires must be tracking us. There's no way they could have known where you and I were so quickly after our flight. I'm thinking they knew our general vicinity, so when I blew our cover, they knew it was us."

"So?" Andre asked.

"So, we go by boat," I said.

Andre's face lost the color he'd managed to gain overnight. "We don't have a boat, Karolina. It's a stupid idea."

Roman shoved Andre. "It makes perfect sense."

"Down, dog," Andre said. "If you want to follow the lead of a woman who can't even keep her coffee in her cup, fine by me."

I looked down. Not only was I still wearing the cute little floral nightgown, the left side was spotted in coffee.

"At least I'm wearing clothes," I said. "I'm going to get dressed, and if you want to come with us to Russia you better be ready by the time I'm at the door."

Up the stairs and in the privacy of my room, I gave into the smile I held back downstairs. Mission complete meant I would meet my uncle Loukin. Warnings from Miruna aside, Loukin had gone to a lot of trouble deploying his top man to locate and escort me home untouched. I refused to believe the circumstance of our meeting could be completely disastrous.

I triple-checked my pack and all my belongings and rifled through my clothes. I decided meeting Loukin was a formal occasion and picked a tight shirt of layered mauve and black lace. For the rest of my outfit, jeans would have to do. I clutched my necklace and opened the door.

The men had both managed quick showers and had their stuff ready on time. My guess at the formality may have been right, as Andre had opted for a collared shirt. Miruna stood by them, and when I got closer, she stretched her arms out to me.

"If you change your mind at any time, just come home." She kissed my forehead. "If not, remember you are Dalca *and* Albesuc."

"Thank you. Either way, I know I will see you soon," I said.

She turned toward Roman and Andre. "Take good

care of my niece." Then she crossed herself with her index and pinkie finger pointed down. "Grace be with you." A faint glow of white light flooded out over the three of us.

We thanked Miruna for her hospitality and headed out the door. As I crossed the threshold, I felt the hum of power again. From what I learned from the book, once invited into her home the ward allowed us entry. Until Miruna rescinded our invitation, we could enter as we pleased. When we got to the car, Roman walked to the passenger's side and I braced myself for another awkward ride.

Andre held up the keys and looked at Roman. "What? Too eager to share a seat to ask me to drive?"

Roman ignored him and got in the car, sitting in the sharing-a-seat position we'd developed. He wrapped his arms around my waist, but then ran a hand down my thigh when Andre started the car.

"Ro," I whispered and swatted his hand away.

He played at an innocent smile in the side mirror and held up his hands.

"How long to the harbor?" I asked.

Andre checked the rearview mirror. "About five."

"Okay. Do we know what we're doing for a boat?"

"I made a call. There's a fishing boat stopped at port for trade. The owner is doing me a favor," Andre said.

When we arrived at Constanta harbor, the sunlight reflecting off the water blinded me. The sea sprayed up into the air as the waves crashed up against the docks. I got out and the wind slapped my hair against my face. The seagulls cried out over the water. Amid them there was the white bird I saw on the drive here. It stood out, like a misshapen pebble amongst the others. It was small. Its shape too elegant to be a seagull, similar to the rare albino falcon I saw in the shop back home.

"Where to?" I called to Andre.

He popped the trunk. "Far end of the harbor."

The old, salty wood creaked under the weight of our footsteps. I looked out at the horizon. I'd never seen an ocean or a sea before. The Black Sea was more blue than black. The water changed from cobalt to bright marine once it touched the shore, making the colors of the harbor more vivid. Even chipped boat paint looked lush and energized.

"What's the name of the boat we're looking for?" I held up a hand to shield the sun.

"*Mopenah,*" Andre said in a pronunciation I didn't recognize.

"Mo-pe-nah? What does it mean? Is it Romanian?"

"Sealord. Nah, it's Ukrainian. We're traveling with my people."

Roman scoffed. "Great. Slow down, Karo. You'll attract attention."

I looked at the names mounted on the backs of the boats as I walked past. Most were powerboats, but some had sails and halyards which wacked against the mast in the wind. At the far end, some crusted paint read something similar to *Mopenah*, if some letters weren't missing.

I jogged ahead and heard Roman and Andre calling out behind me. The rickety finger dock swayed with my weight as I ran up the side of the boat. I skidded to a halt at the edge. Three handsome men stopped securing the deck. We looked at one another other for a moment, then I scrunched my nose as the smell of fish wafted off the boat.

"Hi," I said.

Andre caught up behind me and maneuvered me back. A language foreign to me poured from his lips as he stepped in front. My view was shielded, but I peeked around him in time for their faces to light up with smiles for Andre.

Roman stepped to our sides.

"English, please," I said.

"Karolina, this is the crew of the *Sealord*. Some old friends of mine." Andre brought out a large wad of cash and slapped it into the hand of a tall, blond man.

Blondie's smile widened as he clasped down on Andre in a rough hug. "Come!" He waved us onto the boat.

Roman boarded, and I was close behind him.

"Oh!" A robust redhead flashed to me and caught my waist midair, moving too fast to be human. He lifted me onto the boat. I got firm footing, then studied the crew. They could all be vampires, but I would assess for more obvious signs.

"Come," Blondie said. His accent was thick. "Sit down, we have drinks while we depart!" He slapped Andre on the back. "Should help your fear of the boats, no?"

Andre grimaced. "Thanks."

His crewman jumped to life, untied the boat from the dock, and hoisted the buoys onto the deck and bow. Blondie, who I now knew was the captain, climbed onto the steering platform and threw the shifter back. The boat shuddered and reversed toward the open sea. As the captain steered us out, his crewmen produced a jar of pickles and a bottle of vodka.

I knew exactly what those pickles were for. My friend Nicholi, who lived two doors down from my dorm, had me drinking vodka pickle shots one night. It was a night of both fun and remorse.

Andre dodged an oncoming spray of seawater, as the boat charged forward. He sat down and rolled up his sleeves. "So, Anton, how's your sister doing?" He grinned at the dark-haired man, who replied in Ukrainian shaking his fist in playful annoyance.

"You must join us!" Red said to Roman and me. "It's bad luck if you don't."

"When in Rome," I said to Roman and sat down. I took a glass from Anton on his way back up from the cabin.

"Come on, Wolfie," Andre said. "Don't tell me you can't hold your vodka."

"All right, I'll take a free drink," Roman said.

Red clapped his hands and poured shots for the five of us. I held my hand out in front of him once he was done. "Karo," I said.

"Fedir," Red said and clasped my hand in his.

Anton saved the jar of pickles from more saltwater crashing onto the deck. "So. We all know what the pickle is for?" he asked.

I fought to stay on my stool as the boat broke through a wave. "You smell the pickle, take the shot, then eat the pickle," I said.

"Yah!" Fedir and Anton clapped again, celebrating I was in the loop on their tradition.

"When in Rome, eh?" Roman asked.

The face I gave him said I didn't owe an explanation. I took a pickle and the others followed suit. "Why do sailors always drink? And why aren't we drinking in the cabin?"

"Sea sickness," Andre said. It's worse if you stay in the cabin. Try to keep your eyes on the horizon until you're used to the movement."

"I see," I said and readied my shot glass.

"*Ura!*" Anton called out and toasted me.

We clinked our glasses and continued as I directed. The pickle cooled the burning sensation of the vodka. The combination of the fiery drink and salty air was invigorating. They refilled their glasses. On the third refill, I covered the top of my glass with my hand.

The crew of the Sealord shared tales of what got them into fishing. The common theme was to be their own boss. They'd grown up with Andre as kids and worked as part of the fishing trade on the Black Sea. On occasion they did favors for the vampire underground to earn extra cash.

"Not all of us started in the underground when we were eight." Fedir nodded at Andre. "And what about you, wolf?" The more drinks he had the thicker his accent got. "What type of vampire business carried you here? Not that we don't appreciate an extra drinking buddy."

"I'm here for her." Roman nodded toward me and downed his drink. "To make sure she's not carried off into oblivion, locked up in a dungeon somewhere," he counted the mental list on his fingers, "or loses her sanity in blood lust."

"The lady is free to choose her outcome herself," Andre said, "and she was already in good company before you showed up."

"You and I have different definitions of good, leech."

Our companions halted. It was like they'd been flash frozen, making them unnaturally still. The type of still you would expect from an inanimate object. All three of them were not human.

The captain held the wheel still in his hands. The boat rocked through another wave. Sea water splashed onto the deck breaking the eerie quiet. I glanced at Roman and Andre's tense stances, ready to pounce at any brisk movement.

"Ro?" I gingerly touched his hand. "Will you come get some air with me on the bow?" I kept my voice low and calm.

Roman got up without a word, keeping his attention on Andre, and once far enough away headed for the side stairs.

"Oh, Smoke." Fedir shook his head. "It's always a girl."

I followed Roman and to my relief, our hosts regained their casual demeanor. My footsteps echoed against the steel stairs. "What were you thinking?" I asked.

"He started it. Karo, we don't belong here. This type of floundering could get one of them killed."

"*Floundering*? Ro, I'm half vampire. They're not my enemies; they're helping me. Half my family may be in Russia, and I am going to meet them." I glared at him. "Whether you like it or not, it's who I am, and it's happening."

Roman looked down to his shoes.

"Why, Ro? Why follow me?"

"Because, Karo, I would never let you go through with this alone. We've always been a team, and that night in the woods—" He caught my chin as I looked away. “It doesn’t change anything.”

My palms were sweaty. I hadn’t realized how much of me ran away from the intimacy of our sex. He drew me closer and anxiety turned into a ball in my throat. My inaction let him bring his lips to mine.

“I told you, I waited for it for a long time. Waited for you to be ready,” he said.

“I didn’t know. I knew you were always game for ramping up my sex life, but I didn’t know where you wanted it to go.”

“If I had it my way, Karo, we wouldn’t have left home. I would have taken over my father’s business, and I would have built us a house.”

I took a step back. “But that’s not our reality. I’m a fugitive back home. I can only go forward and take the leads I’ve been given. I’m doing this, Roman, and you need to respect my decision.”

“I will, if you’re not at risk,” he said.

Sounds of a low melody caught my attention, I looked around the bow and saw we were still alone. I turned back to Roman. “I wasn’t at risk down there. You have to trust me to make the right choices.”

“Fine,” he said.

“Okay,” I said then turned toward the chanting voices which erupted from the deck. It was the same song from a moment ago.

Andre and the crew stood against the afternoon sun. Anton and Andre swayed with arms interlocked. Vodka swashed out onto the floor from their glasses. Fedir sat with an empty bucket in his lap and drummed it while his baritone voice rang out over the makeshift drum. A high-toned voice echoed Fedir’s, which sounded like it belonged to the captain. He stood, drink in hand at the wheel, swaying with the rocking of the boat.

By the number of empty vodka bottles rolling back and forth on the deck, it was a wonder they could stand at all. The four of them, in tone, sang out in what I presumed to be Ukrainian, in rhythm with the beat of Fedir's drum.

"Hay!" Anton's glass flew through a splash of seawater.

They took respite breaks to sit down and enjoy each other's company. Periodically one of them would start up again at random and the others would jump in. In time, Roman ditched the tension he carried in his shoulders, and when he started dancing, he was forgiven for insulting our hosts.

The boat jolted upward as it battled a new stray wave. Back and forth it rocked, as the inky waves smashed against the boat with a deep shudder. My stomach turned. We rocked backward, only to be sucked forward and downward again. My stomach inverted and my vision spun.

"You okay?" Andre asked. "You're turning green."

"I lost track of the horizon," I said and groaned when my stomach summersaulted again.

"Blood?" Anton asked.

"No." Andre ran down the stairs and disappeared into the cabin, while Anton poured me a drink. The idea of having a drink and pickle when I was about to throw up made me cringe. Andre reappeared with a platter of sandwiches. I took one off the tray before it hit the table.

"Fedir loves food," Andre said.

Anton held a drink out for me. "It helps." He

nodded. “You’ll see.”

I slammed it back. “Whatever works.”

They all cheered. Even Roman started to smile again. My stomach relaxed, and I decided joining the party was the best way to avoid seasickness. By the time I poured my fourth drink, I accomplished learning most of the words to their drinking song. As the sun started to set, we were all three sheets to the wind, including Roman.

“Storm!” The captain’s voice thundered over the ruckus. He clutched his hat and pointed ahead.

Anton and Fedir leapt from their seats and climbed the rails to peer out over the quickly darkening multi-colored sky.

“It’s moving too fast!” Anton called as he snatched a handful of rope. He tied a strand around his trunk and the opposite end onto the railing. With a swift toss, he threw the large mass of rope to Fedir. He caught the bundle of rope as his eyes bulged.

“Rogue wave!” Fedir’s voice reverberated through the air.

“To the cabin!” Andre screamed as Roman jumped from his seat.

My stomach slammed into the railing. Mist dusted my face as I froze. The wind and sea roared in front of us, coming to a menacing head with a colossal forty-foot wave.

“*Karolina!*” Andre’s voice echoed distantly in my ear.

I clutched the rail, as the massive wall of water surged into me.

Chapter Twelve
The Storm

I clung to the metal bar. The saltwater rushed by me. A salty taste leaked through my tight lips as I held my breath against the turbulence. My ears threatened to explode from the pressure of the wave rolling in on itself. I peeled my eyelids open against the rush of the sea and saw only the vessel I clung to and the blue storm of water. The ship rolled over in the power of the wave. I looked down to see vast, dark, murky sea. The sky above the surface must have matched the color of the bottomless water, as I couldn't tell which way was up or down.

A shape stirred overhead. I looked up to see Andre clinging to a rope that swirled with the boat as it spun. He climbed hand over hand in the rip of current. The water clouded with bubbles as the boat twirled. The continuous motion was sickening. My lungs burned. Andre glided closer with each spin. He seized my middle and I clutched the rope. With each turn of the vessel the rope wound tighter around it, drawing us closer to the cabin.

Blackness crept inward from the corner of my eyes. My lungs prickled with heat from holding my breath. I looked at the mound of sinking steel we were entangled with. Water thrashed through my hair. I gripped the rope so hard I couldn't feel my fingers. Pure fear kept me with the shipwreck, as it offered the immediate safety from being washed away into the oblivion of the sea. But what was the point? Be it the wide blue sea or tied to the wreckage, there was no air here.

My lungs fought against me, urging me to take a breath of water. My body started to shake. My eyes stared blankly at the cabin door. As it darkened from my view, belongings flew past the window and crashed onto the floor. It took a moment for my brain to register why they stood out to me. They fell. The debris didn't glide weightlessly, the way they should have in water. There was no water there. There was air.

My hand thrust forward feeling blindly along the rope. I felt myself leave Andre's arms. My muscles seared with the moment, deprived of oxygen. I yanked myself toward the cabin against the current. I stretched my arm out. My fingertips grazed the metal handle.

I jarred backward.

Andre's steely fingers were clapped down on my ankle. He must have followed me up the rope and was now dragging me back. *No*. I fought mercilessly against him, kicking out with my free leg. He tugged on me harder, his grip unmoving. My final thrust of energy called my vision back in a rush. I contracted my legs to my chest and pumped them outward. They hit Andre in his chest.

Bubbles burst from his mouth and he recoiled his rope hand. He swung free, loose in the powerful rip of the wave's current, dangling from my ankle. My grip on the rope vowed to let go with the added weight. My strength was depleted. My hands slid down the rope farther away from the cabin, air, and survival.

I looked down at him in the swarm of bubbles. I

could shake him free…I could make it. Andre shook his head at me and screamed some inaudible words. Then blackness took me again. My chest ached, and I knew the burning in my lungs was in his too. The idea of letting him go then seemed horrible, because my pain was his.

My fingers found their way down to his other hand. He climbed up me, then wrapped his arms around my chest. It was just in time. My body let go. I started to convulse. My lungs swelled, and I felt the water trickle in through my nose.

The vessel turned, and with a rush of saltwater the weight of the sea around me was gone. My ears abruptly popped, and a cool gust of air hit me in the face. Gagging up seawater, I gasped for breath. My lungs felt heavy and labored, but the breeze—it was beautiful. Seagulls cried out to one another in the background. My hands trembled as I left Andre's arms. I heaved and slumped over on the soaked deck.

"Anton!" Andre called through hoarse staggered breaths.

A rope tied onto the rail grew taut. "Over here!" He climbed up the rope and over the railing.

Andre rushed to his side "Where are the others?"

"They made it to the cabin."

I rose to my knees and dragged the wet hair from my face. "How?" I asked. "How are we even here?"

"The cabin is airtight," Anton said.

Andre walked to the steel cabin door and rapped on it loudly. "So long as the cabin door stays closed to lock in an air-pocket." He banged again. "It will surface top up, when capsized."

"The door has to stay closed," Anton said, "to keep

the vessel buoyant."

"The air pocket makes it rise to the surface?" I asked.

Anton nodded. "Slowly. Depending on the strength of the wave."

"What if the door opened under water?"

"Then we'd be on the sea floor right now."

The cabin door swung open and Roman, Fedir, and the captain climbed out. The three of them were covered in sandwich and cabin debris.

"Hail the *Sea King*!" Fedir thrust his fist into the air.

"She's old," the captain said, "but unsinkable." He slapped Roman on the back with a laugh. I looked at Roman, covered in mustard, lettuce, and motor oil. I couldn't help it. I laughed. It wasn't just Roman wearing lettuce; it was the whole situation. I almost killed everyone. I crunched down and held my stomach. At first everyone had joined in, but when I didn't stop laughing, the deck started to quiet.

I cleared my throat and the jitters passed. "What do we do now?"

The captain climbed the steering platform and turned the ignition. "So long as she starts, we get the hell out of here."

The first few times the boat wouldn't start. After air-drying the spark plugs, we finally had ignition. Then we waited ten minutes for the pumps to purge the engine. It sputtered to life, and we were in motion once more.

"That wave was too big," Anton said. "The sea was too calm for such a wave to appear out of nowhere."

"There's magic afoot," Fedir said and turned to

Andre. "To conjure a wave that size, it takes power. The wave was made to drown anything in its path—meant to kill." Fedir's words hung in the air as he met Andre's gaze.

"We intended to travel by air," Andre said, "but we thought being on the water would throw off any tracking spells. I didn't yet have confirmation; it was just speculation. I didn't think they would come after us here." He looked at the faces of his friends. "I'm sorry."

The crewmen surveyed Andre for a moment, then nodded their heads. Fedir patted Andre on the shoulder.

"Either way, friend, its magic meant to kill. Best to stay on the move," Anton said. "This has gone beyond a favor. I assume this is underground business?"

Andre nodded his head.

The captain looked over his shoulder. "Then we'll get you to Russia, quickly. Better Sochi than Novorossiysk. They'll be watching Novo for certain. I'll find a small harbor. Andre can spell the boat, so our arrival is undetected. We'll sleep in shifts for the night, one to man the wheel and the other to watch for anything awry." He looked down at me. "This way everyone will have time to make it to the cabin."

I gave him a nod. Guilt turned into a rock in the pit of my stomach.

The boat rocked through the waves once more, as we continued east. The waves felt choppier than before. The captain and Andre took first watch. Roman and I headed to the cabin where Fedir and Anton would join us once they'd secured the deck.

"We should turn back." Roman said once we were inside.

I looked around for a spot in the cabin which

wasn't covered in sandwich bread. "If it was quicker to turn back the crew would have said so." I decided there was no clear spot and took a nearby broom and started sweeping up the trash. "Plus, it's obvious the wave was only sent because whoever is tracking us saw us disappear on the coast. They probably didn't know our exact location, so they sent the wave." I knew I was presumptive, but it served my point for the moment. "With any luck, they'll think no one could have survived it."

"We shouldn't assume anything. They may have known exactly where we were," Roman said. "The crewmen were right. There was an intense amount of magic behind that wave spell." He sat down on the horseshoe bench which lined the cabin, and the blue vinyl upholstery crunched underneath his weight.

"Yes, so the culprit may be momentarily drained. I can't imagine how much energy it would suck from a person to conjure a spell with so much force to create a forty-foot wave." I blocked out the memory of being thrashed in the surf.

"Fifty. Do you think it was dark magic?" Roman asked. "I mean, for someone who commands Shadow Forged and vampires with the Dark Charm, it would make sense." Roman shifted, trying to get comfortable on the bench.

"It would make sense, but a person can invoke more than one element, Ro."

"Guess we'll never know."

"No, Roman, I intend on finding out. This is why I'm here."

"No, you're here to meet your uncle Loukin. You said you wanted to go to the Russian address, and you are. We're doing what you want. But tracking down someone who summoned a tsunami to kill you, is just plain stupid!"

"Easy, burger kid, we don't need you jumping back into the fryer." I couldn't take him seriously with mustard and shreds of lettuce on his face.

He stared at me. "What?"

A throat cleared, and we turned to the door. Anton and Fedir stood on the cabin stairs.

"She's got a point, you know," Fedir said. "It would be hard to follow your direction when you've got food all over your face." He had a deep, burly laugh.

Roman touched his cheek, smearing it more. He looked down at his hand and flushed red. "Point taken."

"There's a bucket full of water outside on the deck. You can use it to wash," Anton said.

Roman stood up. "Thanks."

Anton and Fedir descended the stairs and stood at the kitchenette to my right. The power of the setting sun was creeping over me. I could feel the tension of the pending night gathering. I imagined the sun would be completely gone in a matter of seconds. It reminded me there were two other vampires in the room with me. Though friendly, not folks I would consider trustworthy. My grip tightened on the broom handle.

Anton put random objects which lay astray back into place. Then fished a plastic water bottle of blood from a cooler.

Fedir busied himself at the kitchen. "So, does your friend always order you around?"

"He's just protective," I said.

"Mmm."

"We've known each other since we were kids," I

said.

Fedir turned back to the fridge and started putting some sausage and peppers on a platter. "In Ukraine, there is the most beautiful flower, the *zozulyntsi*." He spread his hands in front of his face as he said the name. "It grows in the strangest places. It amazes everyone at the places it chooses to grow, the mountain peaks, shallow riverbeds…it can even grow through concrete."

I abandoned my broom and sat down on the bench.

"But!" He placed the platter on the table and sat down. "If you pick it, or you try to plant it in the place of your choosing, it dies."

I stared back, waiting for his next words.

"There are two types of men, Karolina. The ones who can admire the greatness of the little flower." He picked up a sausage in a bun and handed it to me. "Or the ones who try to control it."

Roman wasn't always dominated by the need to be in control. When we were six, he was like a puppy dog—rambunctious and driven by curiosity. We were walking home from the park when a man pulled over on the road. His dirty leather coat looked warm and sticky in the sun. It scrunched while he walked. We paused when he spoke to us, we knew we should have kept walking, but Roman was invincible, a master of soccer and climbing trees. When the man held out a sticky lollipop covered in car lint, the situation felt wrong.

I smacked it out of his hand as Roman reached to accept it. Roman went to scream at me, but I took his arm and dragged him into the ditch. I kept running, pulling him with me. Soon, Roman was so angry he chased after me. Later that week, another child went missing. Neighbors gathered in groups to search the woods for weeks, but she was never found.

Roman and I never truly spoke about what happened, except through innuendos and jokes. I would do him a mundane favor, and he would say, in earnest, he owed me his life.

A crunch made me look up, and I saw Anton had sat down beside Fedir. I was so immersed in thought, I had completely forgotten Anton was even here.

"Thank you," I said, "for the sausage."

Fedir smiled down at me. "Any time."

The cabin door swung open. The light of a lantern on the deck patterned the doorway with amber shapes. Roman emerged from the darkness and stepped down the stairs. He sat down beside me and checked out the food.

"Looks good," Roman said.

Anton left the table and lay down at the point of the U-shaped bench. "Help yourself," he said and closed his eyes. He nuzzled further into the cushion.

"Thanks," Roman said.

To my awe, he managed to put down five sausages before he finally leaned back.

Fedir looked amused.

"What? Almost dying in a shipwreck works up an appetite," Roman said.

"Tell me about it," I said and leaned back against the bench. I adjusted a pillow underneath my head and felt the draw of sleep on my eyelids. "At least you guys made it to the cabin. Holding my breath for such a long time was probably the scariest thing I've ever done."

"Really?" Roman looked at me.

I shook my head. "You have no idea what it was

like. Not being able to breathe, fighting the reflex to take a breath of water. It was torture."

Roman looked down. "I thought you had already made it to the cabin when I ran to it."

With the memory of the water, I felt breathless, like Roman sat on my chest. "I panicked and ran to the rail."

Fedir nodded. "Andre tore past me after you while I was on my way to the cabin."

"It was scary, but I could handle it," I lied and shoved my shoulders back into the seat. It felt good to close my eyes. "Wake me when it's my turn for watch." The boat rocked back and forth in the waves, the motion slowly lulling me into the unconscious.

"Sure," Roman said faintly in the distance.

I drifted toward sleep. My body started to relax—too much. It felt like I didn't have enough strength to expand my rib cage. I struggled to breathe. I willed my arms to rise, but they lay at my sides. Panic pounded in my chest. I tried to roll over, but I remained limp. The faint sound of Roman and Anton's voice echoed in the void. I called out to them, but my voice didn't come. Tears welled under my closed eyelids.

A slimy voice whispered in my ear. "Karolina…"

I shivered and wanted to recoil, but it only worsened my inner struggle against my limp body.

"Karolina…" His voice sounded so close, like he was there beside me.

My stomach twisted. I screamed out in my head. *Wake up! Wake up!*

"Karolina!" the voice said.

The drum of his malevolent voice reverberated through my body. An image of a face slammed into my mind for a millisecond, but it stained my memory. He had dark wavy hair and dark beady eyes. The skin of his face was worn and stretched tight over his jaw and cheekbones. Then the thundering of the water played in my ears and grew to a murderous roar. Images flooded my mind from the horrific experience of the wave—of drowning. My eardrums pulsed and promised to explode. I fought for breath. *Breathe! It's not real.* My lungs stayed stagnant, and the blackness I thought I escaped in the sea embraced me once more.

Chapter Thirteen
The Dawn of a New Era

I awoke with a gasp and shot up in the darkness. I breathed in and out as fast as I could, trying to fill my lungs. It took a moment to realize I sat in the dark cabin. I drew strands of hair from my sweaty face. It was just a dream.

What I'd just experienced was like sleep paralysis, but tenfold. It reminded me of my experience at Miruna's house I'd forgotten. It felt like a dream gone wrong, like being trapped in my own body. At the house, I had felt the overwhelming drag of sleep, but I was safe. This time was different. It was torturous. I held my head between my hands. *The wards*. I was within Miruna's wards, and I had my own fresh ward around me. He now knew I had survived the wave. He'd been so arrogant; he had even shown me his face.

I looked around the darkness of the cabin. It didn't seem like I'd woken anyone up, and I hadn't been summoned for my watch yet either. I wrapped a blanket around my shoulders and slipped off the bench. I felt my way through the darkness and then fumbled with the knob of the door. I stepped onto the deck. The cool wind blew against my skin, blowing my hair back. I let out a sigh of relief.

"Can't sleep?" Anton's voice sounded out in the dark, making me jump. He stood at the wheel sipping from a tin cup.

I sniffed the air. It smelled like coffee. "Just needed a bit of fresh air."

Anton let go of the wheel for a moment to fill another cup from his thermos. I took it from him, and while sipping it, let out a little moan. Black coffee wasn't my first choice, but it was still coffee.

"Thanks," I said and turned up the stairs onto the bow.

The sounds of the waves hitting the boat were calming. I looked out and saw the glitter of starlight painting streaks across the inky sea waves. The moon was nowhere to be found, which meant it would be dawn soon. My foot caught on a bollard. I twisted my leg and stubbed my toe on a mounting rod, making me drop my coffee.

"Easy, princess, we don't need you breaking your neck before I get you to Kislovodsk." Andre sat in the darkness near the rod.

"Just keeping you at attention, skipper. Lookout duty?"

"Yup."

"You didn't wake me up?" I asked.

"Thought you needed the sleep." He passed me up my tin cup he'd managed to take from my hand before it fell.

"Impressive."

"I must be dreaming. You actually gave me a compliment."

I sat down and tightened the blanket around my shoulders. The sky started to lighten to a dusky blue. "I'm up here because I couldn't sleep. So, I'm probably just disoriented."

"Bad dream?"

"Yeah." I looked down. "About that. Thanks for not telling everyone what happened underwater."

"You did better than most would have. Don't beat yourself up about it."

"How'd you know about my dream?"

"I felt it."

"It seems since our blood exchange, I've been at a disadvantage."

"You noticed," he said.

"Yeah." I stuck out my chin. "I *noticed.*"

"When you drink another vampire's blood, you not only taste their soul, it changes you. It becomes a part of you, allows you to feel the other person."

Andre's blood was now part of me. I should've been less calm. "So, when I feel for you, and hit a wall?"

"When you are more skilled at using your new power, you'll learn how to keep a guard up."

The sky was lightening to purple and mauve. Tips of the sun's rays peeked up over the horizon. "So, the guard?" I looked over my shoulder and noticed I could now make out his face. "It fails when you get emotional?"

He laughed. "My guards never fail."

"Oh yeah?"

"Yeah."

"How come I could feel everything you felt after Miruna healed you?"

Andre turned quiet. He took my coffee from my hand. "You may have felt a bit, before I got my guard up." He sipped the cup and passed it back.

"I thought about going to you, but I didn't think

you'd open your door even if I did."

"I don't think I could have seen anyone at that moment."

"What did Miruna do to you anyway?"

"Well, I guess she healed my soul. If you believe in souls…"

"Oh." I tried to keep the look of shock from my face.

The sun's rays broke out over the water. As it rose, shades of pink and red formed in the sun's wake. I turned to Andre, and saw the amber hues reflected on the smooth skin of his face.

"What?"

"Nothing," I said. "It's just…I think this may be the most beautiful sunrise I've ever seen." The light burned into my eyes, but I still stared forward, unable to look away. I could feel Andre's gaze.

"Your eyes aren't brown when you're in the sun. They're more of a hazel…" He cleared his throat. "The last time I saw a sunrise like this, I was here on the Black Sea."

"When? Was it for underground business?"

"In a way. It was right after my parents were murdered, and I avenged them."

"I see."

"I didn't want to at the time," he said. "I was just so angry; I drained the next door neighbor. He was my teacher in grade school." He stared out into the sun. "After I invoked the Dark Charm and did what I had to, they threw me on a boat like this one and sent me to Kislovodsk. I met the Second in Command, Loukin, and worked for him to earn my keep. Ever since then, I haven't really been back on the water."

I slid an arm underneath his and stared ahead with him. "Eight years old is too young to lose your parents. Plus, after what we experienced underwater, I don't know if I'll be back on a boat anytime soon either."

The cabin door creaked on the deck below.

I slid away. "Thank you. For helping me."

"No problem, princess."

"See you down there."

As I descended the stairs, I clutched the banister for balance. Andre had changed. Whatever Miruna had done, healed soul or not, had rekindled a part of him I only saw glimpses of. My stomach fluttered with a mix of hunger and longing to see more. A blood craving hit me full force. I missed a step. I closed my eyes and steadied myself. When I turned the corner, Roman stood on the deck. I put my hands in my pockets to hide their tremble.

The captain and Fedir emerged from the cabin. I followed their line of sight and noticed an earth-toned strand off in the distance. "Is that land?"

"Yes," Anton said. "We'll be to Sochi in an hour."

"Perfect." Getting off the water was a relief but stepping back onto land reintroduced the issue of tracking spells. The memory of a spell in Miruna's magic book resurfaced. Using its principles, we could use any form of magic to rejig the incantation. I climbed down into the cabin and looked for my pack.

Roman called down to me from the stairs. "Karo, what are you doing?" He leaned in.

I had the book in hand. "We need a way to disarm any tracking spells."

"Okay."

I flipped through the book until I spotted the spell.

"Tracking spells." As I read on, I deflated. What I needed to do was switch our sense of identity. The idea was to learn the mechanism of how tracking spells work—to sabotage it. Tracking spells honed in on a person by using their sense of identity. Our self-awareness is what binds us all together. Crazy people were nearly impossible to track. Last time I checked; I still knew I was me.

"What?" Roman leaned closer.

"We're screwed."

"Not exactly," Roman said.

Andre entered the cabin.

"You know how to put my concept of self in a foreign body?" I asked.

"No," Roman said, "but I know how to put a foreign identity in yours."

"How?"

"The spirit of the wolf." Andre shook his head. "So, you're a packmaster."

I looked to Roman.

"As packmaster," Roman said. "I have the ability to make new werewolves. If you start the ceremony, but don't finish it, it will be enough to trick the spell."

"Explain," I said.

"When you take the essence of the wolf, your body and mind will be tricked into being the wolf. You'll be a form of yourself, but not yourself at the same time. So long as you don't complete the change, it will temporarily mask you. It'll only last for eight, maybe ten hours tops."

Andre snorted. "As long as we don't kill anything, or we'll be forever bound to your pack as your little wolf minions."

"This is the most important part, Karo. If you kill anything, anything at all—person or animal—the change will be complete. You'll lose all your powers. You won't have your strength, the vampire inside you will die, and you'll lose your fire and earth magic."

"But I would have werewolf strength, right?"

"Yeah," Roman said, "but it takes years to learn how to control the shift."

"Don't want your breeding stock to lose all the magical abilities you're hoping to pass down to your cubs?" Andre asked.

Roman ignored him and took his keys from his pocket. He untied the bronze and bone keychain—the one I always told him to throw away. He held it out in his palm, and it started to glow.

"Your family talisman is a bit small don't you think?" Andre asked. "You know what they say about guys with small talismans."

The dust around Roman's feet stirred, spiraling upward around him. The glowing light projected outward and turned golden. As did Roman's eyes. His canines lengthened, and a guttural sound emerged from his belly. His thumb bore down on the center bone piece, and a serrated blade jutted out from underneath the disk. Blood dripped from Roman's palm. Then the light faded.

"There, it's charged." Roman said and held it out to Andre. "You go first."

Andre looked at me. "I don't like this."

"I know," I said, "but it's the only option for now."

Andre took the disk from Roman. "What now?"

"Press the button again and the blade will come out. Just make sure you wipe—"

Andre's finger clicked the button before Roman finished speaking, and as a golden light burst from him, so did black smoke. It zigzagged back and forth between the men, until the smoke and light vacuumed inward. Andre slammed against the kitchen cupboards.

Except it wasn't Andre, not his face at least. He slumped over stunned as the smoke and dust cleared.

Instead of a deep growl, Roman hissed.

"Why are you wearing my face, leech!"

It took me a second to register Roman's face was indeed on Andre. More interesting still, Andre's body had widened. His skin color darkened. He looked like a carbon copy of Roman.

"Stay calm," I said and turned to Roman, then gasped.

His lips were peeled back revealing fangs. He crouched low to the ground. Looking out at us through dark strands of hair were Andre's eyes. Roman's voice remained the same, but within his now baggy clothes was Andre's body.

"What happened?" Andre murmured.

"I told you to wipe it first!" Roman yelled and blurred upward. He hit his head on the roof and bounced down again.

"Wow, easy," I said and placed my hands on Roman's chest. "Clearly this is an accident. So, just explain."

"There's nothing to explain! I use my blood to activate it, and usually my assistant wipes it down and passes it to the rest of the pledges."

"So, this has never happened before?" I asked.

"No!"

"Okay, okay, we'll deal with it," I said. "You said

it's not permanent, right?"

Roman leaned against the wall as his nostrils flared. "Yeah."

It was strange to see Andre act with Roman's mannerisms. I took the device from Andre, who was now getting off the ground. He leaned against a cupboard, and his hand drove right through the wood. He turned his head to his hand in a delayed reaction.

"Not yet, Karo!" Roman said and took my hand. "Wipe the blood off first."

The serrated blade had already clicked back inside the talisman. I found a nearby rag, held it underneath the disk, and pressed down on the bone. The blade clicked out underneath. As I continued to hold the button, I wiped the blade down.

"Okay," I said. "Ready?"

"Take your necklace off," Roman said. "It's meant to protect the vampire who wears it from wolf magic."

I slipped it off my neck, hiding the shock that Roman knew a detail about my father's necklace that I didn't.

"You're going to feel weird," Roman said. "The blood lust may be like a vampire's, but your body will feel different. Like you've been put inside a…machine maybe. Something strong and foreign."

"I won't become one of those gruesome monsters in all the movies, will I?"

"No, those abominations are made from a bite during a hunt, not the proper way. You're either born or made this way. If a human is bitten during the hunt, there're usually dead within days. If they survive, it's more humane to put them down rather than let them slay their families."

I wanted to ask Roman if or how often an innocent person got hurt by his pack, but now wasn't the time to explore his comment. "Ready?" I asked. My finger hovered over the button.

"Ready," he said, and held his hands out to his sides like he was ready to catch me or stop me from running away.

I tapped the button. The blade cut into the palm of my hand.

A crippling pain seized me, and I buckled to my knees. The veins in my skin bulged and my eyes pulsed, feeling like they would pop. The air swirled around me, but I couldn't breathe or move. As quickly as the magic manifested, it left.

I sat down on the floor.

"You okay?" Roman asked, as he crouched before me. Andre stood over his shoulder, looking like he'd started getting used to walking in Roman's body.

"Yeah," I said. "Am I still me?"

"Yeah," Andre said. His dress shirt buttons had ripped off with the expanse of his ribcage. His shirt now hung open revealing his chest.

They helped me up.

"Port side!" Anton called.

We all surfaced on the main deck. Andre's footsteps thumped on the ground, while Roman looked like a video which fast-forwarded at random.

I hung my head out over the rail. We approached the dock in Sochi with speed. The algae-covered cement ports glided closer. A sea boat more salt battled than the *Mopenah* coasted by. Beyond the harbor was a deep city center speckled with palm trees. The sun shone over the mountains which loomed behind the city. On the other side of those mountains was Kislovodsk.

Chapter Fourteen
The Parade

I stepped on the dock. A fuzzy sensation overcame my body. There was magic at work. Lots of it. Going onto solid ground felt like emergency training at the station all over again. Then, as a student, the idea of a lockdown was nerve-racking. My exterior was calm, but inside I was a ticking mechanism ready to strike at sudden movement. Now, the feeling was intensified. In a few seconds we'd find out if my idea worked.

"You feel it?" I asked Andre.

Roman gasped when he stepped onto the concrete strip. I hadn't thought about the fact he may have never experienced the sensation of magic before. I imagined shifting into a wolf would be similar, but perhaps not. "You okay?"

"What is it?" Roman asked.

"My guess would be our suspected tracking spell at work."

Andre leaned in to hear, but he crinkled his nose. "You both reek of wolf."

"You're probably just smelling yourself." I had never 'smelled wolf,' but it was likely a scent I was used to because I grew up with Roman. "Let's move before we're spotted."

"Affirmative," Andre said.

The plan for Sochi was to wait for Andre's contact

to approach us near the boat and guide us to our next set of wheels. The ride from Sochi to Kislovodsk was nine hours. Andre had advised Roman to speak as little as possible to the contact, to avoid having to explain our circumstance. Andre didn't want to spook his contact into thinking Andre had been compromised by a spell.

As I skimmed the crowd, a dark-haired teenaged boy approached us. He was tall, skinny, and slouchy. His black hair hung over half his face, to complement his all black outfit. If it were night, dressing in all black may have made him blend in. On a bight sunny day which was heating up fast—his black getup turned heads.

"You gotta be kidding me."

"No, I'm not," Andre said. "Careful, Roman, he's skittish."

Roman skidded forward and blurred three feet. "I got this." He walked toward the contact and slouched down mirroring his posture. "Hey, sup?"

"What?" the kid said.

Roman straightened up and put more moodiness into his tone. "We're ready."

The kid shifted his weight uncomfortably. "What's with the act? Are you on drugs?" He stepped back. "What's with your voice?"

"Be cool." Roman held up his hands. "Look it's been a long ride and I'm tired. I got choked out in a fight and it messed with my voice box." Roman leveled down to his height and looked him in the eyes. "You ready? Or not?"

He reacted to the authority in Roman's voice. "The van is over there. But I don't owe you anything else after this."

"You've done well." Roman clutched his shoulder.

He flushed with the clearly unexpected praise. "It was nothin'. Stealin' the van was easy. Gettin' it back will be the hard part."

Roman turned and gave us the signal to follow. We tailed them to a black van parked behind a dumpster.

"Hi-yah, Tod," Andre said.

Tod flicked his head to Roman. "You told him my name!"

"Just get driving, Tod," Andre said. "We've got a deadline to meet, and you've got a stolen van to return." Andre climbed in. Tod put the van into gear, hit the gas, and stalled it. "The clutch," Andre said. Tod glowered at him in the rearview mirror.

"You got it, Tod. Try again," Roman said.

Tod turned to Roman. "Not from you too!"

The tracking spell would be there lying in wait for when the essence of the wolf subsided. It was imperative to get to Kislovodsk as quickly as possible, but I couldn't tell Tod this. Instead, I let quiet anxiety eat away at me.

We drove down the narrow street, and I took one last glimpse at the glossy sea behind us. The van veered onto the main strip, revealing the city of Sochi. The shiny skyscrapers stretched out between palm trees and manicured flower gardens. Suspended above the city was a chair-rail carting people up to the mountain peaks. The bluffs were huge, and by the time we'd journeyed halfway past the mountains, the hours passed more quickly.

My tormented sleep last night made my eyelids droop. Not even my wolf-like strength could fight the lull of the drive. Every time my head nodded, I would jar myself awake. I wasn't sure if the essence of the wolf would keep my dreams safe from my enemy. I snapped my head up when the van cruised to a stop. There was a gas pump outside my window.

"How much longer to Kislovodsk?" I asked.

"Four hours," Andre said.

I relaxed. I fell asleep and my mind remained untouched, which meant I was indeed shielded. If my dreams wouldn't be protected when I got to Kislovodsk, I would bank as much sleep as I could while I had the chance. I laid my head against the seat and closed my eyes.

"Wake me when we're there."

****

The beeping of car horns jarred me awake. My feet shot out into the front seat, sending it forward off its floor mount with a cracking noise.

"Shit! Shit! Shit!" I leaned around the flipped car seat. If Roman had his werewolf strength and not Andre's, I wouldn't have worried about hurting him.

Roman was quiet.

The honking of horns meshed with the dance music which boomed out into the street. The roads and sidewalks were all crammed with people.

The crumpled passenger's seat rustled. Roman flipped the seat back over and sat back down a little lopsided. "I'm fine."

"Sorry," I said.

A woman bumped into the side of our van. She wore an intricately painted mask in the shape of a bull. "Wooo!" She threw her hands into the air, spilling her drink on the passenger door. There was an onrush of people, and she danced toward the next car.

I looked across the mob filling the streets. Half-naked men and women shouted out in Russian and danced to the music. Many wore masks in the shapes of animals painted in bright colors. Others wore traditional Russian garb. Disk jockeys and live bands were stationed along the sidewalks, next to booths selling drinks and pumping beer from kegs.

"Guys…" I kept staring outside the window. "What am I looking at?"

Andre, Roman, and even Tod, were silent, like they were hypnotized, but I think it had to do with the blonde girl in front of our van flashing her breasts at the windshield.

Tod did me the favor of a response. "Autumn Equinox Festival."

They watched the little doe yank her shirt down and fix her costume antlers as she trotted away to a new group of people.

"I hoped we'd make it into town before the parade started," Tod said, "but you guys got in later than Andre said. We'll be stuck in traffic for hours now."

Andre leaned forward. "Not if I can help it." He pointed to an alleyway off the main road. "Down there. We can try to cut off the parade. Stay away from the main road."

Tod laid on the horn and jerked the van to the left. Pedestrians jumped back. It was a ballsy maneuver, but it was effective. He beeped the horn and turned down the alleyway. More people dodged out of our way and we broke through the main crowd.

I caught flashes of the festival through gaps in the buildings and alleyways. The little girl part of me was giddy to see the floats. I didn't yet see any signs of the parade. What I did see was a little flash of black lightning. I squinted, summoned my vampiric vision, but recalled I only had the essence of the wolf now.

"Ro, how do you improve your sight?" I stayed focused on the crowd as the van sped forward. Through an alleyway, I spotted another flare of black lightning between a tall figure and a dark-haired woman. A bystander would have told themselves it was a trick of the eye. A member of the magical community would have known it instantly. Dark magic.

I slanted forward, waiting for the next oncoming laneway. Another bout of light flared between two people in a different location. One party fell to the ground, then the other hoisted them up and carried them off through the crowd. An oncoming building blocked my view before I could gather more details.

My gut reaction to help the person got my adrenal chemistry pumping, but in wolf form it resulted in a pulsing strength which rolled over my skin. My veins bulged. Deep within my bones a pain broke loose, but instead of crippling me, it hit me like a dose of amphetamines. My hands shook as my muscles tightened. My ligaments threatened to snap.

"You can't, Karo. Not unless you shift, and it would be too dangerous since you haven't mastered the wolf."

"Too late." My clawed hand stretched for the handle and broke the van door open. I leapt from the moving vehicle and rolled onto the street.

My wolf body felt like human steel. I took off, running in the direction I last saw dark magic. I caught glimpses of my claws growing into talons as I ran. The stitching of my sweater tore apart at my elbows.

The man turned down an alley with the woman in tow.

My feet shattered the concrete beneath them. The surge of strength crippled my body into a crouch, and my arms lengthened as I barreled through the crowd.

Men, women, and hunks of stone blew through the air around me, as my claws unearthed the stone and metal in their path. The carnal need to eat, chew, and devour overcame me. Everything I once found attractive in anyone or anything, I now needed to consume. I almost missed my turn at the alleyway. I dove down it and set my sights on the only door visible.

The wood splintered as I exploded through the doorway. I slid to a halt in the middle of the room. Hot air spiraled from my snout, not from fatigue from the run, but from bloodthirst. My vision was tinted with a red hue. Blood surged from my temples to my eyes.

Six men froze, one with a fragile-looking woman lying limp in his arms. Behind them was a large wooden crate, open to the front of the room, and full of limp bodies. The people lay still, except for the steady rise of their chests. They were alive. Behind the closest crate stood four more, packaged and sealed. Ready for departure.

Electricity ran down my spine. A low muffled snarl escaped my jaws. Fighting the change felt like constant nails on a chalkboard, but I had to know who was behind this. My back arched, and my forearms elongated. My shadow unfurled on the floor like a ghoul breaking free from the concrete. I screamed, the sound reverberated off the walls, sounding half-human, half-animal. My jaw contracted just enough to form words.

"W—hat is thisss?" I asked.

The men backed up, one step at a time. The smell of fear oozed from their skin. They all looked to a stocky man with skin like cooked ham. Whispers flew between them like Russian proverbs.

"This is Vampire business," Ham Skin said and squared his shoulders. "This is the First in Command's human stock for the Harvest Festival coming," he leered at me, "and if I were you, I wouldn't come between him and his personal supply."

I snarled, not from his words, but from the little pair of doe antlers which lay before their feet. My gaze followed the droplets of blood trailing from the antlers to the side of the crate. I pawed sideways to increase my view. A pool of blood surrounded pretty blonde hair. I contorted and collapsed to the ground.

My bones broke, and my joints hinged. I screamed, but the sound turned into the horrifying roar of a predator. I felt the vocal cords in my neck snap. All I recalled after the pain was the urge to tear the juicy flesh from Mr. Ham—to make him pay for what he'd done.

They scattered, but I was too close for them to fully retreat. I raked my teeth through his calf, and the skin filleted from the bone. He tasted like pig. The warm blood in my mouth didn't quench my anger, it made it worse, like the first sip of vodka for an alcoholic. I darted forward and cut off the others' escape.

"Karo!" Roman called.

"Karolina!" Andre followed.

Roman charged the cornered vampires. Thrusting his hands outward, he called his new magic forth. A sizzling purple light coursed from his hands. He swung it like a baseball bat as the vampires made a break for the door.

The lightning zapped through the air—about two meters away from its target. The bolt cracked into one of the crates. Pieces of wood tumbled onto the floor. Smoke rose up from a charred hole. Men and women with panicked cries started to climb free from the opening. Roman caught on and started blasting holes in the crates. People flooded the door, crying out as I pounced to pursue their captors.

"Karolina!' Andre slid in front of me. "This isn't you!"

Looking into Roman's face with Andre's voice snapped me onto his wavelength.

Roman blurred forward and tripped on his own feet as he skidded to a halt. "You get the vampires," he said. "I'll walk her through the change!" Roman held either side of my face. "Karo, you're in there. You control your body, okay. Take control. No one else is here but you and me. Concentrate."

Behind Roman, Andre shifted, but only as far as his upper body. Creating massive clawed arms which looked outrageous on his human legs. He raked his talons through one of the henchmen left behind, but left enough of him untouched that he could sprint away.

Some of the crates Roman had blasted with Andre's magic had caught fire and spread to the rest of the building.

The sound of sirens rang out over the crowd.

"Look here!" Roman twisted my head back. "Look at me. You got this, Karo."

The essence of the wolf urged me to the scents of blood and prey, but inside of the wolf's body there was me. I focused on the Karo I knew. Who I was. I concentrated on the thing which gave me power: my free will.

My muscles relaxed, and I felt the power subsiding. My claws started to retract. I shifted into the form of a woman. My torn clothes hung limp around me.

The room filled with smoke, and there were people passed out in the closest crate who hadn't awakened from their jolts of dark magic.

I dashed to the pile of people and started lifting them over my shoulders and carrying them outside. Andre had shifted back and already beat me to the pile. We placed the people down outside in the alleyway. Roman left my side and put Andre's super speed to good use. He zoomed back and forth moving the people outside. I felt around on the ground on my hands and knees to ensure there were no civilians left. The thick smoke at floor level burned my eyes and lungs.

An object in Andre's hand scratched against the concrete floor.

"There's no one left. Let's go!" I coughed and jerked on his arm.

"No! There's someone still there." He headed to where I just left.

I dragged him toward the door, just in time to see Roman's silhouette in the doorframe.

"It's go time," Roman said.

Andre fought against me, this time using Roman's werewolf strength. "There's one more!"

Roman grabbed Andre underneath the arms. With our combined strength we schlepped Andre out into the light of day. The festival attendees had gathered in the street to assist the people we saved. I looked down to Andre's hand to see what he held. He had the set of deer antlers, which had belonged to the blonde doe who flashed the men outside the van. The one who was dead. He fought against me to go back inside.

"She's gone!" I said. "The other vampires drained her before I even got there." I lost my grip on his arm.

He hung his head in his hands and crouched to the ground. For a second, he looked like he'd be sick. "*Fuck*!" He exploded upward and whipped the deer antlers against the wall. "Damn it!" He walked forward into the crowd. "Let's get out of here."

Roman and I followed, and the three of us rushed into the camouflage of the onlookers.

"Where's the van?" I said.

A black van beeped and appeared through the swarm of people. The door of the van gaped half open. Tod hit the gas when I still had one foot left on the ground. Andre hoisted me in and slammed the part of the door that still remained shut. We sped off into the winding alleys.

"What were you guys doing?" Tod turned his head to Roman. "No time to be heroes when you're on a schedule!" He mocked Andre's voice. "Those are your words! Precious Cargo, *Tod*! No stops, *Tod*! The wolf goes running off, and next you guys have set a building on fire for a crowd of people to see!"

"We." The image of the blonde girl flooded my head. "Those people would have been drained dry by vampires if we didn't help them."

"Do you know who they work for?" Andre asked.

"Their leader said it was the First Command's blood stock for the Harvest Festival."

Tod squeaked and veered the van off course, sideswiping the narrow backstreet wall for a millisecond. The side view mirror flew off and clattered onto the street. We all grew silent, letting Tod regain control.

"Harvest Festival? Was it not the celebration today?" Roman asked.

"No," Andre said. "Today was a bit of a pagan tradition, The Autumn Equinox. The Harvest Festival is October first."

"Guys!" Tod made another sharp turn.

"What?" Andre asked.

"Did you let any of the vamps escape?" Tod asked.

I looked around the van. "Why?"

Tod accelerated. "Because we're being followed!"

An engine roared behind us. A jarring impact sent the van skidding onto two wheels. The metal on the other side of the van peeled back, producing a fire show of sparks as it scraped along the wall. Our bodies jolted forward and then slammed back against the seat. Roman took the wheel.

"Hold it straight, Tod!" Roman bellowed.

Andre looked to the back. "Punch it!"

"I already have!"

The engine revved again behind us.

"Then turn!" I cried out.

"They're coming in again!" Tod turned the wheel, but Roman stopped him.

"Not yet!" He'd leapt out of his seat to hold the wheel with Tod. "Hold it straight when they hit." Roman turned over his shoulder. "Hold!"

The van jolted from the impact and skidded forward. The squealing of tires on pavement echoed through the alley over the noise of the engines. My hands flew to my ears to shield from the screeching, which didn't stop. I looked to the back of the van. A large black SUV had fully collided with our trunk and was still driving full speed behind us. I turned to the brick wall ahead. "They're driving us into the wall!" I screamed.

"Tod!" Andre cried. "Get ready to turn!"

"There's no place to turn!"

"There's a small lane on your right!" Andre pointed over Tod's shoulder.

"It's too small!"

"Do it, Tod!" Andre shouted.

"You got this, Tod. You're a bad ass!" Roman inched closer to take over the wheel completely if he failed.

The wall flew to us.

"Now, Tod!" Andre screamed.

Tod turned the wheel into the mouth of the hidden laneway. We soared sideways. The noise of the van's roof crunching inward popped my ears. The screeching of tires and a large crash echoed behind us. I waited for a tangled mess of steel to cave in and crush me, but the moment never occurred. I opened my eyes. We drove down a brown brick tunnel, which looked more like an oversized storm drain.

The large SUV was stopped at the end of the tunnel, much too tall to come after us. Pieces of the vehicle littered the ground, and smoke rose up from its crumpled hood. The driver, when he no longer had our van as a buffer, had collided with the wall once we'd turned. I looked again at the crumpled front end of their vehicle. "They're not going anywhere."

Andre leaned in beside me. "No, princess, they're not."

"Way to go, Tod!" Roman shouted.

The tunnel opened to a highway on the other side of the town. Tod slammed on the brakes and swerved up the shoulder of the road. The van fishtailed out into the highway. The scenery was a drastic change from the old town of brick buildings and narrow streets. The highway ran along green hills which lined the base of the mountain. We had to be directly opposite to Sochi now. I anticipated the view on the other side of the mountains would be bland. I was wrong. The tall stone peaks rose up, high above an evergreen forest. Mist poured down the slopes and spilled into the land, whiting out the road ahead.

"How long to Kislovodsk?" I asked.

Andre leaned back in his seat. "Forty minutes," he said and glanced down at my chest.

My ripped bra and top were hanging loosely and flapped in the breeze of the torn door. "Give me a second, everyone, while I get changed."

Tod and Roman looked ahead. Andre looked out the window.

My next set of lingerie was a black and baby pink number. Only a man would pair a thick lace bra with a thin tank top.

A hint of a smile touched Andre's mouth in the reflection of the window glass.

"Yes, I'm wearing what you picked for me," I muttered. "I have no choice."

Andre leaned into my ear and whispered, "I'll replace your boots again too."

I pulled away. Men who liked to clothe women fit

into one of two categories: men who like to control their women, or men who give gifts to obtain the affection of women.

Roman looked back at me after I'd pulled on a new pair of jeans. "Do you feel the essence of the wolf wearing off?"

I bit my lip. "Not really." Worry turned my stomach like an eggbeater. But as the minutes drawled on, I felt the adrenaline fade from my body. As did the tingle of the tracking spell. I would soon be vulnerable again.

It felt like only a few songs on the radio had passed by the time we drove by a sign which said *Kislovodsk.* The eggbeater in my stomach turned on again full blast. I traveled over an ocean, a sea, and miles of land to finally arrive here. I retrieved the piece of paper from my pocket and unfolded it. *Kurortniy Bulevard 14, Kislovodsk 357700, Russia.* I read the address over and over and studied the unknown handwriting until my eyes strained.

As we drove deeper into the city, I noted the street signs. Kislovodsk was a stone city. The buildings oozed nineteenth-century charm. Smooth rock set into intricate patterns made up the main streets. Any spare piece of land was covered with unruly flower gardens. Tod turned onto a street checkered in a pattern of cream and pale yellow stone. I looked out the window to a sign which read *Kurortniy Bulevard.*

The street numbers slowly ticked down to fifteen. I closed my eyes and thought of Grandpa Dalca. His memory rallied my courage. We approached a pale stone building which looked like the set for an old romance movie. It stretched out four blocks long, with arched windows facing the street. Sports cars lined the strip. The walkways were filled with people, who dressed to show their wealth. I looked at our clothes, which smelled slightly of sea water.

Our crumpled van squealed to a halt in front of the main entrance. Directly outside my window there was a plaque mounted on a pillar. The number fourteen written in gold inlay glittered in my face. Andre and Tod had taken me to the address in my emergency box.

Above the covered entryway, there were big letters mounted on the roof above the entrance. I strained to recall my Russian History class. Piece by piece, I translated the Cyrillic letters in my head, then Russian to English.

"The Grand Hotel," I said out loud.

Andre took the piece of paper from my hand. "You won't be needing this anymore." He ripped it up.

"No," I said. "I guess I won't."

Chapter Fifteen
Home Away From Home

Roman and Andre turned to each other. Tod tapped his fingers against the steering wheel and looked at the hotel.

"What?" I asked.

"As fun as our power swap was, I want my body back," Andre said.

"Is there anything we can do to trigger the change?" I asked.

Roman produced his keychain out of his pocket. "I don't know how to use it other than the way we already have."

"Right," Andre said, "take my hands."

Roman recoiled in his seat as Andre leaned in.

"I'm not going to bite, wolf. I just need to access my power."

They clasped hands. Andre closed his eyes and within seconds a golden light hovered over his skin. The light snaked out to Roman, just as a heavy cloud of smoke puffed from Roman's chest.

"What the hell." Tod scrambled up against the door but didn't abandon the van. I didn't know if he stayed out of loyalty to Andre or fear of attracting more attention to the stolen vehicle.

The light and smoke swirled around us, expanding into the crevices of the van. I couldn't see through the smoke to see if pedestrians saw us. With vacuum-like pressure it sucked inward to both men with a whooshing sound. The air around us was once again clear. Andre and Roman fell back into their seats. They were glassy-eyed and panting but appeared to be within their own skins once more.

"Not too shabby," I said.

By the time we got out and rounded the van, Andre was gone. Tod snapped at us to wait on the street and got back inside the van. A new pair of boots were delivered to me. The battered vehicle rattled to life, and with a painful screech drove from the drop-off point and out of sight. The gilded doors of the hotel sparkled in a come-hither manner.

I emerged from the doorway, not into a room, but into a foreign realm of pure luxury. That which could glitter, glittered gold. The crown molding, the chandeliers, mirrors, tables, and candlesticks all sparkled in the bright afternoon light. Footsteps tapped against the marble floor, adding to the low, sultry music playing in the lounge. Guests chattered amongst the velvet drapes and upholstered furniture.

I locked eyes with a woman in the back of the room. Anger flared in my belly, until I realized her blonde hair and blue-eyed features were just akin to Bronwyn's. She stood behind a desk in a black uniform with gold buttons down the front.

"*Dobro požalovat.*" Another woman wearing the same uniform handed me a flute of champagne.

"Thanks." My gaze drifted to the buffet spread, and I almost dropped my glass when I saw a stuffed leopard mounted to a stand in the middle of the table. I walked over to the cat. It stood with one paw lifted amongst the platters of caviar, its eyes frozen in place and its mouth wrenched back exposing its fangs. I downed my champagne.

"I said to wait."

I turned and found Tod behind me. Roman followed him, holding a glass of champagne in each hand. With a little gesture of cheers, he shot down the champagne, and coughed when he saw the leopard.

"Sorry," I said. "What now?"

He led us to a corner. "We wait." With his back to the wall, he watched the doors.

Poor Tod. Andre had coaxed him into being our wheelman, and now the van he borrowed was totaled.

"So…how did a nice kid like you get all caught up in this vampire business?" I asked and got an eye roll from Tod. "I ask because your accent sounds almost Canadian."

"I'm American."

"Oh yeah? How'd you get here?"

Tod stuck out his chin. "My parents owed a debt, so they paid it with me. They didn't want their perfect little lives disturbed by my presence."

"Oh. I see." It seemed like lots of people made a habit of owing Loukin a debt.

Tod brooded in the silence.

Roman jumped in. "You did great today, Tod."

"A compliment from a wolf is about as rewarding as a broken fang," Tod said.

Andre entered the room. He made his way to our corner, giving greetings to people along the way. One woman trailed a finger across his chest as she passed. When he joined us, he removed some gold paper wristbands from his pocket.

"This is so the staff can tell you're special guests," he said. "Now you have full rein of the hotel. Follow me."

"Full access," I said to Roman. I shouldn't have been surprised by the privilege. Andre had said he was Loukin's top man. He led us through one of the arched doorways, and we wound through the crowds of people. We descended a staircase with crimson carpet down the center. A set of doors encased in stone loomed at the bottom. As we drew nearer, I looked up at the charmed carvings etched in the stone. They were worn and covered with layers of dust which only time could produce.

Andre rapped the brass doorknocker and a sliding panel opened to reveal a set of eyes. He and the anonymous man whispered in Russian and the metal clicked loudly on the other side. The heavy doors swung open.

Andre's hand blurred out in front of Tod blocking his path. "Not yet, mini-me. Your time will come." Tod glared at him, but paled when he caught the bouncer's attention. He backed up and headed into a passageway I hadn't seen.

We squeezed by the bouncer who ran a hand over his lumpy bald head. Our footsteps echoed down the hall which stretched upward into a ceiling of carved stone roses. Vines wound in mounds around chandeliers which dangled crystals in the low light of their bulbs. Sun angled in from slit windows, illuminating long patches of the creamy stone floor.

Three quarters into the room there was a lineup. People spoke softly as they waited. Every moment or so, the line shrank. Only as we merged with it did I clue into the shuffling of feet behind us.

I turned and saw two young men with a small brunette.

Andre tensed. He stepped forward into the line.

Roman and I followed behind him and waited.

The two men in front of us whispered back and forth between quiet laughs. They looked to be around Andre's age, which on the outside, was early twenties. One held the arm of the small woman they were with. Another brunette. She stood with a clenched jaw and nostrils fuming. She tugged her arm back, testing the hold of the man.

I stepped out and looked at the people ahead. The men all ranged in their looks. Their ages maybe between late teens and early thirties. The women, however, were all petite with dark hair, dark eyes, and fair to medium skin.

"Andre," I said. "Why do all these women look the same?"

He drew me to him and whispered, "Don't say anything about yourself."

"Andre!" One of the men ahead of us turned around. He ran his hand through his sandy blond hair which poofed up in the middle from the short choppy sides. His friend snickered, like a joke had been told. The woman with him glared and spat out some words in French.

"Where did you find this one? Let me guess?" the blond asked. "She's a townie whore from some dirt stop in the north."

I recoiled. Not from his obvious intent to get under Andre's skin, but from the fact he'd spoken in English to insult me as well. "I'm from Canada," I said, "and your flat-top haircut is older than the woman you're with."

His dark-haired sidekick turned to Andre and burst with laughter. "Canada! You think Aleksandr's lost daughter hid in *Canada*!"

Aleksandr. My father's name was Aleksandr.

The woman on his arm spoke in broken English. "I not the daughter you seek!" The toe of her strappy sandal flew out and nailed him in the shin. She tried to run free, but he dragged her backward.

"That's exactly what you would say if you were her," he said.

"*I'm* Karol—" Andre held his hand over my mouth.

Roman nodded to the woman. "Where's she from?"

"Paris," the blond said. "We tracked down a lead on a woman in Paris two years before Aleksandr was assassinated."

"When it comes down to the underground spy game, Andre, you're always going to be on the D-list. But hey, baby," the brunet grabbed between his legs, "if you ever want to find out what the A-team is packing, you know who to see."

The woman wormed away again. Her cries of pain shrieked out as she was yanked back to the brunette man.

Roman straightened up in front of him. "You tug on her arm like that again, and I'll break yours."

He took a whiff of the air close to Roman. "Wolf!"

The blond shot in front of Andre and me in a blur of vampiric speed. "You're pathetic. Now you're using wolves to fight your battles?"

My skin heated. It was like booking the flasher in

my internship all over again. Only this time, I didn't have to abide by rules of the law. I yanked at Andre's hand on my mouth and was puzzled to find him using his full strength to keep me from talking.

"You there!" A uniformed man stalked over, dressed similarly to the women upstairs. My senses noticed the smell of human blood on him, before my eyes found the dark stains on his dress jacket.

"What's going on here!"

"Andre thinks he's found Aleksandr's lost heiress. We explained we had her, and he tried to start a fight. It's okay, we understand when you're a bottom of the barrel snake, you'd do anything to change your position, including executing your own. Which is why no one will work with you."

The rest of the lineup laughed along with them.

"Careful, you never know when you'll show up on my retrieval list," Andre said.

The vampires in the line hushed, the chance of a fight holding their attention.

They were all a part of the vampire underground. Andre wasn't Loukin's top man at all.

I had the urge to bite a chunk out of Andre's hand. I would have, if I wasn't a tad impressed he'd tracked down the real Karolina Dalca. The pursuit of my identity looked to be some sort of bounty-hunting derby. The question was what was the prize? Andre was clear that my retrieval was his object. It'd been obvious he acted for his own self-interest, but he'd swindled his way into getting me to comply. It was an ingenious half-truth, mixed with lies. But I wasn't going to lose my chance to meet Loukin now.

I called forth my fire. My skin prickled with heat

and grew to a low flame. Andre jumped back, his burn being nothing compared to the humiliation I felt for falling for his lines at the restaurant. As quickly as the fire was produced, it dispersed. I stepped toward the man in uniform, into a patch of light. "I am Karolina Dalca," I said, "and I demand to see my uncle, Loukin Nabokov."

A fury of whispers rose like a storm throughout the hall.

"Very well," the man in uniform said. "We shall see who is correct. You six follow me."

Andre walked in front, creating more distance between myself and the other two agents. Roman covered my back. We passed by those who remained in the lineup. The ire in the other vampire agents' expressions made it clear this was a competition no one wanted to lose.

We passed through a set of doors onto a sunken floor. An intense prickle of magic draped over my skin. The room was a hexagon with vaulted ceilings. Multiple gold doors between hanging tapestries made it feel like the center of a maze.

A row of women who stood before a rich wooden desk turned their heads at our entrance. The men in the room hovered at the sides of the desk. It was untouched by the light of the chandeliers, but the noise of fingertips tapping the wood lifted my gaze to realize a person was there.

A candelabra flickered to life on the desk, lighting up a man's pale skin and striking dark features. Features similar to mine. He leaned his head against a green leather chair. His gaze fixed on me, lingered on my face, and trailed to my necklace.

He rose from his desk and paced around the women to stand before us. With a wave of his hand he urged the others away from me. Roman and Andre left my sides. He paused a moment for another appraisal of me, and then breathed in the faintest of breaths. Within his slight moment of stillness, his body spewed into a ball of flames. The liquid fire pummeled toward me in a torrent of flame.

In the millisecond I had to react—I froze. The heat blistered onto me as the massive ball of flames rose before my face.

Chapter Sixteen
The Truth

My eyes stayed open. The surge of flames activated parts of me my stunned brain couldn't. My own magic balled forth without being called. Before now, I would have said it wasn't possible. Just as the flames licked at my skin, a fiery mass blew out from my chest.

The force of fire on fire combusted the surrounding air, sending out a broiling shock wave. Everyone dove backward. Furniture flew into the air and crashed onto its sides. The heat wave dissipated, and my hair fell to my shoulders. Light smoke wafted across the room. The smoldering remains of the chandelier above fell to the ground with a clatter. I called up my fire for another attack.

"*Da*!" the man cried. "*Da*!" He spread his arms upward and laughed.

I let my flames die.

"My niece, at last I've found you. Clear the room!"

Everyone jumped to action, climbing over the flipped furniture and heading toward the doors. A few men and women had torn clothing, but most were untouched.

"Stay," I said to Roman and Andre. I wanted to tell them this wasn't the welcome I had hoped for.

"My dear, my name is Loukin Nabokov, and I am

pleased to meet you." He took my hand, placing a light kiss on it.

"I'm Karolina Dalca. Ana Dalca's daughter."

"Ah yes, Ana," Loukin said. "She was here to visit my brother often."

Andre straightened like he was giving a military report. "Ana Dacla gave birth to Karolina nine months after Aleksandr fled to Romania after the assassination attempt. I have confirmation, verbal and written reports, indicating Aleksandr fled to the Albesuc house in Romania and died there from his wounds in the night. After Karolina was born, her mother fled to Canada. I have proof Karolina is Ana Dalca's child with both of their birth certific—"

"That will not be necessary, Mr. Zima." Loukin held a hand in Andre's face. "I can tell she is my niece by just looking at her. You will henceforth cease all contact with Miss Dalca."

"No," I said.

"Not to worry, my dear," Loukin said. "We have plenty of others to assign as your personal guards."

"My apologies," I said, "but they will not be a vampire I trust. With all due respect, Andre found me, not the others. He risked his life to save mine and managed to get me here alive, despite multiple attempts on my life. He's proven himself to me." I didn't tell him I had plans to confront Andre about his lies after he and I were done speaking.

"We've bonded," Andre said.

Loukin snapped his head to me. "Is this true?"

"I needed blood, and I don't drink from humans. I was injured by a spel—."

Loukin held up another hand. "Please, don't

continue." He looked like he had something distasteful in his mouth. "We have willing humans here for feeding, so perhaps this will change your taste." He turned to Andre and Roman. "As you can imagine, gentlemen, I would enjoy a moment alone with my niece. Perhaps Mr. Zima can show you around, Mr…"

"Lupei," Roman said and held his chin up.

"Ah, A wolf. How lovely. It's been a while since we had your kind here. Zima!" His gaze fixated on Andre. "Please show our guest around. Perhaps the dining hall, billiards, and gentleman's room would be of interest. You will, of course, arrange the finest of rooms for our guests. The Princess Quarters would be fitting for Miss Dalca." His face warmed. "It's where your mother stayed when she visited."

Andre nodded. "Yes, Tzar." He turned and signaled Roman toward the door.

"Oh, and congratulations, Mr. Zima," Loukin said. "It seems you've made yourself indispensable."

"No," Andre said. "It's was all the years you commanded me to track down and kill our own which did that."

Roman and Andre left, with Andre slamming the door behind him. A heavy thud echoed against the floor as the wood shook in its frame.

Loukin turned to me. "Well, shall we?" He led me to his desk and gestured to a chair. He flicked his hand and more candles were given flame. The darkness which cloaked the area dispersed and detailed tapestry of portraits enlivened behind him. Of the men which were resurrected on the cloth, the one on the left held my attention.

"Tea?" Loukin asked and shifted an ornate tray

beside a gold samovar. "It's still warm."

My gaze was still hooked on the portrait. I slipped out of my chair and rounded the desk. His face was younger, but the chill creeping over me confirmed it was him. It was the man from my nightmare on the boat.

Loukin stepped beside me. "It's our family tree: your father Aleksandr, myself, and our younger brother Kazimir. I knew you were Aleksandr's daughter from your eyes."

The man who tried to kill me was my other uncle. My fingertips turned cold. I stuffed my hands into my pockets. The center photo was of Loukin. To the right…Loukin was correct…my father and I shared the same eyes. I traced the lines of my father's face on the tapestry, my mind absorbing every detail from the shape of his nose to the texture of the fabric.

"Aleksandr inherited his eyes from our mother. I see her now when I look at you. She loved her firstborn the most. It was only fitting he would share her likeness." He grinned, but the lines of his eyes didn't crinkle. "Your father was a valiant leader, of course. Everyone loved him, the people, our mother…Ana. They loved him for his love. Ironic, I know. You see, your father believed humans, vampires, the whole supernatural community really, could achieve peace. The Grand Hotel was a meeting ground in your father's time—still is. I try to keep it this way."

Warmth stirred in me at the mention of my parents together. "You said my mother was here often? Was it how they met? Were they in love?"

"Oh, very much so."

I always knew there was more to the story. *How*

can you fall in love with a man in one day, Mama? What do you mean that was it? So, you were seduced by some bloody rages and a half-dead man?

Loukin's voice rang out like bells, and I would never have guessed he had such a warm laugh. "Ah! There is Ana. You have your mother's smile."

"Did she live here with him?"

"Your father liked to keep his private life closed to the public, for fear of an enemy lashing out at those he loved. He liked others to believe he had many lovers. Women would come and go and stay in the Queen Suite. I don't know how they met, but I first noticed Ana in the rose garden. She had the look of a teenager in love. It was only after I met her, I noticed Aleksandr had the same look. Ana was always here after, and no one stayed in the Princess Suite but her. Later, Russian politics got more complicated and Ana left." He turned to his desk. "Your father's assassination shortly followed."

I resumed sitting in my chair. "Andre called you Tzar. It's my understanding you're the Second in Command of the vampire underground?"

"Your father was once Tzar, but after his assassination I was next in line for the throne. However, our younger brother unlawfully assumed control as Tzar, First in Command. Now Russian vampires are divided. Those loyal to me, the true Tzar, stay in the south. Kazimir's men remain in the north. We've been warring amongst ourselves ever since."

"You fight for your position back?"

"I try to keep the peace! Kazimir believes the human governments are to be dominated, while your father and I advocated for harmony. We are not so different, except for our moods, strength, and fangs. We need each other." He crossed his hands on his desk and the aristocratic air about him took hold.

"Is this why you've been looking for me?"

"Yes, my dear. You're Alek's only heir, and we couldn't risk losing you in this war."

"Did Kazimir kill my father?"

"Yes."

"Is he trying to kill me?"

"Yes, but we've found you, and on my word, no harm will come to you under my roof."

It was the truth which Mama died protecting me from. Dad was Russian royalty of a vampire organized crime ring. Uneasiness rolled in my stomach. "Is the hotel warded?"

"Surely you felt them?" he asked. "The hotel and all of its grounds are yours to roam."

"That's a lot of ground to cover."

"It's your mother's family which is most famous for their wards. The Albesuc house is said to be impenetrable."

"I have something to tell you," I said. "Mama was killed when my house was attacked by Shadow Forged."

Loukin's face turned into a stone mask. "So, the worst is true. When I noted you were alone, I hoped she'd stayed in Romania." He got up and paced to a painting. "I'm sorry, Karolina. I wanted to hear more about your Great Aunt's skillful wards. And to tell you about the heirloom you wear around your neck. But I'm afraid I need some time. Please make yourself at home." He gestured to the door.

I knew all too well the pain he might be feeling.

My heart bore down heavy in my chest. I outstretched my hand to his arm to comfort him.

He tensed at my approach.

I backed away. Relationships with my last remaining family were priceless, and I didn't want to smother mine with Loukin. I turned to the door, when a thought flashed across my mind. I had the opportunity to extend a kindness to him. I slung my pack off my shoulder and rustled around inside until my hand clasped the book. I lifted it out and undid the security string.

"Here. It's the Albesuc book of the Light Charm." I held it out. "To answer some of your questions about the wards. I just want you to know how grateful I am for your support."

"Thank you." Loukin took the book. "How kindhearted of you."

"No problem." I threw my pack back over my shoulder and turned before I witnessed any more of Loukin's private moments, but when I opened the door, I paused. "Loukin."

He kept his back to me as he clutched the book. "Yes, dear?"

"In sociology class, they say it's natural for all children to feel like their parents love the other more, but it's impossible. They always love their children equally. Just thought it was worth mentioning."

"You sound just like my mother. Thank you, Karolina, we'll chat again soon."

"See you," I said and stepped through the door.

I walked back down the cavernous hall. The warmth I had gained from my chat with Loukin faded when I reviewed what I'd learned about the man who'd killed both my parents. The wide slits of light had traveled across the floor and up the walls. It was midafternoon, and Roman and Andre were probably at each others' throats by now.

A woman's screams rang through the hall.

Chapter Seventeen
Unexpected Friends

I raced down the hall. A woman's voice cried out in Russian. Splashes of blonde hair flew out from behind the wooden door. She fell backward onto the floor. The woman I had mistaken for Bronwyn kicked out at a meaty set of hands. Her body slid from view, and a gold button bounced across the ground in front of the door.

I rounded the doorway and saw a mouth open wide near the woman's throat—fangs about to pierce her flesh. Reacting on instinct, I slammed the door into the vampire's face. He stumbled from the blow, covering his face with his hands and letting go of the woman. She fell to the ground and scrambled behind me.

I recognized his lumpy bald head. It was the bouncer who had previously let us into the hall. It was no wonder a six-inch-thick door to the face barely nudged him. His meaty form blurred toward me. My body lit up with a low glow of flames.

He stopped dead. "Whoa, whoa. I don't want any trouble here."

"Really?" I panted. "Because it looked like you did."

"Ina and I have a little game going. She says I can't feed on her, but she doesn't mean it."

"Sounded like she meant it this time."

"Sure. Whatever you say."

"Okay." It was too easy. He turned to walk away. "Oh, Lumpy," I said. "What are you forgetting to say?" I tilted my head to the woman.

He stared blankly at me.

"Really?"

"Oh! I'm sorry. I'm sorry, Ina."

She rustled around behind me and muttered in Russian. Lumpy took it as his signal to leave and hustled out. I turned back to the woman and looked up. The woman's eyes shared the same shade of blue as the Dyad Bronwyn, but her features were much fuller. She smoothed out the wrinkles of her skirt and dusted off her knees.

"Thank you." She took a small tube from her pocket. Bending down to pick up the button, she squeezed the tube and super-glued the button back into place. Then, as a finale to what seemed like a regular routine, she straightened a little nametag on her bust which read *Ina*.

"No problem," I said. "That happen a lot?"

"It's nothing a swift knee to the groin can't fix, but thank you for your heroism."

This is what my crewmembers would have called resilience. I took another look at the woman. She wasn't a vampire, or she would've been able to hold her own. Yet after her tango with the bouncer, she was calm. She could be a mix of species. Summoning up my senses, I sniffed the air.

"You're human," I said.

She thrust her hand out to me. "And you must be Aleksandr's heiress."

I shook her hand. "Yeah. How'd you know?"

"Same way, Lumpy, as you call him, did. Your fire.

Only the Royal Family wields the Fire Charm around here." She gestured to the door. "Shall we? I'm here to show you around."

I followed her through the doors and felt the light tickle of the hall wards again. It didn't quite compare to the ones around Loukin's office.

"This way," Ina said and climbed the stairs.

"You said the Royal Family. Do you just mean Loukin or others too?"

She led me through a set of arched doors at the top of the stairs and we wound through the crowded halls. "Yes, and his two sons, Alexi and Leonid. Your father had it too." She nodded to a woman across the room as we turned another corner.

"And Kazimir?"

"No. It was ironic really. He inherited the Water Charm." She laughed. "Some thought he would become a priest."

"Sounds like they were wrong."

Ina shoved me onto a barstool. "Not here," she whispered and sat down. "I need a moment." She greeted the bartender and ordered in Russian. Her fingers ran across the bar absentmindedly as she spoke, but her gaze had locked onto a man in the reflection of the mirror behind the bar.

The Bandhgala he wore rustled as he walked to a woman sitting at a table for two. Rings of huge emeralds shone in the light as he placed his drink down on the table beside her. They chatted for a moment and then he left, but the napkin which surrounded his glass remained. There were words scribbled across the surface of the napkin, barely there to the naked eye.

My eyes strained as I read the writing, and my

vampire senses were summoned too late. The woman's delicate hand casually covered the napkin, and a moment later she slipped it into her purse. The thick layers of gold jewelry around her neck tinkled as she glanced around the room. She straightened her woven vest, which could have been made for a Kayanin queen.

I gained a deeper understanding of what Loukin meant. The hotel did indeed seem like a meeting place for people around the world. I looked to the group on my left and wondered if I was in the presence of politicians and royalty.

"Okay, let's go," Ina said. She took two drinks from the bartender's hands. By the time I had slipped out of my chair, she'd already started to snake her way through the crowd. She handed me a drink once I caught up with her. I raised it to my mouth and the sweet scent of human blood filled my nostrils. My fangs glided through the roof of my mouth. A nauseating hunger turned in my stomach. I lowered the cup from my lips. "Sorry, Ina," I whispered. "I don't drink human blood."

"Really? Never?" She raised a brow at my fangs. "Looks like you have a taste for it."

"Another vampire's blood is different. I'm not preying on people."

Ina seized my arm, her mouth aghast. "*No. Way.*" She yanked me to the corner of the room. Her fingers were like steely pincers digging in between my muscles. I rubbed my arm.

"How many?"

"What?"

"How many vampires have you drunk from? Better yet," she hushed to a whisper. "Tell me who. Was it as good as they say?" Her eyes sparkled at me.

"Just one. We ran into a situation where I needed blood. I figured drinking from a vampire wasn't the same as drinking from a human."

"I bet it wasn't." Her grin widened. "Who? Who was it?"

"Andre."

"Andre!" She cut her laugh short, then looked around. "I've heard he's unrelenting."

"It's no big deal," I said. "Andre said it's a solution all vampires use when there's a shortage of blood."

"Oh dear," she said. "That *xep*!" She shouted then dropped to a whisper. "Vampires don't drink from other vampires. Not unless they want to bond. Very taboo. It's supposed to be one of the most erotic experiences a vampire can have. If I'm bitten, it feels good. But a vampire on vampire, much different. They connect spiritually. It's supposed to be epic, but there are side effects."

"Like feeling each others' emotions?"

She nodded at me.

The look on Loukin's face when we told him flashed through my mind, and my stomach turned. I held my forehead in my hand. "We told Loukin."

"How'd that go?"

"He looked like he wanted to kill Andre." I wouldn't have shared intimate details with my mother, let alone my uncle that I just met. "This couldn't be any worse."

"It's for life."

"What!" My hands balled into fists.

"When vampires bond, they've mated for life. Like a sexy marriage, but with no guests and a lot more blood."

I downed the cup in my hand. It tasted warm and sweet. Whoever donated the blood was happy. I, on the other hand, was the opposite. "Ina." My hand shuddered as I put the cup down. "Take me to Andre. Now."

Her face paled. "Yup."

By the time we entered the room Ina said the men would be in, I shook with anger. I anticipated Andre to set himself up to benefit from my retrieval but tricking me into an erotic vampire union was beyond any actions I imagined he could resort to. My face burned with heat. The veins pulsed in my neck as I scanned the room.

Andre and Roman stood by the bar. Andre threw his shot glass into the air and it collided with Roman's spilling on the wood. The loud beat of the music masked the sounds of their laughter. The two of them tossed back two more drinks and held up their hands to the bartender for more. A woman leaned into Roman, with long blonde hair and eyes of blue; she tilted her angular face up and whispered in his ear.

Bronwyn. I could have sworn it was her. I took a step forward, but a couple danced in front of Roman blocking my view. I looked to the side, but by the time my view was clear she was gone. I searched the room. She'd been here. The anger and frustration which steamed up inside of me made my skin crawl.

Andre's head turned to the door.

I jumped back out of view and leaned against the wall. The nausea in my stomach grew stronger as I held the bridge of my nose. *It couldn't have been Bronwyn, Karo; you're losing it.* For once, my inner-self made perfect sense.

"Do you want to get out of here?" Ina asked.

I nodded.

"Come on, I'll show you where the women hang out."

Ina let me in on the loop, for the women, the place to be was the pool. She was easy to warm up to and she told me about her mother and little brother living in Canada. We had common ground there. They had been sponsored to go over and every month she sent half her paycheck to them. It added to the list of reasons why I admired her. On the way to the women's dressing quarters, among the many features of the hotel, she had taken the time to show me the feeding area.

Loukin had told me they had willing donors here, but I expected to find more of the desperate junkies I saw in Romania. The facility was clean, comfortable, and even provided a complimentary glass of champagne. Ina explained the people in the waiting room were pampered and showered with treats. The better their mood, the better the blood would taste. As we walked past the blood barrels in the storage area, I was reminded of a wine ageing cellar. To create a rare barrel of blood, the donor was asked to disclose their heart's desire. If the hotel could grant it, they would, just before the moment of extraction.

The smell of fresh blood carried our walk to the donor rooms. People were hooked up to machines which calculated and withdrew a non-threatening volume of blood. Afterwards, they were provided with snacks and a thick stack of cash. It was more humane than grabbing people from the streets like Kazimir's men had at the parade. Loukin's facility was ethical, and now I had seen it, I feared I would harbor a dangerous predilection for guilt-free blood.

On the way to the pool we passed an ominous looking door. Thorny veins wound like snakes carved into the dark wood. By the way it was set into the floor it looked like it housed a staircase which plunged deep underground.

"What's down there?" I asked Ina.

"We call it the snake pit. That's where the *ispolniteli* get trained as new recruits. The ones who get deployed to hunt their own kind. Other vampires."

"You must not get a lot of volunteers."

"Most don't volunteer. They either accept the position or spend months in the pit. Eventually, they all accept the position. People learn to fall in line around here."

Andre had been called a snake. He'd spoken about killing his own. He was an *ispolniteli*. A draft from below the door blew upward, chilling my skin.

"Let's go," she said.

Ina arranged for a bathing suit for me. The women's change rooms, of course, continued the gold theme. When I stepped out onto the warm patio stones, the poolside garden rustled in the breeze. The rose garden was overgrown and unruly. When its branches caught in the wind it looked to have grown a foot before it settled. Ina called me ahead and I followed her onto the pool deck.

"This way." She walked toward two chaises with a small table between them and a sign marked *reserved*. Ina had done more than show me around. She took time out of her day to cheer me up. I didn't expect the extension of her friendship, but it was welcomed.

We walked by a few men who were sprawled out in the sun with drinks, and the better-looking one eyed up the curves of my body as I passed.

The next chaise was adorned with a naked woman, her legs fully parted. Her fangs glistened in the sun, along with a piercing between her legs. The redness of her most delicate region a clear cry for shade. I averted my gaze. She laughed.

Her companion, also bikiniless, sipped blood while she rubbed sunscreen onto her breast. The man beside her, completely unaffected by their nakedness, reviewed their plans for the evening.

I lay down and Ina took out two sunhats from her bag.

"It's time for drinks." She held up her hand for the waiter's attention.

"Won't argue you."

Ina turned and glanced at the men. "He's the king of Peru," she whispered.

"Really?" I looked over again and caught him looking our way.

"Well, king of the vampire underground in Peru."

I ordered a blood to start. My animal blood diet was derailed the moment I drank a glass of human blood upon the news of my marital union. The blood's sweet, sticky taste wasn't as intoxicating as Andre's blood, but it helped to numb my rage.

A man lowered a silver tray to me. "*Printsessa.*"

I took my second glass of blood and raised a brow at Ina in hopes of a translation.

"Princess," she said.

The whole time Andre had been calling me 'princess,' I thought it was his nickname for me. He meant it literally. It hadn't clicked until now, if my father had been a king—I would be a princess.

"*Spasiba,*" I said to the waiter.

Champagne was my second drink and my third. I rolled my shoulders and focused on the warmth of the sun on my skin. As I relaxed, my mind did too, and with the relaxation snippets of Andre's deception slipped by my mental blocks. I forced myself to think about Roman instead. He'd also lied to me.

The experience of being a werewolf swamped my memory. My strength had been incredible, but the beastly need to devour took over my freewill. It had been worse than any blood craving I ever had. All this time, Roman suppressed the beast, every moment of every day. A shiver clawed up my spine, which not even the warm sun could dispel. I now understood what he meant during our night in the woods, when he feared he would consume me.

Andre *had* consumed me. I let him drink my blood. Taste my soul. Entering into an act so intimate, with a man I'd just met was a gamble far more unnerving than my indiscretion with Roman's monster. I dipped my fingers in the pool and swirled them in the water. *Trust me*, he'd said. I let him touch my body, bond with my soul, and he'd used me. The blood and alcohol in my stomach churned into my mouth.

"Karolina," Ina whispered.

The anger in my chest reared, burning the vomit taste in my mouth.

"Karolina!"

I flicked my eyes open and glared at her. "What!"

She nodded to the pool beside me.

I turned my head and noticed a curtain of steam. I

looked down and saw the pool water bubbling around my hand. Nearby a woman cowered in the corner, trying to get away from the patch of water I'd raised to boil.

I gasped and yanked my hand from the water. "Shit! I'm so sorry!"

The woman looked at me wide-eyed.

"So sorry!" I looked at Ina. "I can't be here. I need to blow off some steam."

"Steam, really?"

I rolled my eyes. "No pun intended. You must have a training room of some kind?"

"We do."

"Great. Where am I going?"

"I'll have the king of Peru show you." Her eyes did that spark thing again.

Chapter Eighteen
Fight It Out

I opened the training room doors and walked down the steps. It was a large, square room. The high ceilings rose up from massive stone pillars which framed the sunken floor. An assortment of weapons lined the walls behind the pillars, giving the room an air of a medieval armory.

I inhaled the silence of the empty room, finding a moment of calmness. Then, I dove into a lunge and drove my hand into a fist. I flowed through each move of my martial arts routine. At the last second of every graceful position, my body flexed, and within the moment of force exertion, I dispelled a tiny piece of my anger. As I continued to fight my imaginary opponents, my senses electrified, and my thoughts dulled.

The sound of a sword unsheathing rang out through the room.

I tensed and spun around. The room was empty. I studied each pillar, waiting for a person to jump out.

A voice spoke in Russian, echoing into the square. "Show yourself!" I called.

A man stepped out from behind a pillar with a sword in hand. He had dark hair and an angular face. "I would know your style of fighting anywhere. You're a Dalca." His gaze grazed my necklace. "And Aleksandr's heir." He readied his sword. "Attack."

"You have a sword. The match is hardly fair."

"Life isn't fair. So, you must attack it."

"Sparring against a sword unarmed is suicide."

He charged, swinging the blade down to my shoulder. I dove to the ground and rolled. He slashed at my belly as I sprang up to my feet. I jumped back avoiding the range of his sword and an attempt to sweep my feet. My feet hit the ground. I thrust my hands upward and caught his forearm midair, halting the sword. "Listen, bud—"

His other hand hammered into the side of my ribs.

The wind was knocked out of me. My teeth ground. I didn't retreat but dropped a hand to seize his other wrist. With all my strength, I yanked his free arm across my abdomen, twisting his torso. I had both wrists. I hauled him backward onto my flexed knee and rammed it into his spine.

He grunted in shock. His sword rattled to the ground.

I glided back from him putting distance between us. He kneeled to the ground for a moment, clearly feeling the injury. Then he rose, looking exhilarated. "Good. Very good."

"You weren't so bad yourself." I panted. "But if you come any closer it's going to get really fiery in here." I'm usually up for a good sparring session, but this man was more than a little overzealous. I called up my vampiric agility for stamina.

"My name is Gerel Petrov." He laid a hand over his chest and bowed. "I trained your father and lived in the shadow of your mother's father."

"And the sword you use?"

"Mongolian."

"You have a Russian last name."

He sliced his sword through the air in a figure eight. "I am both Mongolian and Russian." He reset his sword into position. "Shall we go again? You can show me what other Dalca tricks you've inherited."

"I can, eh?" I tossed my chin up. "Where's your technique inherited from?"

"The origin of my technique is a secret you have yet to discover. Much like the purpose of the crown jewel you wear."

My hand clutched my pendent.

"He wants it, you know." He paced forward. "And I think you are not the type to give up what is yours so easily."

I glided back.

"If so, then you must protect yourself, little Nabokov."

He dove toward me again, and we began a dance in which only two martial artists could engage.

****

Hours later, I beaded with sweat. Exhilaration was pounding through my veins. There were moments in our training when I almost called Gerel Grandpa, out of habit of all the years I trained with Grandpa Dalca. My time with Gerel had been intense, but fun. With a few of his words, all my experiences with the Fire Charm clicked into place.

My family had kept fire lessons short: don't use it. I knew my emotions made my fire hard to control, but he'd confirmed the magic stemmed from my spirt. Fire users were rare due to a massive genocide of our kind. Society had decided such power was too dangerous to be put at the whim of the human emotion. When one factors in the volatile ups and downs of a vampire's mood, especially at night—it was catastrophic. Only select Royal families had managed to hold onto the fire genes, though it'd be possible for the genes to resurface again.

Gerel had taught me to focus on both my emotions and target. If my feelings overwhelmed me, my fire would do the same. If I pictured what I wanted to strike and held the image in my head, I could focus my fire into a precise attack, like the wick of the candle Loukin lit when we first met. The pitfall was I had to maintain focus, which wasn't an attribute of mine.

When Gerel left the training room, I opted to stay and continue my practice. I found a music player set into the stone wall and selected a top forty station on the radio. Techno dominated the dance chart favorites in Russia, and the combination of music and endorphins had me feeling renewed.

Andre walked through the training room doors.

I kept going with my training routine like he wasn't there. My fist flew out for a punch so hard, my knuckles cracked.

He turned the volume down and sat down on the steps. "Hey. Can we talk?"

I continued through the motions, but my balance teetered. "I'm busy."

"I have some explaining to do."

"You do?" I round housed my imaginary opponent, and decided I blew him into oblivion. "I'm surprised, I thought pawns didn't get explanations." My fist flew out like rapid fire. "You know, since they're busy being used by another for their own purpose." I pivoted and slammed into another strike.

He rose and crossed the distance between us. “Can you stop?”

“No. Move.” I shouldered past him, but his hand extended to my lower stomach, stopping me.

“The goal was to find you. Prove myself…if we could bond then I would ensure my new position.”

I shoved him. “I don’t want to talk!”

He grasped my outstretched hands and pinning them against his chest. “I wasn’t prepared for how I would feel about you.”

I twisted his hands out to the side.

“Or how Miruna restored a lost part of my soul.”

I twisted farther. He let go, but he closed the foot of distance between us and pressed against me. His hand gripped my back and slid up into my hair. His weight bore into me, causing me to stumble backward up the steps and against a pillar.

“You used me.”

“I know,” he said. “I wasn’t whole.” Smoothly, like the unseen force of a magnet, his face drew close, and then halted, restraint leaving him teetering just before my mouth.

The anger I had bottled up inside of me dissolved—leaving only my swirling stomach. Blood rushed to my skin, increasing the feel of his touch. Like he felt my heartrate spike, he leaned deeper against my hips, cupping my face in his hands. His cologne filled the short span of air.

“Please,” he whispered. “I don’t want to fight.” He took the wall he had between us down. The sensation of his affection flooded into me, starting at my toes, and crowning at my head. “If I could go back in time, I would change the way I treated you. But I wouldn’t change being with you."

His genuine admiration, lust, and need swirled within me like a storm. Those feelings grew, until they peaked and stunned my senses. The room around me spun. I felt intoxicated.

He found the edge of my shirt, then the top of my jeans. His fingers glided across my hips. I tilted my head back and bit down on my lip. Blood flavored my mouth. In the fog, my mind slowed on my memories of the dorm. Where we left off, what we didn't do.

He tugged at the edge of my jeans.

I met his gaze for the first time since he entered the room. His eyes were very, very blue, like a beacon for me to focus on in the haze, while my senses climbed higher.

"Please forgive me?"

My anger at him was gone. It had evaporated with the world around me. I was angry about how I felt about him. Not what he'd done. His deception had been real and calculated, but he'd put his plan in motion before he'd changed. I knew it, and in the daze, I could no longer lie to myself.

A steamy heat turned inside which wasn't my fire magic. It rose up and turned unbearable. My back arched, and I kissed him. He parted my lips with his tongue, then reached down and hoisted me into the air, wrapping my legs around him. Hot air blew out over my face. I was pinned between him and the pillar.

I ran my hands over his skin, feeling his excitement peak at my touch. I felt the hardness of him between my legs. His pleasure bled into mine, making me feel like my body was spilling into his.

A tiny rational part of my mind buzzed at me like a

bee. *Is it the bond or is it real?*

A sound escaped Andre, as he jerked my pants down to my thighs. The warmth of his skin slid between my legs.

No, no. I had a thought. Something important. The bond. It was the bond. I spread my hands against Andre's chest and forced him back. His mouth parted from mine, allowing a gust of the cool room air on my face, sobering me just enough.

"I can't," I slurred.

Andre backed up enough to let my legs slide to the ground. He looked shaken, leaning against the pillar with both arms on either side of me.

I jerked my jeans up. "I'm sorry."

"What is it?" His breathing was still labored.

"I just. I can't. I'm sorry." I ducked under his arm, and bee-lined it to the doors. Andre whispered inaudibly just as I left the room.

By the time I found my suite, I still hadn't cooled off. I closed the hotel room door, whipped off my clothes, and hunted out the shower. At the risk of the cold water being counterproductive, I banned all thoughts of Andre. The ice water numbed my skin, and slowly the furnace inside of me cooled.

I toweled dry and explored the hotel room. The Princess Suite was various shades of light pink to deep crimson. The characteristic gold accents continued. Loukin or perhaps Ina had some essentials laid out on the couch in the living room for me. Next to a warm set of pink pajamas, there was a cell phone and laptop. Ina had to be the culprit.

I pounced like a cheetah. Hello, social media. Hello, texting my friends again. Hello, celebrity gossip and countless hours spent with online videos. I sprang to action on the keyboard, but my fingers froze after I started keying in the internet access code. I couldn't do any of those things. I was still a wanted fugitive in Canada. The risk of my accounts being flagged for activity wasn't one worth taking. I slapped the laptop lid closed.

A cold chill cascaded down my back.

I turned my head to the hallway door. The lock was in place. A chilly breeze blew inward from underneath the door. I sat in silence as a shadow flickered across the bottom of the doorframe. A white envelope slipped under the wood and glided across the carpet on a gust of air.

Chapter Nineteen
Blood for Blood

The cracks of the hallway door lit up fluorescent white. I shielded my eyes. Then, the light was gone. I slid off the couch and prowled to the door. I looked through the peephole, then flung the door open. The hall was empty.

I stepped out, fists clenched and ready for a fight. A squeaking noise traveled along the carpet behind me. I spun around. A bug-eyed bellboy with a trolley stopped. He stared at me as the suite door behind him clicked closed. I tightened the towel around my torso and backed up into my room.

When I walked toward the couch, the white envelope crunched underfoot. I summoned my Charmed senses. There was no tingle or abnormal feeling to signal any magical tampering. I scooped it up and held it to the light of a chandelier. There was a note inside. I tore into it.

Dearest Karolina,

I am requesting the honor of your presence for a formal introduction. With so little family left, we must cherish our precious moments while we have them. I would come to you, but I thought your friends may not favor my visit…and then I would not favor them. I hear the wolf introduced himself to my men in Romania, and now Russia. I thought it was a lovely gesture. One so lovely, I would like to return it to his parents in Canada. That is, if I'm not preoccupied by our visit. My men will be waiting for you in the main park at 11:00pm.

Sincerely your Tzar,

Kazimir Nabokov

I crumpled the letter. If I didn't meet Kazimir then he would go after Roman's family. The majority of ransom notes ended in death; it was just one of the cold statistics of policing. I would be lying to myself if I believed I'd be excluded. I remembered Roman's mother, and how his father retired from carpentry work as his body got older. Now that I knew Roman was a werewolf, I wondered if his father's charismatic strength passed down to him. Why else had Roman gotten so strong in adolescence, and his father suddenly so weak? With Roman here, both his parents might be defenseless.

Kazimir also referred to my friends. Werewolves and vampires could fight for themselves, but the civilians at the Grand Hotel had no abilities. Loukin said he was at war with Kazimir. He would have prepared for an attack. The hotel was warded. But he said it himself; his wards were not Miruna's. I considered how weak his wards were in the hotel lobby. I hadn't even felt them. The hotel might not survive a massive assault, and if it didn't, its occupants wouldn't either.

His wards also couldn't protect the surrounding towns. I weighed the events of the parade. Kazimir's men were confidently venturing into Loukin's claimed territory and abducting people from the streets. When I questioned the war for title of Tzar, Loukin snapped at me. It wasn't obvious at the time, but it was now. His irritability was more than anger birthed from betrayal. His resources were draining. Could it be this was a war Loukin was already losing?

The clock on the wall read ten-twenty. I picked up the phone and dialed zero. With a ring and a half, the operator answered.

"Ello," a woman said.

"Roman Lupei, *spasiba*."

The call beeped to voice mail. "Hey, Ro, I guess you're out and about." I twirled the phone cord in my fingers. "I just wanted to tell you; I'm going out for a bit. I may not be back for a while. I just wanted to let you know, I love you. Thank you for being my best friend."

I rolled my neck, and with a large crack the tension eased up. I walked through the living area to the bedroom and found the closet. As I hoped, arrangements had been made for clothing. I rifled through the hangers and gambled Ina wouldn't fail me now. At the back, there was black spandex. I took the pieces of clothing from the hangers and ripped off the paper tags. It was a training outfit.

I climbed into the skin-tight fabric and caught a flash of my dark silhouette as I passed by the mirror to get a set of runners. In the current setting, I looked ridiculous. I recalled the image of Tod dressed in all black during the daylight. But once I was out in a park at night, I'd blend into the shadows. I found my key card and tucked it into the safest place for a busty woman: the inside of my bra.

The main hotel level had filled with more people. As the evening was still new, the crowds would get worse. I squeezed my way through the throng into the main lobby. As I hoped, it thinned out the closer I got to the door. People were heading in rather than out. I wove into a group which had stopped to ask for directions from a babushka telling fortunes. Just when I was about to celebrate my escape a hand took my arm. But Lady Fortuna had still given me an edge, as the hand belonged to a cute young man.

"Excuse me, Miss Dalca. But we've been advised not to let you leave the grounds tonight."

"Oh, but you wouldn't deprive a girl from her workout routine, would you?" I touched the muscle of his arm and sloped my back, letting my natural attributes shine. "It looks like you keep up with yours pretty regularly."

He took the opportunity to check out what I was selling, but he didn't buy it. "I'm sorry. I can't let you leave."

"Look, I've had the worst day and all these people are smothering me. Please. Even if I just jog along the ward line, I need to get outside for a run."

"Fine," he said. "You've got ten. But just before the ward line, like you said."

"Thank you."

After a few minutes of jogging, I figured I kept up the ruse long enough. When I was clear of sight I dove through the bushes. A twig scratched my face, but I kept going at a full run across the street. There was a tourist park in the center of town, which we passed on our drive in. It was logical to think the main park would be the largest. I tracked beams of moonlight on the tree leaves up into the northern sky. When I found the moon, I got my bearings. If I hoofed it in this general direction, I'd eventually stumble across the park. I dumped all my vampiric strength into my run, covering as much ground as I could within the seconds I had.

A sign confirmed I chose the right direction. I kicked up turf and sprinted off the sidewalk across a neighboring lawn. My sights narrowed on a grouping of trees. I stopped at the mouth of the park entry. The last light of twilight disappeared. The town was immersed in blackness. The quiet filled with the sound of crickets and my shoes squishing on the freshly watered lawn.

I prowled the park. The smell of freshly cut grass masked any other scents. What looked like the outline of a man in the darkness now appeared to be a tree. I called up my vampiric eyesight and focused on the surrounding noise. My eyes adjusted to the night. Shrubs surrounded me.

A twig snapped and I reacted by calling my fire. It was a mistake, as I started glowing.

Lady Fortuna was known for being a fickle bitch.

"*Vot!*" A man's voice called from a shrub no more than three meters from me.

The sound of thunder clapped. A dark bolt let off a sinister glow as it streaked through the air. The bolt blew into my shin before my fire grew. A searing pain snaked around my ankles, entrapping my other leg. I slammed into the ground. The whiplash knocked the air from my lungs. More pain screamed up from my legs as the lightning bonds charred deeper into my skin.

The silhouette of a man streaked before me against the backdrop of the night sky. There was a crack and his face lit up with an eerie light.

Another dark blaze of lightning shot toward me.

I shielded my face. I called my fire again, but I felt

the dark magic on my skin block it from my access. The bolt slammed into my wrists, snaring them in a blistering pain. It coiled up my forearms. I cried out as the smell of burning flesh wafted to my nose. The echo of my screams cut off, as I gagged down the contents of my stomach.

A fist hammered down into the side of my face.

****

The pressure in my temples pulsed into my eyes. My head pounded. I considered rolling over, but even the idea made me nauseated. I lay still, barely conscious, trying to get orientated to my surroundings.

A swift kick landed on my gut.

It took me off guard. My muscles didn't flex, and I hadn't even recoiled. Either I was still way more asleep than I realized, or I had put up with a beating for a while. My face felt hot and swollen with fluid. Patches of swollen skin thumped with each pulse of blood. Some areas of me felt warm and wet. Other parts of skin ballooned with pockets of cool blood. A new welt started to form on my stomach.

My ears filled with the sounds of droplets hitting the floor. My hearing was back. I focused on the drops. They fell from my abdomen to below. My head rested on the inside of my outstretched arm. The loud slapping of the drops continued, so loud, they had to be falling on a surface made of metal. In front of my eyes was dark, but I could make out a faint slit of light. I was blindfolded. I kept my eyes closed and focused on the floating feeling of being in motion, the wind whooshing. The odd bump below caused the area I was on to jostle. I was in a van.

A group of voices laughed, and a woman's high-pitched cackle pierced the air.

I flinched this time. Which told me I was back, as much as I could be, and so was the pain. The pain I felt when I first awoke was a massage compared to what it was now. My teeth ground together, and I started to count the voices in the room around me. One, two, three…the pain broke through and I lost my focus. I had to remain calm. I knew my survival depended on it.

Weight shifted on the floor and my focus was redirected back inside of the van. The sound of heavy boots paced toward me. A few of the voices murmured in Russian. The sound of the last footstep hovered around my ear. The heavy breathing of a man hung in the space above me.

I recoiled. My wrists tugged hard against the crispy bonds which had charred into my skin. I cried out, yanking them deeper into the raw burns. It was another mistake. I gave myself away; they now knew I was awake. Though the dark magic was depleted, I lost any edge I had.

Two hands clasped around my shoulders, hauling me up into the air. The others in the room screamed out together. My panic flared, in an instant, the thought of exploding into fire crossed my mind. I could lay waste to this van and those in it—but it wouldn't get me to Kazimir.

His breath touched my skin a second before his fangs tore into my flesh. He ripped into my shoulder sideways and flayed my skin from the bone. Pain sizzled up the nerves in my neck, and my fingers contracted. I screamed as the warm liquid trickled down my arm. The endorphins from the vampire bite arrived way too late to counter the carnage he started with. He wanted it to hurt.

He lapped up the blood from my neck, until his mouth jerked away. His hands jarred from my shoulders and I fell to the ground. The blindfold around my eyes slid off my hair and onto the metal floor. I squinted against the fluorescent lights of the van.

A meaty vampire knelt before me, his eyes glazed and blood dripping from his chin. A second vampire stood behind him holding him by the neck and screamed into the side of his face in Russian.

"*Mne zhal, mne zhal!*" the underling cried. He put his hands into a praying position. "*Mne zhal!*"

The second vampire threw him into me, and his knee landed on my bloody arm. I looked down at my black clothes now turned garnet-red and gasped. Blood pulsed from the bone exposed on my shoulder and splashed to the floor. In the latent effects of bite euphoria, I hadn't felt the blood loss.

He leaned to me, letting his putrid breath fill my nostrils. His fangs sank into his wrist. He held his arm to me.

I closed my mouth. I would rather let myself bleed to death, than drink his blood. The room spun wildly.

He pried at my lips. The blood from his wrist dribbled onto my chin as he fumbled with my mouth. I held my lips tighter. The bright lights above grew hazy. The vampire in command rushed over and flipped me onto my back with his boot. He tried to open my mouth and the watch he wore caught my sticky blood-soaked hair. I winced. He leaned his weight on my jaw, and the muscles of my mouth strained.

"Drink," he said.

When he glared at the vampire who'd bitten me, I

understood the vampire had done so without his commander's consent. The goon had too much wiggle room. He'd bitten me and indulged himself, but I lost too great a volume. If they presented Kazimir a dead Karolina, instead of a live one, the fear on their faces told me they'd regret it.

My jaw gave way.

They shoved the goon's bloody wrist against my lips. The taste of his blood made me shrivel. Rotten capers. The bitter flavor washed over my tongue, full of blind anger and numbing regret. As I swallowed down the foul-tasting salvation, I could feel the tiny shreds of muscle fibers in my shoulder rejoining to themselves.

The goon jerked his hand from my mouth the moment the wound on my neck formed a raw scab. He denied me any more blood than I needed to survive, making my half-healed injuries come alive with new zeal. My nerve endings exploded and screamed messages to my brain, shrieking for relief.

What was worse was through all the bodily pain, the feelings of the lout who'd bitten me started to creep into my body. It was what I feared. When he drank from me and was forced to feed me his blood—the bond was formed between us. I shuddered at the self-loathing and hatred which trickled in.

This would be my breaking point, like a crack in a breastplate, which would let the next blow shatter it to pieces. This was the chink in my armor. The optimism I had in my strength would be gone. No. He couldn't be a part of my soul. Not now. Not ever. I glared at them all and a coldness fell over me. With a sweeping bout of strength, I slammed an icy barrier between myself and the man.

His head jolted back like he was punched in the face. Others caught his arms to stabilize him.

The van doors flung open, making some heads turn. We'd come to a halt while I was fetched back from the brink of death. The lone woman in the crew kept her gaze on me. It must have been her shrill laugh I'd heard. She surveyed me and the hairs on my skin prickled. Women had to try harder in a man's profession. I'd experienced it myself. She was a woman looking to prove herself.

The men bustled out the doors. Their boots smacked down onto a hard floor. It echoed like concrete in a garage. The man I presumed to be the leader was last to leave. He jumped out and turned to me, seizing me by the bonds around my ankles. Pain flared up from my burns. He dragged me to the van doors. My hair caught in the coagulating blood. The van's uneven metal floor dug into my wounds. The fluid from my blood blisters popped.

His other hand took my wrists' bonds. He tossed me out of the van. I took the impact on my forearms and shins. The twinge from my funny bones shot up my arms, but I got a view of my surroundings. We were in an armory. The room was built like a giant concrete bunker, one built to house all the weapons one needed—to be a Russian vampire mob boss.

Metal rattled behind me. I looked back just in time to see the industrial-sized garage door close on the mountain landscape. The glimpse of detail I collected stood out in my mind. Miles out in the darkness was a low glow from the cluster of lights in a city. It was the closest civilization.

Dozens of vehicles filled the loading area.

Blackened trails of old blood streaked across the floor to a set of lab doors. Computer screens lined one wall, displaying live security feeds of a modern mansion, but what stood out the most were the guns. Some of them were out on tables, others behind metal fencing secured by large keypad locks. Anything from a hand pistol to an assault rifle was at my captors' disposal.

I had no idea how much money was poured into this place, but I knew one didn't have security like this unless one had a treasure worth protecting, like a dynasty. This had to be Kazimir's.

Two of the men walked toward me, one being the lout. Fire turned in my belly as he grew closer. I had a few mere seconds to form a plan. The woman hung back against the wall. Her hand rested close to a thick automatic. The leader hovered to my right, leaving only one man and the woman out of proximity. If I took the three closest to me out at once, it would only leave two. The added possibility of a wall of bullets wasn't good risk mitigation. In any case, I was too weak.

I needed more blood.

"Move!" shouted the leader. He slammed his foot into my thigh.

I scrunched and toppled over.

The other two men stepped forward.

"Get up," said the lout.

"I can't." My voice fluttered out as a pitiful whine. I strained meekly against the floor, letting my arms buckle and closed the distance to the ground.

"Grab her," the leader said as he started to walk toward the door.

The lout scoffed at me and bent down. His colleague remained at his side.

I squished my chest against the floor, drawing the lout farther down, creating more distance between the man beside him. I drew my senses up. My fangs poked against my tongue. The moment I felt his rough hands around my shoulders, I pivoted. My face rushed toward his neck.

I ripped into him with a ferocity which sickened even myself.

Chapter Twenty
Kazimir

The bitter taste of rancid capers which was this man's soul washed over my mouth once more. I swallowed the blood. My flesh sprung to life, fostering new connections between the tissues of my muscle. My wounds repaired. My vampire senses invigorated. Strength sailed through me, revitalizing me with every second.

The two vampires closest to me blurred forward, but they were too late. The charred bonds were broken. I unleashed a wall of fire from my outstretched palm. The air of the room sucked inward with a whoosh. Using the focus Gerel had taught me I kept the rest of myself from igniting.

The two men who charged skidded to a halt, their boots squeaking on the concrete. Their silent silhouettes disappeared behind the thundering flames, just as the first gun shot rang out through the garage. Within the same moment, the lout lashed out catching me in the jaw.

I jerked my head, gouging my fangs deeper and stripping his muscles from a tendon, all the while straddling him tight between my thighs. He froze in shock. I threw all my weight into a tuck and roll, carrying my new meal along with me. The world blurred as I traveled at a rate not humanly possible.

The bullets missed us by an inch, whizzing through the air. With a series of booms which deafened the ears, the shots rained into our trail as we rolled. Caught between our rapid escape and an all-consuming thirst, a monster awakened within me. I never felt more powerful, more formidable. The thirst intensified with every second. I needed more. His body grew limp. I heaved against his shoulder, syphoning more blood into my mouth. His body jerked. Like rapid fire, bullets tore into his legs, traveling up to my thighs wrapped around his torso.

I had to let go, but my fangs dug deeper. I felt the whoosh of the bullets cutting through the air above my skin. I yanked my face from his flesh and shoved him in front of me while I dove to the side. The bullets peppered into the lout as a momentary shield.

My sights set on the remaining man. A feral instinct overtook me. I could feel my mouth forming into a snarl above my fangs. Power from the fresh blood coursed through my veins. I crouched low, just as the woman with the automatic rifle was correcting her sights. In my split-second window, I sprung from the concrete and soared toward the man.

The vampire had called for his magic the moment before I sprang, and with a clap a dark bolt of electricity was sailing where I once was.

He had expected me to charge him like a human—I hadn't.

I collided with his shoulders, taking him to the ground. His neck snapped. I rose. The woman opened fire. My fire plumed, hissing as it expanded into the air and melting the concrete ceiling above. The rounds sizzled into vapor when they hit the inferno.

She dropped the gun and flashed toward the door, moving with a speed days ago I never could have matched. Now, with a belly full of vampire blood, my strength felt godly.

I flew after her, my flames licking at her heels. Just as she made it through the door, the fire around me bore down on the doorway. The concrete it touched liquefied and dripped down, making cracks streak into the structure. The ceiling crumbled as I dashed through the hole.

A dark and empty feeling seized the pit of my stomach. I stopped. I turned back as the icy fingers of fear trailed up my spine. My teeth chattered as an unexplainable force dragged my gaze to the lout—the vampire who'd been forced to bond with me. My gaze met his just as the last bit of life drained out of him. A shudder reverberated within me, dropping me to my knees. Tears clouded my vision, and an unbearable loss filled me. I hadn't cared about the lout. The pain he inflicted on me would plague my dreams. What I experienced was magic at work. I experienced the bond being broken.

The rest of the concrete wall crashed to the ground like drumfire. I climbed into the hallway. The woman turned a corner at the far end of the lengthy foyer. I didn't chase her. I looked at the football field sized aquarium at my side.

My initial view was blocked by a raised iron platform, but as I looked up, an array of tropical fish swam by. I peered through the tank into the luxurious interior of the mansion on the other side. Large dark shadows cut through my view. Inside the aquarium were sharks. The oceans' most famous killers cruised above studying the shapes below. The sharks' black eyes stayed fixed on me as they sliced through the water.

The trickling sound of water nearby originated from spouts in the wall, which formed tranquil streams of water lining the hallway path. The manmade creeks formed streams and fountains throughout the decor.

A stir of silhouettes pulled my gaze to the right. The opposite side of the hallway was lined with modern clear glass cells. At a glance, it looked like they housed the dead, skeletons strewn in a heap, until one moved. She was cadaver-thin and covered in bruises. One by one the corpses rose, like a chilling movie scene where the dead rise. Their frail faces fixated on me. Some ghosted forward and limply banged on the glass. From underneath the dead, more people revealed themselves. They looked plump enough they could have just arrived.

In the middle, a young boy in a red baseball hat smacked a photo against the glass. Tears streamed down his cheeks. The picture was of himself and his twin brother. The boys stood in a baseball field wearing wide grins. The Tzar's personal bloodstock. I knew what I'd found, and I knew I had to help them. My fire, along with my blood lust, diminished.

Rubble from the wall had crashed down onto a nearby cell and scraped the glass, telling me it must have been shatter proof if it could withstand a concrete slab. I looked at the locks on the cells. They were the same electronic keypads which were inside the armory. I extended my hand to the lock and let loose a wave of fiery heat. It melted away.

The glass door swung open and the people inside

flooded to the rubble of the downed wall. They didn't head inside the mansion, which told me they had entered the compound the same way I had. They climbed over the debris and gathered at the garage door. I turned back to a row of at least twenty cells.

I ran and repeated the same action to the second cell, and then the third. By the time I had sprinted to the fourth cell and melted the lock, the female vampire rounded the foyer corner with a group of reinforcements. The people behind me cried out. The vampires ran at me.

I planted my feet.

A ghoulish shadow of a shark glided across the ground, and as the mass of vampires sprinted, their screaming jaws were painted in the lurking shadows. The faint glistening of dark magic oozed from some of their palms.

I gave up more ground.

The seconds rolled by, and with the lout's blood in my belly, the vampires' movement no longer blurred in my sight.

A man's outstretched fist flew to my face.

My forearm met his, and in a flick of my wrist I took his arm and ripped it off his shoulder. Sidestepping his body, I ducked and flipped a vampire over my knee. His back broke in half. My unearthly strength hijacked my mind. A blank bliss. I struck with the lightning fast precision I'd trained for my whole life.

I downed three more vampires before I recognized myself.

They regrouped and attacked again at the same time.

I dove into the air, twisting a man to the ground by

his neck with my feet, just as a dark bolt of magic grazed my belly. The woman's fangs rushed to my neck. I shattered her jawbone. A gargantuan blow to my side broke my ribs as I landed. I wasn't the only one drinking vampire blood. Pain ignited with every breath I took. I clenched my jaw and scrambled back.

They flowed toward me like a stream, and I retreated up the iron stairs of the platform before the aquarium. A shark skimmed the glass beside me, kicking up debris in the current. A small red baseball cap tapped against the tank. I looked to the boy who still beat against the cell. He wore the same hat. It was the hat the missing boy wore in the picture. Vomit burned into my mouth. Kazimir's empire was fed from the blood of innocent people, and once they were drained dry, their remains were shark food. No bodies to be found. No charges could be laid for the missing persons' cases.

It was too insidious to bear. My fire flared out. As quickly as the mob advanced on my retreat, the blaze engulfed them. I leapt from the melting platform, incinerating the vampires beneath me. Blasts of fire soared through the glass cages, melting huge holes which served as escape routes for the terrified prisoners.

I kept going, cutting into the vampires with a fury which rivaled the pain of Mama's death. As the last remnants of the group scattered, I ran to the boy in the cell.

The water from the stream which lined the walkway trickled upward defying gravity, forming a mass before me.

The boy backed up from the cell wall trembling in

fear. I held my hand to the glass, hoping to melt it once the boy withdrew far enough. I wanted to tell him it would be okay—I wanted to hold him.

The water shot toward me in a pummeling stream. At first it evaporated on contact, and with a hiss steamed into the air. But more kept coming. It flowed like a fifty-pound broken water main. The torrent of water bore deeper into my flame, and in every second the water evaporated, it was replaced with more. The fluid carved deeper into the inferno, and closer to my face.

I dug deep, trying to channel my emotions. I had to save the boy. I dodged to the side, but it followed with the quick reflex of human life. The tidal flow of water hammered inches from my face. Sweat beaded from my brow and I forced my last bit of strength out into the flame. As quickly as the energy was spent, the colossal pressure of the water hammered into my face.

I was hurled into the floor. Water filled my nose and mouth. I opened my eyes. The spouting stream cut like sandpaper against my upturned eyelids. Shiny black shoes paced toward me, kicking ash and metal out of the way. They stopped at the pool of water, keeping the soles dry. A man crouched down, his hands moving rhythmically in front of him, like the fluid motion of water.

I looked onto the face I'd seen in Loukin's office. His black eyes cut through the flow of liquid like the angular features of the sharks above us.

My vision spotted. He drifted away.

****

I awoke shivering against a cold metal table. My eyes flickered but I squeezed them closed. A voice I assumed I'd dreamt spoke in whispers which bounced off the walls.

"Come on, Kazimir. What are you waiting for? Kill her already. Secure your position." She put sultry inflection on the word kill, giving it a convincing appeal, one even I felt spurred to act upon. I diverted my mind from her incantation, only to be lured in again as her voice lulled on.

"Loukin's claim will be demolished. Not only will he be overthrown, but his desperate attempt to appeal to vampire Russia with Aleksandr's heir will be squashed."

The temptation was too real. I opened my eyes a sliver. I wasn't dreaming. Bronwyn stood at Kazimir's side. Her long blonde hair shimmered in the dark low light of the room, like it had magic of its own. She looked down at a white bird on her forearm. It was the albino falcon from the shop in Canada. She'd been the one tracking us.

"Yes, I'm finishing what you couldn't," Kazimir said. "You forget you failed me originally."

Her melodic voice took on an edge. "If it wasn't for Lukas, I would have finished her then and there. You forget; I have a cover to maintain."

"The boy's an issue."

"Don't worry about him. He's in love with me. He thinks we're ridding the world of its evil, one righteous little battle at a time." Her laughter chimed out, sounding like it was made of sunshine.

Kazimir scoffed.

"Oh, you aren't jealous, are you Kazy?" She traced circles on his chest. "You know no one could ever be you…"

Kazimir took her wrist. "Save your magic for a *svolotsch* it will work on. She's up. You know your way out."

"I want to watch," she said.

Kazimir walked toward me. "So be it."

I opened my eyes. The walls of the room were dark and moving. A mass of Shadow Forged rippled above me, like tormented mounds of people covered in tar. The eight appendages of the misshapen arms and legs scuttled by along the walls in their spidery forms. By a sconce close to me, one reared its head and mouthed a soundless scream.

Kazimir flicked his hands like a maestro and water flowed up from a moat lining the room. The liquid formed tidal waves, and with a swish of his hand they rolled toward me. I jumped at the rushing waves and felt slimy bars against my skin. Fire flared up from my skin with a whoosh. I wrestled against the restraints expecting their incineration.

They remained.

Steam wafted into the air where the water crashed into the edge of my fire. The waves halted just before the table, raining down speckles of water as they towered overhead. The ceiling stirred like a dark cyclone above me. More Shadow Forged gathered in the mound. Claustrophobia set in. The memories of being smothered resurfaced.

"Karolina." The waves parted for Kazimir to appear at my feet. "Welcome."

Sheer motor reflex took over. The veins in my neck bulged as I screamed and used all my strength against the bars. They fought back. Like an eel they wriggled and tightened against me.

"Don't bother. Bronwyn forged those bonds. Her light magic is impenetrable. Thanks to her, my whole compound is."

"Great. Then our bonding time won't be disturbed," I said.

With my fire dispelled, the metal I lay upon cooled, chilling with the moisture in the air. He wanted me to feel cold and alone.

"I see you inherited my sense of humor. How flattering. You also inherited my pious nature. Were it not for the boy, you would have seen me coming. You know…I thought I would be a priest. Like you, I wanted to save as many as I could." He remained polite, but his face looked both calm and disturbed, like the man I'd seen holding the detonator in a bomb de-escalation video. "They demeaned me. A water user born into a family where fire reigned. A man of my skills could only be useful in the church. But as I studied my powers, and God, I realized I was God. Water…is…the…most…powerful."

He signaled to Bronwyn.

She stepped forward and stretched out her palm. Her hair whooshed back as a rush of frigid air blew to us, freezing my skin. An eloquent twirl of Kazimir's fingers, in a second of time, separated a wave from the pack which barreled toward her. The wave thundered as it met the gust, forming barbs of ice mid-air. But the water rumbled onward. Chunks of ice tossed in the wave, rushing into her, and swallowing her from view. Water splashed to the ground, leaving a human-like statue of ice.

"It can outlast you all, like the strength of the ocean tides grinding down the earth over time. And if you face it head on, you'll be snuffed out."

Bronwyn stepped out behind the ice statue.

"And I will eat your soul."

The walls of water collapsed in on me with a force so great it snuffed my burst of flame. The circle of fire around me shrunk to a mere pocket of air around my chest. I focused, imagining my spirit, and forcing power into my blaze. It flared for a moment, only to collapse inward, closer to my skin.

Crushing weight bore down on my legs, uncovered by my protective cocoon of fire magic. The electric burn of the nerves in my ankles sailed up my spine. The water turned like rapids above my face, methodically delving closer to me. The bones in my legs cracked as I gathered more will.

Kazimir's voice boomed into my ears. "You are mine." Images of his face flooded my mind. His laugh, his grin, the tail end of his whisper tore through my chest like a blade. Water crushed downward, compressing my stomach. The strain of the blood gushing to my head was unbearable. The protection of my fire retreated to my throat. The water spun like a meat grinder inches from my face.

"Breathe." The word echoed through me, robbing my body of any part it touched. My muscles contracted as they were momentarily crippled. I felt barren. The water constricted my last inch of precious air.

"Breathe!" Every aspect of the word hurt, tormenting my flesh. Images of Andre and me within the murky blue of the Black Sea drowned my mind. The burning in my lungs. The bulging of my veins. The blackness which consumed me. An image of Kazimir's face morphed into my burning house. Mama's hand exploded into flames. An image of myself setting fire to our house and Mama tormented my mind. I wanted to vomit, to scream, but instead I froze. The moment played over in my head, each time inflicting more grief, until it felt like my soul was being ripped from my body. I wanted to crumple up and die.

Mama's face flowed into my mind, and I wanted to save her like I had wanted to save the boy. All the people still locked in the cells in Kazimir's layer still needed my help. I had failed them. A tiny spark inside of me was fanned to light. The water had overwhelmed me, and my fire would surely fade. My earth magic would be no use against the tidal flow—but it didn't have to help me. So long as I still had breath, I could help the people captured.

I didn't try to fight the pain of Mama's death. I let go of the things I had no control over. Kazimir's voice still screamed through my head, but it was distant like speaking from the far side of a theater. I set to my purpose and summoned my earth magic, its tingle mixed with the screaming nerves in my toes.

This is for you, Mama, because you taught me well. I gathered the warm sensation of the magic in my chest, letting it build within me, and imagined the electronic locks on the glass doors. My eyes winced closed as the colossal flow of water pummeled onto me.

I released my spell. The warmth left me, and through the clear mound of fluid, a golden light scrolled through the water and up into the air.

Chapter Twenty-One
A Hero's Call

A white light glowed warm against my face and the darkness which surrounded receded. The pain cascading through my body turned to jelly. I rose like a balloon toward the light. An unseen force drew me to it, like the glowing sensation which comes from the voice of a parent when you're an infant. A being out there loved me more than I ever knew—and they called me home.

Hesitation tugged at me. My airy thoughts weighed the prospects of the people I'd just released. I'd forgotten them completely until now. Did they need me? I hovered in a pause. Andre. What was he going to say to me at the hotel? Roman. A warmth radiated on me. The sunny memories of a picnic with his family elevated me higher, only to arch and weigh me down. The thoughts filling my head weighed on me, and as they quickened, I drifted farther away from the light.

The heat around me faded, like draining a bathtub. Slowly the sensation of my body flowed back to me, the hair in my scalp and the nerves of my skin tickled to life. With a tiny shock, my heart thumped. Its beating rose and played musically in my ear. The spark grew and danced with every beat, like each one was a pluck on the strings of the universe—like it held the secrets to life itself. Each beat sent waves of magic through me, and with every pump of blood I grew stronger.

The momentum built. I felt like I could no longer contain the energy of life within me. *Karolina.* Mama's voice grazed my ear. My eyelids flickered as I inhaled a breath. I caught a glimpse of the room and saw Kazimir's back as he walked to Bronwyn. I should have wanted to incinerate them, but it wasn't about them anymore. It was about the prisoners, and I would ensure their escape.

I chanced a second look at the ceiling, then lay cadaver still. The Shadow Forged still stormed above me, but a faint glow of silver strings of light lined the ceiling. I was seeing the ward bonds Bronwyn forged. Kazimir's wards were made of light magic, but he wasn't the type to let people pass through his compound freely. If people were out of their cells, the wards had to come down for them to get outside.

I searched the inner corners of my mind, looking for what I learned about wards from Miruna's book of white magic. As my thoughts puzzled together, the new power inside me was kicking at the door to let loose. For a moment I dared to think I may have invoked the Light Charm.

I pictured the strings of light I saw on the ceiling and imagined them woven together throughout the whole complex. According to Miruna's book I had to look for the misplaced thread. My new senses spread out, feeling the weave. I continued until a single thread end stuck out in my mind. In my head I could see my hand pinch the thread and pull.

A mass of the energy flowed out my chest with a whoosh. My eyes shot open. A sonic boom reverberated above. Forks of lightning snaked down the walls in a fire show. The Shadow Forged fled from the chunks of ceiling which tumbled down from the electric blasts.

Kazimir whirled around. With a furious sneer he flicked a rolling wave my way. It thundered toward me with savage speed.

The voltage in my heart broke forth. It blew out from my chest in a blaze of light, frying my bonds and tossing me from the table. As I crashed to the ground, the stream of lightning zig-zagged through the water toward Kazimir.

He gasped. His head rapped against the concrete as the force of the lightning drilled him into the ground. A dark spot grew on his breast where the electricity zapped into his chest. A cloud of vapor emerged. The pungent odor of rotten meat drifted through the room.

Bronwyn's voice pierced into a scream. She charged me. Balls of light gathered in her hands as she leapt into the air. The electricity in her hands sucked together into a massive stream.

I covered my face with my forearms. I jumped to a lunge. My heart swelled, loosening another stream of power. The electrical charge exploded and caught her blow mid-way. Sparks flared out over our shoulders.

She dodged me and threw a short punch into my ribs with a glowing hand. Flares of light sprawled from the hit. The electrical burn jolted through me, but not like before.

I threw an uppercut into her jaw.

She grunted with the impact and recoiled. Except her elbow silently glided to my jaw within my peripheral vision.

I slid back and caught her wrist with mine just in time. I gripped her second hand and locked my elbow with hers.

She was trapped in a deadlock.

Sparks cascaded around us from the contact of our skin, encircling us on the concrete. Her leg swept at mine, but I held the hold. Shoulder to shoulder, she stared me down. I held the gaze of the woman who killed my mother.

"Why?" I asked.

An ember of light glimmered in Bronwyn's eye.

"Why!" I screamed.

Piercing light exploded outward into the room with a thunderous crack. The redheaded man she'd called Lukas dropped down from the orb with his sword drawn. He plummeted into a heap of Shadow Forged, which had silently swarmed behind me.

Dyads hunt Shadow Forged. I disassembled the ward of light magic shielding Kazimir's compound, and accidentally exposed Kazimir's horde of Forged to the Dyads. It was a happy coincidence…exposing Bronwyn to her own.

She shifted the moment we caught sight of Lukas. She had abandoned her grapple with me and was already charging toward the misshapen forms. But Shadow Forged were always controlled by a master. I glanced back to Kazimir. Not only was he still breathing, he'd crawled away from the charred spot on the floor. His haggard form leaned against the wall, moving his hands like a drunken orchestra conductor. Only instead of music, he was conducting a lethal horde of Forged.

I ran toward him.

A Forged glided into my path. It reared on its back legs, like a wolf spider, and sprang. As it soared through the air, its human belly was exposed along with two conjoined human heads. Panic triggered a bout of light magic from my pounding heart. A stream of light beamed a hole through the Forged in a huff of ash, but gravity kept it on its collision course.

I tucked and rolled. As the world whirled, I glimpsed Lukas and Bronwyn battling a group of the Forged. Two more stormed at me. An indigo charge of electricity blazed in the corner of my eye, followed by the heinous snarl of a wolf. The charred body of a Shadow Forged fell to my feet. The familiar jaws of a werewolf clamped down on the second. He shook it like a rat caught in a terrier's jaws. Andre and two vampires I'd never seen before streaked to my side.

"Get ready!" Andre called.

The smoky tail end of Kazimir's jacket disappeared behind a door arch.

"He's getting away!" I bolted from the group. The scene around me distorted as I used up the last of the blood I'd consumed to run freight-train fast. My knees buckled with the force of each step. My body couldn't maintain such speed while my inhuman strength depleted.

Down the hall, Kazimir's singed patches of hair jerked up and down. His outstretched hand clung to a strap wrapped around a Forged as it dragged him along the floor. The Forged bolted at arachnid speed from the sound of my footsteps. Kazimir's ragged body kicked up dust as he skidded along.

I couldn't let him get away. Deep down I knew it was wrong. To chase him down. To pursue an unarmed man. Kazimir was no longer a threat, or else he wouldn't be running—but he would be one day. He wouldn't give up. He wouldn't yield. In his mind, he was God.

I ran him down and let loose every ounce of white magic I had. There was a whoosh. Then an explosion of light filled the hall. Kazimir's voice cried out in the abyss. Cloudy spots overwhelmed my vision. A ringing barreled from ear to ear. The vague outline of shapes in the corridor slowly darkened back into view. The world was once more.

Kazimir lay half scorched in a crater of black ash which stood out like a pothole in the white marble.

I crept closer. A tremor rose from my ankles to my knees. I told myself it was from the running, but when I looked at the damage I did, I knew it wasn't. The electric blast had practically cooked Kazimir. Chunks of his flesh screamed out an angry cerise color or had crisped to black completely. Its pungent odor added to the sickness brewing in my stomach.

My cheeks were wet, but I couldn't look away. To know a life—evil or not—had ended, hurt my soul. I extended my hand subconsciously, like I could grab hold of the life force which was once there and keep it from escaping.

Kazimir's hand shot out. His sticky fingers closed around my wrist. He jerked me closer, with strength which was startling for a dead man. "So brave," he croaked out. "A hero, are we?" An unseen force knocked my head back. An image hijacked my mind. It was my father's face, captivating in all its glory.

Over nineteen years of dreamy sleeps I never imagined meeting him. To see him now in the flesh was beguiling. If I put my hand to his face, I would feel the warmth of his cheek and the patches of stubble breaking the smoothness of his shaved skin.

My father looked down as a voice pleaded, and the ripples in his face smoothed to alabaster. “If the public wielded fire, the world would burn.”

“Please!” A man on his knees clutched his son. “He’s only two years old!”

“His powers would corrupt him as a man, in the worst ways. It’s better this way.”

“But you yourself are not corrupted?”

My father’s gaze changed. He no longer looked at the man, but through him. “A Tzar forfeits his life for his people. As such, he no longer exists as a man.”

Fire scorched through my mind enveloping the man’s cries. Among the flames, his screams took root in my own mouth as the pain of burning flesh and my father’s words engulfed me.

A gurgling noise sputtered from Kazimir’s mouth, and his fingers around my wrists relaxed and fell away. I looked to him in time to see his eyelids close. The room became ghost calm. A feeling of loneliness hung in the air. I rolled my shoulder against the chill, as if composing myself would undo the irreversible act I’d just committed. Looking down at the empty vessel which was once the most frightening person I’d ever met, my mouth dried.

“Goodbye, Kazimir,” I said.

A yelp echoed down the hall. Screeching followed, clawing at my eardrums. I buckled to my knees. The noise sounded like a human scream played backward through an old transistor radio. A noise not of this world. I raced down the corridor clutching my ears and skidded through the door arch.

The Forged had gone berserk. They no longer

moved in calculated masses or battle formations. The masses of them swarmed like wasps, hive minded in their direction, but individually they were crazed. Each one thrashed its appendages like it was caught between a seizure and excruciating pain. The closer I got, the more trans-dimensional their screams, like a rift had been torn through matter itself.

The Forged were no longer controlled. Kazimir had finally died, and now the Forged were loose upon the world.

I caught sight of Roman's tail lashing under a mound of screaming Forged. Their legs looking like black slimy snakes coiling around him. A group of shiny new Dyads charged to his rescue, torrents of light blazing. All together they bore down on the horde, sending a veil of smoke and ash across the room. Roman's wolf form emerged, rolling sideways as he shook a Forged from his back.

Darkness flashed just behind my side. More Forged came up my flank. I turned to face them, and Bronwyn's luminescent blonde hair shined as she battled in the distance. Fire ignited from my palms. I became a human flame thrower. I drove the flames into the attacking Forged.

It wasn't true. It couldn't be. Kazimir would have done anything to hurt me. The group of Forged vanished behind the wall of fire. A moment in time was all it took to wreak irreparable destruction. I had the ability to destroy, but no one had the power to change time, or to bring life back from the ashes.

A Forged rammed into me from behind. Black disjointed legs wrapped around me. I plummeted to the ground. A dead looking human toe just missed my mouth as the Forged lashed out at my head, and a darkened toenail flicked to the ground. Would my father have thought me as evil as the Forged I was battling? His words played in my head. Corrupted. I twisted underneath the Forged, letting its sandpaper skin shred through my clothes and tear my skin. A tiny human head twitched between two massive pincers which snapped open and shut right before my face. Oily goo splashed across my cheek.

I brought forth my fire magic. The ruins of the Forged rose to the ceiling in the vapour of the flames. An amber light encircled me on the floor. The insect mind of the horde retreated, like bats from rising sun. I charged them and they exploded into ash like flash bulbs. The ceiling of the room clouded with residue and smoke. The ground grew hot beneath my feet like the concrete itself was melting.

Bronwyn's nimble form glided between two of her own kind. They blasted beams of light into another fleeing wave of Forged. A rogue beam glanced through the remnants of the horde. The light of it glittered the faintest shade of gray as it traveled. The tint was barely noticeable, had I not been looking for it and saw who it originated from.

The bolt sizzled into my flames. My magic flared. The floor flew out from under me. I smashed into the wall. Then I hit the floor. Blood leaked from my forehead. I hauled myself off the concrete. This was the last time Bronwyn's aim would misfire. She would know what it was like to be on the receiving end of her well-timed accidents. Mama was gone, and she was never coming back. I wanted Bronwyn to know such permanence. More than that, I would give it to her.

I ran at her.

A brown form hit me like a wrecking ball from the side. It pinned me down by my shoulders, and I struggled to roll it off. My mind raced to understand why it didn't get toasted in my fire.

Its hairy form started liquefying into human skin.

"Fuck," I said.

Roman's form finished its transition to human, unscathed by the heat of my flames. His naked body held me down while I pummeled against him.

"Get off me!"

He took hold of my wrists. "No, Karo."

"Ro! She's evil! You have to let me go!"

Roman applied more tension to my hips and shoulders, keeping me successfully pinned.

The memory of Roman's steel strength raced back to me and being pinned under him turned terrifying.

"Ro." I gasped. I looked through the sliver underneath Roman's shoulder and saw Lukas rushing to Bronwyn's side.

"Please, Ro. She killed Mama!"

"Karo, Dyads are the good guys. It's okay, your saf—"

"She's evil!" A shriek balled in my mouth and cut into the air. "She's Evil! She's Evil! She's Evil! Let me go!"

"Get her out of here!" Roman called to Lukas.

"No!" I screamed.

Lukas stepped out from the others and balled his hands together. In a whirl of light from his palms a large electric disk formed in the air from head to toe. Wind whooshed from it blowing in the faces of the Dyads who stood before it, like it was a doorway to another dimension.

Bronwyn couldn't get away. It wasn't a possibility I could fathom. A crushing weight paralyzed me as Lukas rushed Bronwyn to the portal. Snow blew out over her in slow motion, like time had frozen just enough for a small smile to touch her lips. A thought trickled into my mind too late, and when I called forth my earth magic, she stepped into the orb of light and vanished. More of the Dyads followed, and with a whoosh of Lukas's hands the portal collapsed in on itself.

"No…" A tear rolled down my cheek as I fell silent.

"I think she's lost it," a voice said from behind Roman.

"Dramatic outbursts are genetic in this family. You'd know, brother."

"Karo?" Roman asked. He looked at me like he was afraid I would grow jaws like his and bite his head off.

I appeared out of control, and she appeared the victim. Kazimir's image of my father's words slammed into my head. I shoved them into the cobwebbed part of my mind, telling myself I'd deal with it another day. To get ahead of Bronwyn's deceit, I must partake in her ruse long enough to ensnare her. If I told them all what she did now, they would just question my sanity further. She'd gotten away with it—for the moment. The bitter taste of this reality rivaled the foul taste of the vampire blood on my tongue. I swallowed the need to blurt out the truth, and it burned all the way down.

I closed my eyes and forced my face to relax. When I opened my eyes again, Roman shifted like he'd caught a glimpse of the side of me he recognized. He eased up the tension against me.

"You've got a habit of tackling me with no clothes on," I said.

"Mmhm." A one-word answer, but it was the closest I ever saw to Roman's face flushing. He backed away and popped up to stand at my feet, seemingly unconcerned with those in the room seeing his nakedness.

Andre stepped to Roman's side and stared down at me. "You okay?"

I could feel his relief and fear. The cold wall formed before I could go probing any further, but I was grateful he didn't slam it into place. My headache was torrential. Andre's face had a calm guise, but underneath I could sense uneasiness. He leaned down and hesitated, like touching me now might provoke me into another fit.

I threw both hands into the air. "Help me up."

Chapter Twenty-Two
Sugar Daddy

Half the Dyads took my meltdown and attempt to kill one of them as their cue to leave. The rest were now outside the compound assisting any of the prisoners who got caught in the rubble during their escape.

The outside damage was a disaster. The blast from the wards coming down was an outcome I hadn't considered. I did a three-sixty to take in all the wreckage. The outer walls of the compound had crumbled to the ground. The local townspeople had ventured up into the mountains with all the commotion and were now assisting to free the remaining prisoners from the ruins. Many hugged each other like they'd just been reunited with lost loved ones.

Roman had gone to help some of the Dyads with extracting a young woman trapped underneath a beam. She seemed lucid and unscathed, and she was the only one I could see who required immediate assistance. The Dyads worked fast. I wondered what disaster they'd zap into next. Which posed the question, where in the world was I?

The rubble which littered the mountainside framed a view of a quartz blue body of water.

In the distance a stone castle of southern Slavic style stood on a cliff crashing with seawater. The sun shimmered off the waves in a hypnotizing rhythm, making everything I'd just faced seem like a tragic dream.

"Over there!" a little voiced cried out.

The pattering of feet approached at my left. When I turned, a little boy had jumped into my arms. It was the boy from the cells who was missing his twin.

He made it.

I dropped to my knees and wrapped my arms around him in a hug. His little arms encircled my middle and threatened to squeeze the life out of me. Knowing one small innocent made it out into the world again warmed me more than any hot bath, chocolate, and increased length of parole for repeat offenders ever could.

A throat cleared just above my ear.

I jumped, giving the little guy around my waist quite a jar.

"Isn't it impolite to pet someone's dog without asking?" Andre asked.

I turned, ready to lay into him, but stopped. He was smiling. Not a sarcastic smirk or sneer, but a real heartfelt smile. My words died on my thick tongue. The sun shone on him as he looked down at the boy and messed the kid's hair. There was a happiness in him, and he wore it well.

"Incoming," he said.

A woman, wearing an expression only a mom could, approached us. I got the awkward sense one gets when one is treating a stranger's child like one's own. I loosened my arms around the boy, but he remained as a little cling-on. Not having the heart to shake him free yet, I gave his mom an apologetic smile.

The woman chastised the boy in a language

unknown to me and took his hand. He whined and gave his mom some lip while she peeled him off me. His mom picked him up, clearly taking every moment to get one of his special hugs. She held my gaze with a gratitude which could have shaken bedrock.

"*Spasiba,*" she said. "*Spasiba.*"

Then she carried the boy away to the life they had before and to all their happy moments yet to come. When they'd disappeared, I turned to the rest of the scene.

The Dyads had finished, and they were all gathered around Lukas. He looked up and caught me looking his way. He nodded. His look was simple and strong. A way of acknowledging my contribution to the fight, without invading my space. He was okay—for a Dyad. He certainly didn't seem like the type of person who deserved Bronwyn's deception, and I had half a mind to tell him so. But today wasn't the day. He'd earned the admiration of his peers. No doubt being first on the scene, besides Bronwyn, for a horde of Forged this big had earned him some stripes. I couldn't take this moment from him.

"Where's the police?" I asked Andre.

"This is no man's land. The police don't travel up the mountains. Vampires have made deals to govern their own jurisdiction."

"Then let's get out of here."

Andre walked me to the car. The two vampires I saw inside were smoking by the passenger door. They turned my way. They shared the same jaw and eyes, but the hair was different: one sandy brown and one chestnut.

"How you doin', cuz? You got yourself put back

together?"

"Alexi and Leonid?" I asked.

"Pleased to meet you, just don't go throwing fire at us," the dark-haired one said as he opened the backseat door.

"Very funny," I said. "So, who's who?" Climbing into the backseat felt like I was lying down on a cloud. The sandy brown-haired one called himself Lexi. I almost drifted off to Leonid saying his name.

"You're lucky your werewolf friend could track your scent. Once the wards fell, we could come in after you," Leonid said.

"I had it under control."

He laughed in response.

"Where are we?" I asked.

Andre sat down next to me. "Crimea."

I managed to keep my eyelids open long enough to see Roman walk toward the car.

****

I awoke with a feeling of panic, trapped and held down by a band across my chest.

"Hey, whoa, whoa." Andre held his hands up in the air. "You're safe. Everything's fine."

The strap against my chest was my seatbelt. We were the last ones left in the car. We were in an underground parking garage, with a sign which had a golden arrow pointing up a stairwell. The quiet hum of neon lighting around us told me we were alone.

"Thanks. Where is everyone?"

"They're inside. You were in and out the whole twelve hours, but they didn't want to wake you for good until you were ready."

"I doubt Roman would have a problem waking

me."

"You were asleep on my shoulder."

"Oh." I looked down. My leg was thrown over his lap in a snuggle.

"Yeah," he said.

I shifted to take my leg off him, but his hand touched my thigh. "I didn't have a problem with it." He touched the skin of my leg exposed through the tears in my body suit. The rips in the clothes were there, but the wounds were gone. He must have let me feed off him when I was half-asleep, which explained the dreamy look he had. The sweet salty residue of his blood clung to my tongue. He leaned in, and my heartrate spiked.

The wall stayed between us, letting human touch guide the way. His hand traced my thigh, and the skin on skin felt better than any magic or bond.

My fangs broke through the roof of my mouth.

His mouth hovered close, but not close enough, giving me a chance to catch up or back down.

Excitement made my belly clench. But to taste his lips right now felt like jumping into a dark void. He blocked the bond. If I kissed him now it was because I wanted him in a very human way. I didn't know if I could navigate back from that.

Roman was here. He had followed me. Despite the fact his life was back in Canada and mine was now anywhere but Canada—he was here. Our relationship hadn't made it to a title before I left, and it was impossible now, but I owed him more. More than continuing with Andre without telling Roman how I felt.

"I can't," I whispered. "Not yet."

"Okay," he said.

He slipped a hand into my hair and kissed me on the cheek.

A shudder zinged through my lower stomach.

After I slinked out of the car and put some meters between myself and the parking lot, my head started to clear. Fugitive of the law, most of my family gone, heiress of a vampire empire, and about to crack open my lifelong comrade's heart. The latter was the only one capable of rattling me at this moment. Roman was my last remaining connection to my previous life, and I was about to give him up.

But I didn't have to. I could choose Roman. We could leave the Grand Hotel and stay with Miruna in Romania. Roman would leave his family behind in Canada, maybe make visits. My rational mind killed my hopes before they took hold. The police would watch a known associate of a fugitive traveling in and out of the country. If Roman chose to stay with me, he would trade his life in Canada for a life on the run.

My inner monologue had carried me to the hotel front desk without me noticing. I clued in by the time I walked into the counter. "Roman Lupei's room, *spasiba*."

The concierge's bangle-packed wrist jingled as she jotted down a room number on a piece of paper and handed it to me.

The elevator wait sabotaged my attempt to keep the debate from continuing. I could think of nothing more selfish than making Roman give up his life. But part of me needed him. At the same time my feelings for Andre were confusing. I stopped myself there. I had to leave him out of this. This was about my feelings for Roman. I either loved him or not. If I did, it meant I valued his happiness equal to my own. This much I knew.

I found myself staring at a number plate which read *6696*. The paper in my hands read the same. I knocked on the door. Silence. I knocked again, harder. The wait felt like it would induce an anxiety attack. I leaned my forearms above my head on the door. *Where are you, Roman?* Then I chastised myself. Roman didn't live to answer my every call. If the sunrise was over twelve hours ago, Roman was probably having dinner.

I was a grown woman, and I would do what was right. I wouldn't ask him to give up his life for me. I'd ask him to go back to Canada.

Heaving off the door, I dragged myself down the hallway and smacked the up button. I'd order room service…and maybe a bottle of wine to solidify my nerve. The doors opened at the top floor and I walked out of the elevator. Midway down the hall there was a beeping. It was the sound Andre's beat-up flip phone made when he dialed. I stopped outside a door marked *Hotel Personnel Only*.

I hovered my ear to the door and listened for the confirmation of his voice. When he spoke, I braced myself to leave, but his tone kept me still.

"I told you to give me time! I will fucking die before I go back to the pit! Do you hear me? I've tried! She's incorruptible. You don't know what she's like. Every time I try, she pulls back. It's going to take time to build her trust and even then, she's like Mother Teresa with canines!"

My mind shut down—then slowly jump started. She. He said she. My thoughts raced to make a possible list of whom he could be talking about. Frantically, I searched for any name but mine.

"She was raised Dalca. Instead of sparking the Dark Charm she sparked the Light! It's going to take months, years, before she's ready. I'll need more time." He paused. "What do you mean you found another way?"

I swung my back to the door and silently leaned against it. My eyes glossed over making the hallway watery. I stepped away and the room spun as I teetered on my feet. I vaguely caught a glimpse of my hotel room door. With each step I took, I told myself I was almost there. I clutched the door handle and turned. Locked. Leaning against the wall I fished into my bra for the new keycard the lady at the desk has given me.

The door swung open and I slipped inside. When I closed the door, I dropped the card to the ground. I fell onto the sofa cushion and my eyes overflowed. Slowly a thought seeped into my mind through the shock. I've been a fool. Everything I just heard washed over me, even though my heart was still denying it happened. The high I felt with Andre was ripped away. I collected my hands neatly into my lap. He had been trying to manipulate me for a person who wanted me to spark the Dark Charm. He'd wanted me to give up part of my soul, just like he had. The part which was supposed to have returned to him. Had Miruna's magic failed?

It was all an act. A show. He hadn't changed. He hadn't cared about me the way I cared about him. My stomach wrenched. Or the way I cared about Roman. Andre hadn't put me first. He was trying to maneuver me, like a puppet on a stage, lining me up for the final act—whenever it occurred. But he had just revealed it wasn't him manning the strings. He was following a superior's orders, one on the other end of the phone, and with Kazimir dead there was only one other person in Russia I knew with that type of power.

The phone rang, making me startle in my seat. Shock gave way to the familiar charge of adrenaline. My hand smashed into the receiver knocking it off into the air for me to catch.

"Hello?"

"Miss Dalca, the Tzar has requested a private audience with you immediately," said a female voice. "Can you accommodate?"

I had to find Roman and get out of here, but not before I confronted Loukin. Confirmation of his involvement in Andre's conversation was necessary to know who was plotting against me. I also needed to know why. I would act my part until I got more information, and if my theory was true, Loukin would see just how much damage a rogue police intern could do.

I smiled into the receiver. "I sure can."

The walk to Loukin's office gave me valuable moments to reanalyze days' worth of intel I'd overlooked. A tiny voice of shame wanted to break out and scream. My thoughts snapped back and forth like firecrackers.

A king and military leader doesn't let it slip he's losing a war. Loukin wanted me to know. He'd wanted me to take it upon myself to end the war with Kazimir. I took out his main adversary, which had a chilling resemblance to my father's assassination, done by another but to Loukin's benefit.

My hands pumped with blood as I stood at the thick arched doors to his office. I turned the handle and stepped down inside. I now had the feeling of stepping onto a spiderweb. The multiple gold doors of the hexagram room looked inward, like the strings of a web which met in the center. It made me wonder how many people he'd caught in his web before, and if I'd be drained of blood before I left its grasp.

Loukin looked up from the papers he'd been studying on his desk and waved me to a chair opposite him. His face glowed from the candles on his desk, split into light and dark.

"Ah, Karolina, please sit."

I dragged the chair out an extra two feet and sat down, away from his arms' vicinity. "You needed to speak with me?"

"I wanted to congratulate you on your victory."

"Really?"

Loukin smiled pleasantly, waiting for my response, but his face faltered when he looked at me. No doubt noticing the dried tear streaks down my cheeks and puffy eyes. A flash of softness broke his professional manner.

"Here I thought you were the victor." I knew I looked like hell. I hadn't showered after a night of battling for my life, and with Kazimir it'd been a battle for my soul. Not only had I left alive, I'd left on a bliss point. Only to come back here and face more lies and deception. The painful shock Mama would have called heartbreak rippled into an emotion far more dangerous—and I could feel it seething onto my face.

"Well," Loukin said. "I have good news for you. We had our police department file a report on your kidnapping. It explains your questionable disappearance after Ana's, I mean your mother's, death. It states you were abducted from Canada after your captors set fire to your house, and the Russian police apprehended your kidnapper's body after a violent hostage negotiation. Your wolf friend's effort to find you and track you down is also included to explain his absence, and it's stated his work with the Russian police was invaluable."

I paused. Maybe I had misjudged this whole situation. Here I was throwing shade at Loukin, when he was the only person who had given me a solution for getting my life back. He'd cared enough to know what I truly wanted: to go to school, to be a regular young woman again. A light stronger than the Light Charm itself shone in me. Hope. He'd come up with a way to clear my name. No, bought a way to clear my name. The buy-off for the Russian police must have cost him.

Like he'd read my mind he said, "You are no longer a fugitive. You and the wolf can return home. Your father's inheritance held in trust for his heir is now yours. I've called your university and explained the unique circumstance. They've accepted you to begin classes shortly after your return."

A sickly feeling crept into my innards. It was too good, too perfect.

"And," he continued, "with my political connections, I was able to get quite a prestigious internship for you within your Canadian Government."

I fought the urge to squirm in my chair.

"These things do come at a price, of course. These are the types of favors which money can't buy. Only connections can…and once you take a favor you owe one."

There it was. The drop. He'd set his terms.

"We will be expecting information in return. From the internship which has been arranged for you."

"Where's my internship?"

"The House of Commons in Ottawa."

He was asking me to spy.

I dove across the two-foot distance to the edge of his desk and swiped all his belongings to the floor.

He leaned back out of range.

I hunched over his desk, palms planted. "If you think for one second, I'm going to spy for you, you're wrong. Terribly wrong."

"Funny how fast Ana's features can disappear from your face."

"I'm only half my mother."

Another twitch surfaced, and I knew I hit a nerve. Loukin's posture recoiled for a moment and I prepared for a firefight, but he relaxed back into his professional indifference which he had practiced while playing a diplomatic Tzar. He was nothing of the sort.

"If you want your freedom, it's the price. It's the price for Roman's safe passage."

"Roman can handle himself, and I'm starting to like it here."

"Oh, Karolina. I hoped it wouldn't come to this." He rose to match my gaze. "You will do this," he whispered. "Or Miruna's wards will be dismantled and I'll end the old crow myself."

I scoffed. "No one can pentrat—"

The book. I gave him Miruna's book of white magic when I pitied him for hearing about Mama's death. Now, I see I might as well have petted a viper. He had me the moment I gave away the book of Albesuc secrets.

"You would hurt my mother's family?"

The look on his face confirmed my answer and made me wonder what Miruna could have done to make him hate her so much.

"What makes you think I couldn't just take the book back?" I asked.

"You don't know where it is, and even if you escalate this to a fight, you'll never know who has read it or who could be heading to your aunt's door at any moment."

My shoulders clenched down on my spine. I wanted to break his desk in two. I wanted to kick down the fancy gold doors of his office and tear apart his web of deception which trapped me into this position. But I couldn't. The tension in me rippled down my back. The fire within begged to break free and obliterate the whole damn building.

Instead, I slithered back into my chair, crossed my legs, and mimicked his demeanor, but it couldn't keep the fire from my voice. "I have terms—in addition to what you've done."

He sat down. "Go on."

My mind was blank. I wanted some control, any power over my situation, and the child in me wanted to make demands in return, but I didn't have any requests in mind. The length of my pause bordered on embarrassing.

"Ina," I said.

He looked at me sideways.

"Ina comes with Roman and me to Canada. I will need a roommate who won't be suspicious, and her guidance has been useful. If she agrees, of course."

He studied me. The clock I threw from his desk

still ticked in the pile, even though its glass had shattered to pieces on the ground. Each tick felt more weighted than the last.

"Done." He stood up and stuck out his hand. "I'm glad you've made a friend here, Karolina." As we shook, he said, "This really was devised for your benefit. You'll see in the long run."

Half of me wanted to laugh, the other wanted to cry. I took my hand from his and headed for the door, but as I was leaving a thought made me stop and look back over my shoulder. "The greatest monsters in the world are the ones we ourselves have created." I didn't know if I was his monster, or if the greatest one he'd created was the one inside himself.

"Tell me, Loukin. What was it in your soul that prevented you from killing Kazimir yourself? It must've been bad, if you had to send me instead."

"You and the wolf make a cute couple. Too bad he won't age like a vampire."

I turned and headed for the door, hoping I would never be in this room again.

Chapter Twenty-Three
Leaving on a Jet Plane

I was packed, but Ina reopened my bag to shove in more designer clothes from the closet with the tags still on them. My pack looked like a colorful stuffed snack cake.

"It's full! I've got enough in there to break my back."

"Your house burnt down, and you have nothing to your name but a bank account and a rucksack of clothes. One more outfit won't kill you."

Even the backpack wasn't mine. I borrowed it from Roman when I ran away but mentioning it would just further her point. She rammed another outfit in, which was impressive. Ina agreed to leave with me to Canada and be reunited with her mother and brother. I was grateful for her company, even though she'd most likely be spending the majority of her time with them. I looked up when she stopped moving. She stared at me, catching me in a moment of thought.

"You ready?" I asked.

"Yup." She struggled to pick up the bag.

I crossed the room and took it from her. I under-calculated how much it would weigh. "Thanks," I said, "for everything."

She nodded. Like Lukas, it was short and simple, but it still relayed she understood what her thoughtfulness meant to me. "My bags are downstairs. I'm going to do a final sweep of my room, and I'll meet you in the lobby."

"Sure."

After she left, I took her advice and did a final check of my room too before I retrieved the package left for me at the front desk for my new place in Canada. I walked through the glittery pink and red room and wondered if my mother had encountered as much heartbreak here as I had. Maybe she had, and it was why she'd left the Grand Hotel to be with her family in Romania.

Loukin said she left just before my father's assassination. My dad would have sent her away to protect her. One of the blessings which arose from my journey was I learned my parents loved each other. Enough to sacrifice themselves for one another and their child. Me.

I turned with my pack on my shoulder and headed into the hall. The elevator lights flickered between the seventh and eighth floor. It screeched to a halt. When the doors opened, lighting up the darkness, I decided to jump out while I could and walk the rest of the way. Six flights of stairs later, I rounded the corner and passed the elaborate entrance which lead into the stone great hall. In the shadows there was a narrow passageway I hadn't noticed before. It was just another path I hadn't taken, but the snake emblem on the door made me pause.

I headed to the main lobby, but a figure appeared from a connecting hallway.

"What's the hurry, Princess?" The nickname I used to smile for now just provoked a wall of cold. "Hey," he said and reached for my arm.

Staring ahead, I kept walking.

He raced behind me, just missing my arm again. "Karo?"

That nickname from his voice felt like an insult. I clenched my fist, combating the urge to turn around and face him.

Andre took hold of my shoulders and whirled me around. "What's wrong?"

I couldn't meet his gaze. I looked at the wall instead. His hands glided from my shoulders over my body, like he could find an unseen wound which would cause me so much pain. He stopped. He turned my head to his. I settled for staring up at his chin.

Panic spread across his face. "Tell me what's wrong." His thumbs stroked my cheeks trying to coax the words from my mouth. When it didn't work, he plunged his lips against mine in a desperate kiss, like it would breathe the life back into me, and I would be the Karolina he knew.

I stayed as straight and rigid in his arms as a corpse.

He withdrew, holding my face before his, and I finally met his eyes. The wall crashed down between us. Even if I wanted to tell him how I felt, I couldn't. I had no words to say. Instead, I let the numbing mess of confusion and rage flood into him, leaving a hurt I hadn't known existed.

Realization hit his face like a bomb. His hand trembled on my cheek, and he looked down to the ground, no longer able to hold my gaze.

"Goodbye, Andre." Turning from him, I walked to the lobby, leaving him frozen to the floor. I heard him find his voice again and start to call my name—but I never looked back.

My cousins were waiting with Roman and Ina on the front steps of the Grand Hotel when I stepped out. The first day of fall carried a crisp breeze even in Kislovodsk, which made me wonder what weather we'd be facing in Canada.

"Thought we'd come to help you with your bags," Lexi said.

Leonid looked at my pack. "But looks like you got it covered."

I smiled and tried not to feel like a cartoon hobo with my only possessions slung over my shoulder. "Thanks. But I think you may be of more help to Ina." I looked to Ina and her small mountain of bags she sat upon.

They laughed and started loading the luggage into a black limo, which appeared to be our ride to the airport. Roman helped them, being the ever-steady white knight. After my cousins were done, they hovered in front of me looking down at their feet.

Lexi was the first to break the uncomfortable pause. "Come in here, cuz." His arms shot forward and wrapped around me, causing me to lose my footing.

"Thanks." I had a little more warning for Leonid's hug. "And thanks for the bags." I didn't bother asking if their reptile of a father put them up to it. I knew he had, but my cousins had managed in our few interactions to treat me like genuine family. Recent events showed my judgement could be flawed, but so far, I surmised they weren't misleading me. I wouldn't hold their parentage against them, but neither would I assume it would be wholesome to cross them.

"See you around," Lexi said.

"Don't set the plane on fire," Leonid said.

The two of them stood by and watched us get into the limo.

"Your uncle really hooked us up, eh?" Roman said as he perused a basket of brightly packaged snacks. He hunkered into his seat and opened a bag of peanuts. I would have made the same choice.

Ina cleared her throat, expressing her discomfort at Roman's ignorance, and signaling this was my moment to tell him. I had considered it, but I knew Loukin's threat on Miruna would have roused a fury in him which would have unleashed his wolf. We would have to take on every agent in the Grand Hotel, and it still wouldn't have secured Miruna's safety. White lies, they say, are a long fall through the mud. But my way meant leaving with the situation intact without starting an all-out war. It gave me time to strategize a way to egress my new occupation.

I rolled up the tinted window on the Grand Hotel as the limo trailed away, darkening the view of glittering gold, intricate stone, and royal windows. For all its beauty, this was a place of duality. The place my parents fell in love and the place of my father's assassination attempt. Now it was the place I lost the bargain for my freedom. I had no idea if Loukin's fire power could overtake mine, but he won our battle without magic. That scared me more.

"Yeah, Ro. Loukin really hooked us up." I rested my head against Roman's arm and closed my eyes.

The ride to the airport had been long and boring, giving my mind time to ponder what was to come. When we arrived at the gate, I worked my way to imagining being tarred and quartered for treason. The plan was to take a regular plane from the airport to Canada, to keep the contrivance of two kids caught up in a kidnapping nightmare alive. Still, it was uncharacteristic for the boarding line to be this empty. Loukin wielded more power with the Russian government than I anticipated.

Ina's excitement took some of the sting out of it all. Her family was waiting for her in Canada. She'd arranged for them to meet her at the Ottawa airport and to stay with them in Toronto for a few days. I knew they had catching up to do, and agreed she'd meet me at our new condo in Ottawa afterward. Roman wasn't one for cities but had made a list of all the things she had to see in Ottawa.

When we boarded the plane my ruminating was no different, and no amount of airplane food and action films with subtitles could keep my mind from the bargain I was bound to. The numbness I felt helped with the initial shock, but it couldn't last forever. I was traveling a thousand miles an hour toward the bleak reality of my mistakes. I had no idea what it meant to be a spy. Slipping intel on the Canadian government seemed darker than any battle. I was betraying my country.

The information I would be blackmailed into giving had the potential to hurt millions of Canadians. I looked at the pamphlet before me which showed how to use the oxygen masks and felt like the room was out of air. With every second, we flew closer to my new duty, and the weight of it crushed me.

Roman touched my hand and squeezed. I looked up at him. His hand felt hot and rough from his calluses. I remembered the scratchy tickle they'd left across my skin in the warm wake of his touch from our night in the woods. I'd traveled through the dregs of humanity since then, and he'd followed me.

"I still haven't thanked you."

"Karo, you never have to thank me for being with you."

I looked down to the emblem on his shirt. "I left you behind. At the time, it felt like the right thing to do. And I knew you were keeping the truth from me. That hurt, Ro."

"You have every right to be pissed. I get it. But my family made promises to your mother to keep you away from those people. And I didn't know everything. I knew who they were, and that your mother didn't trust them fully. I also knew if I said you still had family, the first thing you'd do was go charging out to find them."

It was exactly what I did. How many times did we need to have this conversation for me to finally accept he was right? Miruna was right. Even Gerel had warned me. I always thought regret would taste bitter. The taste in my mouth remained the same. What changed was I couldn't stand the taste of myself, because I had no one to blame but myself.

"You're right. Nothing could have stopped me. But I'm still thankful you were there, Ro."

He looked down at me. "I know."

"I know there were things you wanted. What you said on the boat, in the woods. But with the circumstances, things just got complicated"

"I know, Karo. You don't have to say it."

Looking up at him, I wished I could make things different. Going back on my decisions was an impossible dream, like I could save Mama. Like I never could have met Andre or Loukin. Miruna would be safe, and Roman's parents wouldn't have been threatened. I'd be free. At what point did my fate leave my own hands? When I lost control.

Control. I found Grandpa Dalca's words in my head, like I lost them ages ago. Andre had made losing control so seductive, and the most threatening thing was I hadn't wanted to come back from the abyss it created. Now Miruna's survival depended on me. Losing restraint made me easier to influence, and I was exploited. All my mother had warned me about in our last conversation proved true. The hard lesson I learned was now mirrored in my destitute situation. But things could still get worse, quickly. I was alive, and Kazimir was dead. I was a spy, but I was alive.

Roman was still watching me. "I didn't ask you. Before you left."

"What?"

"Should have said it better, before you left, I should have asked you."

"Ask me what?"

"To be my girlfriend."

He wanted to talk about Andre, about what happened between us. My tongue fell dry. For a moment, my courage wanted to shrivel. "I needed blood and we bonded. I didn't know what it meant until after. The cravings took on a new role, and the feelings they gave me complicated things."

He nodded. "You'd never had human blood before, let alone a vampire's."

"I don't know if I can go back to animals. It's so different, so real. Like what it's supposed to be." I caught my gaze trailing down his neck.

"Is it a sex thing? When you feed?"

"Yes and no. It depends on who it's with."

Although feeding off Andre had felt like drinking the nectar of the gods, I managed to stay in control. Feeding in the midst of battle, I had lost control completely. Memories of the lout's final moments still itched my skin. Was it my feelings which kept me in check with Andre? It was a formidable question. If I dropped the wall between the bond now, would I feel him miles away?

A cough sounded out on the mostly empty plane, reminding me we weren't alone. Ina stirred beside me, waking up. She took a sleepy sip of water.

Roman and I continued the rest of the flight holding hands. We stopped talking for the moment, but it felt like there was less of a rift between us. The simple comfort of knowing he was there for me gave me the courage to brainstorm my plans.

When we arrived in Ottawa, we headed to the baggage collection for Ina and walked to the pickup and departure lobby. Amongst the crowd, a blonde woman with eyes like Ina waited with a young redheaded boy. In his tiny hands he held up a makeshift sign with Ina's name on it. Ina ran to them, her purse flying back in tow. She scooped up her younger brother, whirling him around in a hug. Her mother dove in and wrapped her arms around the two of them as tears soaked her cheeks.

Roman and I stayed back, giving them their moment. After, Ina introduced us, and we had a chance to say hello and chat. Just when they were about to leave, Ina swooped to my side.

"Karo, I don't know how to thank you."

"Thank me for what? You know Loukin was the one who forced you on me," I said. "I'd be a lost cause without you."

She threw her arms around me. "Thank you, Karo."

I squeezed her back. "No. Thank you."

She lowered her voice. "Whatever you've done, just know it was worth it. Don't think we all don't know the Northern Russian Organization has been disbanded. Often, people doubt what a woman can do, and those people can be women themselves. I want you to know I'll never forget what you've done for me, and neither should you."

Well, Ina, the thing is when you kill people, you can't tell the difference between yourself and the villains after that. Instead I said, "Thanks."

"And be careful with wolves. I hear they bite," she said with a wink and turned to her departing family.

"I bite too."

A nearby man stepped back from me, pulling his backpack farther up his shoulder. I turned back to the departure pickup. Roman waited at the curb.

"You ready?" he asked.

"Yeah, I'm ready."

His hand found mine again as we waited. "Did they tell you who would be picking us up?"

The fall air was cooler, but not shiver worthy. The pickup lane was full of buses and yellow cabs, which was why a black unmarked cab entering the roundabout had my attention.

"I have an idea of who our ride will be."

The cab stopped in front of us. I yanked open the door and sat down in the backseat. "Hi-ya, Nick."

He let out a gruff snort. "Where to, kid?" He had spoken to me, but his gaze was stuck on the mirror, watching Roman get in the backseat.

Ottawa's lights ahead looked the spitting image of the night I left. Memorizing every twinkle seemed a necessary, but impossible task, since at the time I thought I would never see my home city again. I was wrong, and my memory was closer than I thought.

"This address." I took a page out of my package from the Grand Hotel and handed it to Nick. "And Roman will be heading to his place about an hour and a bit north of the city."

"You're not coming home?"

"It's gone, Ro, burnt down."

"You know what I mean. My parents will be worried sick. I thought you would at least be staying with us. Maybe see some of our friends?"

I hugged my package against my chest. Not bearing to go through it at the time, I still had to read the thick stack of papers and prepare for my new occupation. My first mission could be tomorrow for all I knew. Miruna depended on me, and she didn't even know it. Moreover, there wasn't much for me in my hometown anymore. Mama was gone, the home we built was gone, and I wasn't ready to face it yet.

"Most of our friends are in Ottawa for school. I have to read the syllabus for my courses and enroll in a few more. Plus, I need to see where I'm going to live now."

I didn't blame him for wanting me to come home and be with his family. I would too, if I were in his position. I leaned my head against his shoulder. It was my way of telling him there was more to the way I felt, but I wouldn't be sharing it. My old life was gone. Every breath I took from the moment I gave up the book was under the heavy weight of extortion. I just hadn't known it until now.

Until I found a way to escape this, I had to live with my secret. The more people who got involved in this conflict, the greater the risk of them getting hurt. Loukin had a talent for winning wars with words and a pen, and I was living proof.

"Yeah, I guess the commute would be too long." He looked at me, and his face reflected the sadness I felt. "I miss your mom too."

He credited my sorrow to Mama's death.

I almost broke the bargain I just struck with myself and told him, but I noted this was just temporary. He could know the truth after I made advances with my position under Loukin's governance. I produced a phone shaped like a silver brick from the package and handed it over. "Here, key in your number. I'll call when I get things sorted out."

He took it from me and flipped it open to punch in his number, not commenting on how outdated my new phone was. A true saint. He kissed me on the top of my head when he handed it back to me.

It felt good to have a phone and an address again, like I had rejoined society. The cabbie stopped at a condo building in downtown Ottawa on Sussex Street. The modern glass building shined like a totem against the classic architecture of old Ottawa. The green copper peaks of the government buildings stood tall on their acreage beside my new home. Convenient. Everything must have been planned long before I was blackmailed.

"Here you are, kid," Nick said and handed me back

the sheet.

We wheeled up to the curb with a bump, the car stopped outside the building. A few droplets of rain hit the windshield. I turned to say goodbye to Roman, but my gaze soaked up his face instead. "See you around."

He leaned toward me, but I took the door handle first. As I climbed out, the rain poured down, soaking my sorry ass before I made it under the covered entrance. Fitting. One last kick to the gut from Mother Nature.

I handed the piece of paper to the woman behind the marble counter.

"Ownership documentation, please." She spoke between the smacks of her chewing gum.

I opened the package and skimmed the next document in line. It was indeed an ownership. Curious. Renting would give Loukin more control over me. Whether one was a prostitute assigned to Johns or an agent owned by the underground, the business was always about control. My soaked fingers made little water marks as I handed it to her.

She skimmed it and gave it back to me without looking up. "What are you, seventeen? Must be nice."

"Yeah, I've got a real sugar daddy."

She handed me a set of keys from the drawer. My pack weighed on my soggy, aching shoulders as I stepped inside the elevator. My fingers trailed over the keyring marked PH3. I tapped the PH2/PH3 button and realized there was half a floor dedicated to my new condo.

I told myself not to get too excited. I was still in a cage, no matter how much Loukin dressed it up. But when I opened the door, the allure of my new home was almost bewitching.

The place was huge, covered with glossy red mahogany. The floors reflected the chrome lighting which sparkled throughout, giving it the feeling that the floors themselves glowed. Floor to ceiling windows showcased the view of the heart of Ottawa, right beside Parliament. The panorama continued out sliding glass doors which led to a big wraparound balcony.

The door swung closed behind me as I dropped my bag. A kitchen with white marble counters and matching wood cupboards revealed itself, while a chrome stairway twirled upstairs. I kicked off my boots mid-step not wanting to dirty the floors any more than I already had. I passed the first bedroom and ascended the staircase.

A modern study led into the master bedroom and ensuite, but the balcony opposite the bed caught my attention. I walked out into the brisk air and faced the Gothic rooftops of parliament. If I called up my vampiric hearing, I'd hear every word spoken in parliament near an unlatched window. This is what it had been about all along. The moment the thought entered my head, the night air carried whispers from a few floors down.

I turned inside and saw a white envelope on the dresser. Written across the envelope was *Karolina*. The handwriting was very sharp, impatient for the gothic style. An unusual style of handwriting, which I saw scattered across Loukin's desk in Kislovodsk. I opened it.

Dear Karolina,

I hope you are enjoying your new place. I wanted it to be as comfortable as possible.

Please review your package and be ready to receive word on your first mission. Things will start slowly to give you time to catch up to the others. I do wish we could have left things on a better note. Lexi and Leonid give their hellos.

Warm regards,

Uncle Loukin.

I crumpled the note. This was not a happy ending. Scribbling a few warm words and dangling an idea of family wasn't going to soften the blow. This was what giving me property had been about—to give me a semblance of independence. Loukin made the decision to blackmail me, and he would face the consequences. He started a war for my freedom, and I was determined to win it back.

Chapter Twenty-Four
Dark Eyes

I tore through the whole apartment over the next few hours: every cranny, every light, and under every surface. I even had half a mind to rip open the pillowcases. I found a few spy cams, but they had been set up on the balconies and the perimeter of the front door, allowing me some privacy.

Next were the black boxes called frequency busters. They had been placed on the ceiling of the condo, scattered inside the lights. I hadn't read the package by then and smashed them the moment I found them. Unfortunately, as I read, they were there for my benefit.

The busters scrambled any type of mass surveillance frequencies—IMSI devices—that were sent in my condo's direction. Which meant any text, phone calls, or any electronic forms of communication were blocked from getting picked up. The busters effectively made my condo a protection zone for data. Only one had survived mass extinction at the hands of Karolina.

I carefully placed it back into the center of my living room, hoping the one remaining box would protect me. I would have to use the landline now or stand directly under the buster.

The next piece of equipment my package explained

was the eighties style answering machine which looked like it'd sputter and die at any moment. It had a buster built into it and it functioned on an encrypted hardline which ran signals directly to and from Russia. The purpose of the encrypted line was to redirect the primary source to a mundane location. In my case, it was programmed for tracing to Carleton University.

My answering machine could be accessed through direct contact only, which meant I had to meet 'code check in' prior to accessing any messages, and I had to damn well ensure the environment was secure. This was the main source of communication for my assignments. When the light on the bottom blinked red, it was the ominous sign my slaveholders had given me an order. For the moment the light was just unlit clear glass, but every few seconds I'd eye it like it would detonate.

The rest of the package explained my new resources. My new cell phone also had a buster in it, which is why it was an incredibly old model. There was a firearm located under the desk in the study and under the sink in the kitchen. I couldn't help but scoff. If Loukin's staff didn't catch the firearm pun, he was employing idiots. As I finished reading about tools, I neared the end of the package. At the bottom of each page there was fine print which read, *Burn after reading.* It felt good to defy the little voice that belonged to the paper. I flipped to the next page.

My father's inheritance was held in trust, true to what Loukin had indicated. I now had full access through a debit card and account opened in my name. The card was placed in a pocket inside the package with my birth certificate and passport. A balance sheet was printed, and the eight-figured number written across the page stood out like a broadcast message. I slowly slid off the couch and plunked to the floor.

Sixteen million. It had been dumped into my account in less than forty-eight hours.

Everything I had now manifested out of thin air—and could disappear just as quickly. All of this had been given to me in the blink of an eye, and though many would be overjoyed, I couldn't shake off the hands of fear that had seized me. They could reduce me back to nothing as fast as it appeared. Maybe they could make me disappear entirely, with a vampire like Andre. What had Ina called them? The *Ispolniteli*. The ones who hunt their own.

Andre had said it the day I met Loukin. *When you made me hunt my own.* The other vampire agents hated him for it. It was clear through the bond and the look on his face he hated it. It made it easier to forgive him, the first time. Now, his role had changed. He may no longer be an *Ispolniteli*. If it were the case, surely another would take his place.

I wondered how much I could fall out of line before I truly exhausted Loukin's patience. But he'd strong-armed me for a reason. Loukin had spies already. He needed me especially for a certain task. I had to find out what it was long before his plans materialized. For my strategy to be feasible, I would have to get out of his control before he realized I knew and secure Miruna's safety. To succeed, I would need money and a way out. Surely, they'd be watching the massive account they'd given me. The account could be a test, to see if I'd run. I could stash away small amounts of money at a time, in an account they couldn't trace or touch. But I'd have to find out if both even existed first.

Another item on my list of tasks.

I found myself pacing. I walked over to a metal waste pail in the corner, seized the pail, and tossed it down beside the coffee table. For a moment, my mind drew a blank. It was overloaded. I shuffled the papers into the bin and walked to the refrigerator. The door was one of the fancy ones which lit up when you touched it. Inside there were two lonely bottles sitting on the shelves. The minions who set up my condo had the graceful courtesy of leaving a few beers behind.

I popped the cap off and took a swig. The bubbly liquid rolled over my tongue, and the familiarity of one thing from my past felt good. Beer was still beer, the sun would still rise and set, and I was still here.

I walked to the papers in the garbage and held out my hand. I released my control and flames jetted from my skin onto the papers. It didn't fume up to the ceiling like it had when I lit a fire with Mama. Gerel had taught me well, and his lessons along with the warning about my necklace wouldn't be forgotten.

The amber flames traveled in a line across the paper. I rested the bottle against my lips. The dance of flames huffing to life reminded me of the ninjas from the movies I watched as a kid, almost like two lovers entwined in a battle neither would win, until the flames reduced the pile to ash.

A knock on the door made my body jerk and I spilled my beer on the couch. I roused my vampiric agility to walk silently to the door and looked through the peephole.

It was Roman.

I threw the door open. "Ro? What are you doing here?" It was a quarter past five, a little over two hours since I was dropped off. He must have left home the moment he got in and checked on his parents.

He stepped through the threshold and blustered past me, and it reminded me for anyone but Roman and Ina, I would want a ward in place. I followed him as he traipsed into the kitchen and the door clicked closed behind us. He opened the fridge and helped himself to the remaining beer. His hands shook as he popped it open, and the cap rattled to the counter. Only after he drank half his beer, did he turn to face me.

"Bit early for a bonfire isn't it? At least when we had them, they had been outside."

My gaze darted to the can and smoke which had billowed up against the ceiling.

"Shit."

I ran to the glass sliding door, picking up the can along the way and chucked it onto the balcony. The smoke sucked out the doorway, as the smoke alarm silently blinked. Maybe the alarm was a pretense? Loukin's lackeys must have known I was a fire user. If they didn't, they weren't worth the money.

Roman downed the rest of his drink.

I slipped in front of him and leaned against the kitchen island. "What's up, Ro?"

He looked down at me, eyes warm and bright enough to glow. The wolf beneath the surface stirred underneath his golden baby browns.

"I need to know something," he said.

"Wha—"

"Do you trust me?"

"Sure, Ro."

"What were you burning?"

Even the smile on my face felt wrong. I must learn how to lie but lying to Roman seemed like skipping university and training, and joining the Special Investigations Unit. I needed more time, just a couple more weeks of my old life with him. I felt so brittle I could break, and when I looked up into his eyes, so fierce with the heat of deception, my façade was breaking.

"There are things about my…new life that I can't tell you yet."

"Oh?" he mocked. "But you trust me?"

"Yes."

"Yes?" He leaned in. "But you can't tell me. You have me key in my number. Tell me you'll call me later. So, what? I'm dismissed. What am I? Your pet? You want me to go away until you need me again?"

"No." My hands shot to his chest. I wanted to tell him I'd never do that, that I respected him too much, that it wasn't true. But again, he was right. It was exactly how I treated him.

His expression changed like he'd read my mind. For a second, fire flared inside of him, not like mine, but the fire of a man about to lose control.

"Don't lie to me, Karo!"

His muscles rippled under my hands and I should have feared him, but the memory of how this situation began made me fight back.

"Is not telling you everything lying, Ro?"

"Yes!"

"Then now you know how it feels. You know how it feels when there is no one on your side but you. When you are the last person to know because no one trusts you. When you can't be trusted to even know how to control your own power! When you hurt people because of the ignorance you're trying to be rid of!" Tears I didn't want to acknowledge started to flow. "I have to learn to trust myself. I have to be better, smarter. I have to deal with the situation I've created. I'm doing this on my own. Because I know I can, and because I have to."

His arms moved with the primal grace of his predatory form, but the human side of Roman trembled. The usual warmth of his hands wasn't there. They chilled my skin as they slipped to my waist, and I realized he was scared.

"I can help. You don't have to do it alone," he said.

I wanted to hold him and tell him the thought of never seeing him again in Russia had torn me apart. I wanted to tell him I was trying to fix my circumstance, but I needed him to hang on.

"But I do," I said. "The more people involved, the worse it's going to be. For me and for you. You have to trust me, Roman. I can fix this without hurting anyone." Part of being a woman made me want to protect the people I loved, but what I said was a veil over a much deeper truth. I *wanted* to do it on my own.

Roman saw it too and dove for the jugular.

"What? You think I don't realize Daddy's inheritance had a price tag? You think I don't know what Loukin's operation is? Or how vamps run their matters in the underground? You think I'm just some wolf pup who has no weight in my own community?" His smooth skin rippled again, threatening to release the wolf. "To even think that is an insult to the name Lupei—"

"I'm not involving you!" My hands smacked against his chest. "I have a choice! I get to decide! I'm not some China doll. I have sovereignty! I'm a Dalca, an Albesuc, and Nabokov—and I have a right to choose how I handle my business."

"But you involved him."

I deflated. There it was. The real reason why he'd shown up. The reason he was so angry. The reason he trembled before me. Like he'd exposed a raw wound, he turned his face from mine, and collapsed into me resting his forehead against my cheek.

"Do you want me?" he whispered.

It was a simple but loaded question. The answer, like it could remove all anguish from the past few weeks, stood out in my head. *Yes.*

"I followed you, I protected you, and everything I have done was for you. Do you want me? Or him?"

No. Not him. Never again. "You."

His grip tightened, and he jerked me against his chest. "Me?" His breathing raced, with his ribs flattening into me with each inhale.

"Yes."

His lips touched my cheek, then traced the streaks of tears on my skin. His hands swept across the muscles of my back, gripping me like I'd slip through his fingers. "I'm sorry." He kissed underneath my jaw, his tongue sliding to my neck, and the heat I felt transferred to pleasure.

"Me too." I found the sweet spot behind his ear and sucked.

He heaved me up onto the countertop, entwining us together. His mouth crawled to mine, kissing me hard. My fangs slid into my mouth, just grazing his tongue. A drop of blood in my mouth swelled with the burning flavor of brandy. *Ţuică.* It was a Romanian plum brandy, but the flavor of Roman's blood was stronger—fiery—with the sweetness of a mouthful of brown sugar.

I sighed against his mouth and shivered with the taste. He withdrew from me, and my heart lurched. I was always afraid of what he'd think of my fangs, and it was no different now.

His eyes were glossy, in a haze from the small cut of my fang. He wiped a smear of blood from my lip with his thumb.

"Where's the bedroom?"

"Upstairs."

He scooped me up and carried me to the stairs. Midway, he shifted my weight onto his shoulder and turned the dial of the nearby music player. We passed through the office into the bedroom as the radio host introduced a song. The beat of the music thumped to the rhythm of my heartbeat as he tossed me onto the bed.

Roman's body followed, starting from my feet. He pulled off my socks and tugged at my jeans. Hovering over me, he removed my clothing one article at a time, making his way up my body. When his lips grazed my mouth, he was lifting my shirt over my head.

I shuddered as I yanked his shirt from his shoulders, not having the control or finesse he had with undressing me. I ran my hands over his skin, and let my mouth find his as we finished taking off the last articles of clothing. Then there was the smooth feeling of his skin.

My fangs slipped deep into Roman's shoulder

muscle.

He cried out, not in pain but in pleasure. The euphoria which Andre had worn when I drank from him hit Roman's face tenfold.

"I'm sorry," I said. "I'm so sorry." I backed away, but he gripped me and turned on his back, positioning me into a straddle above him.

"Shushhh. It's okay." His words slurred together. "You can't hurt me. Werewolf, remember." He guided my head down into another kiss. The sweet burning flavor of his blood rolled over my mouth and I was rigid with hunger. Temptation tugged on me. Roman's strength was unfathomable, it was true. "But it won't stop me from draining you dry."

"Karo." His hands ran up my body, placing my cheek on his shoulder. "You can't overpower me." The warmth of his mouth was on my skin again. "I'll stop you before you take too much. Let go, Karo."

The heat of him moving against me, the wet of his mouth and touch of his skin were all too much to ignore. I did as he said and let go.

Eventually, in the turn of our bodies, I tore my face from his bloody shoulder. I nibbled a finger, letting my blood dribble into his mouth to heal him. But the euphoria surging through him wasn't over, and he took over the dominant role I had played with.

"You're mine," he breathed.

I spoke between gasps. "I'm yours."

****

The sun hung low now, and Roman was still entwined in the sheets of my bed, passed out for a total of two hours from the ecstasy of my bite. I looked at the clock. At first, I was afraid he wouldn't wake up, but I relaxed when I considered he was at least breathing. By now it was apparent my bite affected him more than it would another vampire. He wasn't waking up until he had slept off the effects, and I was tired of waiting.

I got dressed and walked downstairs, telling myself I could make the whole spy thing work while still being Roman's girlfriend. My half-empty beer was still on the coffee table where I'd left it, and it was a welcomed treat to my lips. Heading to the balcony to watch the last tip of the sun go down, I stubbed my toe on a massive black box along the terrace and almost fell over.

It was a hot tub. This whole arrangement seemed like a really bad joke, or B-list episode pilot. A woman, a vampire gypsy, and a wolf all hang out in the hot tub—cue the opening scene.

Leaning against the banister, the wind hit my face, blowing my hair back, but it couldn't blow away the thoughts trickling back into my head. The pleasure of sex could only keep my mind blank for so long.

I took a swig of beer and stared out at the streets of Ottawa. *This is my city.* If I called up my senses now, I would hear the mesh of voices and city noises blurred together like a collective consciousness. And it called out to me. I meant the words I said to Roman. I was the last of the Dalcas, the second last of the Albesucs, and heiress to the Nabokov empire, and I'd be damned if Loukin made me betray my home city.

I felt like a super-hero looking out over Ottawa from a tower and swearing to protect it. Helping people was second instinct for a lot of heroes, but there was an aptitude inside me which I loved more. The power of choice. And no amount of manipulation, seduction, or guilt could take it away.

I had a choice—despite what Loukin wanted me to think—and I wouldn't fall into one of his well-orchestrated traps again. I knew how to use my power now, and I would take down Loukin's network of spies and protect my country. I would have to learn about the connections around me, and whose side those I encountered belonged to. Any info Loukin requested must have equal importance to the other side. Which meant finding a way to share the Canadian intel with the right people and distorting the message for my Russian contact. It'd be a dangerous play.

The colors of the sun shone coral in the dusk before the coming night, and for a moment I was back on the boat in the Black Sea. Turning my back on the view, not bearing the reminder, I walked inside.

A blinking red light on my answering machine commanded more attention in the quiet room than an air horn. My body glided over to the machine, and the glass beer bottle slipped from my fingers. I looked over my shoulder and listened…to the hum of the refrigerator. Roman was still passed out. With trembling hands, I clicked the button.

An electronic androgynous voice sounded out from the machine.

"Key in sequence." Three high-pitched beeps rang through the air.

"A—Roma equals R. Mirrored in kind. Product. You. State the missing component."

Another three beeps hit the air, and I covered my ears.

"A—Roma equals R. Mirrored in kind. Product. You. State the missing component."

The beeps rang again, and I frantically looked toward the stairs, anticipating Roman to walk down at any moment. *What does it want me to say?*

"A—Roma equals R. Mirrored in kind. Product. You. State the missing component."

High pitched noises filled the air this time, and I started to panic.

The machine was set for me. The code had to be one I knew. Something familiar that only my mind would register in a matter of seconds. A—Roma. Ana. Romania. The next part of the message. Mirrored in kind. A and R were to be repeated. A and R would be the missing component.

"A and R," I said into the machine.

The high-pitched noises grew in intensity. "Incorrect answer. State missing component."

A and R, A and R. Product me…Aleksandr! I was the product. "Alksander Nabokov," I said.

"Incorrect answer. State the missing component, or self-destruct sequence to be initiated."

Ringing sounded through the room and it felt like my ears would bleed.

"A—Aleksandr Russia," I squealed.

The air in the room silenced.

"Welcome, Dark Eyes."

I leaned against the table steadying myself. With cold shaking hands, I walked to the couch and sat down to listen, still getting over the fact my condo may have been seconds away from exploding.

"Assignment. Bunny ears. Commencement. Fortnight. Partner operative. Smoke."

My head hung limp in my hands.

"Stand by for further instruction."

I didn't know if it was an hour or ten minutes, but when I finally looked up, the red light on the machine was gone. I was left to the silence and my thoughts. Anyone but him…

A word about the author…

M. R. Noble has played tug-of-war between science and art her whole life, but the rope broke when she wrote the first line of The Dark Eyes Series. Immersed up to her keyboard in paranormal romance and urban fantasy, she enjoys blending the real with the surreal. The only drawback is she misplaces her mug while dreaming up her next scene and soon finds herself six cups overpoured.

Keeping to her Lake Simcoe roots, she is a member of the Writers Community of York Region (WCYR), where her muse is made not found…over a hefty cup of coffee.

Thank you for purchasing
this publication of The Wild Rose Press, Inc.

For questions or more information
contact us at
info@thewildrosepress.com.

The Wild Rose Press, Inc.
www.thewildrosepress.com